into the wilderness

into the
wilderness

a novel   DEBORAH LEE LUSKIN

White River Press
Amherst, Massachusetts

Into the Wilderness

First published February, 2010

White River Press
P.O. Box 3561
Amherst, MA 01004
www.whiteriverpress.com

Printed in the United States of America

ISBN: 978-1-935052-20-3

Book design by Jocelyn Edens
Cover photo by H. W. Richardson, Vermont Publicity Department.
Courtesy Vermont Historical Society, Barre.

Author's Note:
While I've aimed for historical accuracy, this is a work of fiction, and all the characters and events are my invention; any resemblance to actual persons, events, or locales is entirely coincidental.

Library of Congress Cataloging-in-Publication Data

Luskin, Deborah Lee., 1956–
Into the wilderness : a novel / by Deborah Lee Luskin.
p. cm.
ISBN 978-1-935052-20-3 (pbk.)
1. Widows--Fiction. 2. Bachelors--Fiction.
3. Vermont--Fiction. I. Title.
PS3612.U786I58 2010
813'.6--dc22
                                                         2009047973

ACKNOWLEDGMENTS

David and Joan Spikol introduced me to Vermont; it has made all the difference. Lucy Gratwick graciously told me about the early years of the Marlboro Music Festival; Chongyo Shin taught me about the piano; and friends too numerous to name maintained faith in my voice even when mine faltered—none more than Mary Pinard.

Writing the book was easy; seeing it into print was not; it is unlikely I would have persisted had it not been for equally persistent encouragement from Karen Hesse and Castle Freeman Jr. In addition, I thank Randy Hesse for his counsel, and Linda Roghaar for her expertise. Thanks, too, to Hilly van Loon, who helped prepare the typescript.

Finally, I thank Miriam, Naomi, Ruth, and Tim Shafer— but for what, I can't even begin to say.

O love is the crooked thing,
There is nobody wise enough
To find out all that is in it,
For he would be thinking of love
Till the stars had run away,
And the shadows eaten the moon.

—W. B. Yeats

For Timo

into the wilderness

1 | theme & variation

She'd be like Jackie, stoic in her widowhood, even though Dory was already an old man when he died in his sleep after a terrible illness, it was a blessing and not a national tragedy, like the murder of a president right on TV. And Rose was hardly a Jacqueline Kennedy, though she did know how to sew a tailored suit and make a pillbox hat, if it came to that. But where would she wear such an outfit? In Miami, it was shorts and cotton skirts, shirtwaists and sleeveless sheaths. You didn't need good millinery to play canasta or walk on the beach.

Nu? So? Maybe Jackie made widowhood look good, but Rose knew better. After all, this was her second time. And she was no First Lady with young children and a small fortune. At sixty-four, two husbands dead, it was enough already. Maybe she'd just amuse herself by reading about Jackie's goings-on. They always reported in the paper when she dined with her brother-in-law, Bobby, who was running for the Senate in New York, even though he was from Massachusetts and lived in DC. No one was going to put in the paper that Rose Mayer was going out to dinner with Stan Samuelson. Stan would ask her, like he asked all the new widows, but Rose didn't plan on accepting.

It was a shame, assassinating a president. And so handsome! A thousand days, they said. If he'd been Jewish, maybe a hundred. But she'd been lucky. Twenty years with Sam, another twenty with Dory. She should complain? No, Rose was going to make a career out of being a widow this time. From now on, she wasn't going to do anyone else's laundry or fix anyone else's meals but her own. Not even Manny's. He was married; let his wife take care of him.

He and Jeannie had both asked her to stay. The kids, Wendy and Marty, too. "Grandma, won't you be lonely if you go back to Florida?"

What? It's a crime to be lonely? New Jersey is lonely. Where they live, everyone's young, married, raising kids. There's no place for an old lady in the suburbs. Besides, it's freezing this time of year. Who wants all that snow and ice, it's dangerous to walk outside, not everyone clears the pavement. Enough already. "Manny," she told him, "Manny, I got my own life and you got yours. I'll come visit. Maybe *Pesach*, for Passover, in the spring. Besides," she kissed Jeannie on the cheek, "a woman doesn't want to have her mother-in-law in the house."

"Mom!" Jeannie protested. "We'd love to have you here! Really."

"Well. I still got to go. I got to go home and think."

So here she was, back in Florida and everyone finally cleared out of the apartment, maybe she could start. Rose sighed against the door after locking out the last of her well-meaning neighbors. It wasn't enough to sit *shiva* in New York? Her friends here had her slippers and a basin of water waiting outside her apartment when she arrived from the airport, and boxes to sit on, as if five hours on an airplane wasn't penance enough. Sadie September wanted to tear her collar like you're supposed to. "Not to worry. I'll do it along the seam, so you can mend it next year."

"Sadie, I'm not wearing torn clothes for a year," Rose said, shrugging her off. Later she overheard Sadie tell Essie Rothman it was on account Dory was her second husband, after all.

What would a meddlesome woman like that know, anyway? Three days of weeping, four days of eulogy. *Gevalt!* Enough is enough. Rose found herself in front of the open fridge filled with enough food to feed all the starving children in China. "Good," she spoke aloud. "So I won't have to cook." She shut the door and stood in the dark. For the first time since Dory died, Rose was alone, with only the flickering light of the memorial candle for company.

The *yortzeit* candle lit the soft night. Instead of the Florida humidity oppressing her, Rose was embraced by the damp air. She unbuttoned her housecoat, so the moist night kissed her neck, and sat at the kitchen table, hands folded as if in prayer, watching the shadows from the flame dance around the kitchen. The room lost its Formica edges in the candlelight; instead of a workplace, it was a sanctuary.

Rose sat late into the night, and before retiring, she pulled the shroud off the bathroom mirror to unveil her widowed face. How did she ever get so old? She didn't feel the way the woman who stared back looked. How was it that she never felt her hair turn silver or her skin crease? How was it she could look out her pale blue eyes and see as clearly as if she were still a keen-eyed milliner stitching hats for Mrs. Mercedes? Inside, she still felt—well, not *young*, not the youthful Rose of urges and lusts—but spry and smart and as if her whole life were still ahead of her.

"But you're sixty-four, sagging, wrinkled, and widowed—again." She stopped her words with her fingers and peered closer into the mirror. "Look how pale your lips are!" She chomped up and down, pleased that she didn't have to worry about slipping dentures, like Gertie Rosen. The poor woman could barely eat sponge cake without her teeth coming loose. Rose straightened her shoulders. "Rose Mayer," she told her reflection, "for an old lady, you're doing okay."

The next day, Rose cleared all the *yortzeit* candles off the supermarket shelf. She'd have to speak to the manager, order them by the case and maybe get a deal on the price. For now, she had thirty-two of the small, paraffin-filled glasses, each guaranteed to burn twenty-four hours. So what if you were only supposed to light one on the anniversary of someone's death? Who was she to follow the rules? And what did it matter how she spent her nights, now that she was a widow?

Each evening, after the chatter of the day's gossip faded from her ears, Rose lit a new candle, even when the flame from the previous day's still had an hour to burn. For a little while, Rose sat in the glow of two flames, the bright eyes of fire seeing into her heart. She had no words for this nightly vigil. She uttered no prayer, constructed no story, reconstructed no autobiography, and experienced neither urgency nor regret. She just sat bathed in the light blessing an old lady in Florida, dislocated from wifedom and the world of her former work.

When the supply of memorial candles dwindled, Rose returned to the supermarket for more, but now that the reduced pension check of her widowhood had arrived, she scrutinized the cups of paraffin and wondered why they cost so much. More exploitation of the poor no doubt, for who else would buy such a modest thing as a memorial candle? The well-to-do had better talismans for their grief. Rose pushed further down the aisle and purchased a box of seventy-two Holyland Candles, the kind the religious used to illuminate the Sabbath. They were the same short, white tapers the *goyim* bought down at the hardware when a hurricane was predicted. Holyland was a better buy, and if the *goyim* could burn them because the electricity failed, surely she could substitute them for the twenty-four hour *yortzeit* without attracting God's wrath. Why would He be looking after a lonely widow like her, anyway? He had other things to do, though Rose was never so sure God was really as good as His billing, given all the world's *tsuris*. If God were really paying attention, maybe there wouldn't be so many troubles in the world.

And so what if she never lit the Sabbath candles before? She didn't treat Friday night or Saturday any different from any other day of the week. What did she need with a day of rest? Now she was widowed on top of being retired; she had all the rest she needed. But she didn't sleep well without Dory's snores keeping time for her dreams. Burning the candles wasn't about God or the Sabbath. It was about having company during the long night.

The evening the last *yortzeit* flickered in its clear pool of paraffin at the bottom of the glass, Rose climbed on a chair to reach down the candlesticks she'd carried with her from the Old Country to Manhattan, from the Lower East Side to Brooklyn, and from Brooklyn to Miami, not even offering them to her daughter-in-law when her son married, because she'd been saving them all her life for this very moment, as if all along she knew it was coming. Despite the Saran Wrap, the silver was tarnished. Polishing silver was a job for daylight, not now. Rose kept to her task as if she were a housewife rushing to meet the Sabbath by sundown.

The Holyland candles wobbled in the silver holders. Rose dripped wax into the holes to glue the candles upright. Without ceremony, she lit them. The flames danced high above the table, spinning new shadows around the room. The light penetrated Rose's heart. Her mother's voice came out of her mouth in the fluent Hebrew of the Sabbath prayer, even though it was Tuesday evening, even though Rose had forgotten she knew these words, as if she could forget. They were part of her tongue, formed the roof of her mouth, stuck between her teeth and filled her ears as if the Blessed One spoke in the modest kitchen of her retirement flat. From then on, she closed her eyes, bowed her head, and hummed the prayer as she lit the candles each night.

One night, it was Sam who flickered out of the shadows instead of Dory.

"Sam?" It was like they were back on Brighton Twelfth Street, after Manny was born, and Sam would clamp his lunch box down on the drain board before washing his hands at the sink after work. "Sam. What are you doing home at this hour?"

Sam dried his hands thoroughly on the roller, always careful to pull a freshly pressed surface around.

"Sammy, you're not laid off, are you?" But she could tell by the way his shoulders slumped as she sewed by the window that that's what had happened. "So, now it's us." Rose stuck the needle in the seam and sighed as she laid the sewing down. "I'll make us some tea."

Rose bustled water into the kettle and struck a match for the gas. Already, she was taking inventory of the Frigidaire. A quart of milk, six eggs, maybe half a pound of butter, some farmer's cheese, and some herring on the *milchedig*, milk, side. Leftover pot roast and the chopped meat on the *flayshedig*, meat, side. Flour and salt, they had plenty, and Cream of Wheat for the baby. Four bananas, perfectly ripe, and the last of a loaf. "Did you bring home bread?"

"I forgot."

"Your last chance for free bread and you forgot?"

"*Shoshana, Rosela.* Beauty, Rosie. Stay calm. Mr. Boyer said I could come in and have bread. It's not like he wants to lay off his

6

delivery routes. You think all his customers is gonna come to him?"

"Sit down already," Rose said. "Here's some tea." She filled two glasses from the pot and placed a bowl of sugar cubes on the table.

Sam was about to pick up his glass—he always drank it piping—when his hand took a detour and covered Rose's, the steam from the tea drifting into their faces as they sat in this tender embrace.

A moist, Florida breeze shook the candlelight and Rose sighed. "Oh, Sam. Those were good times." She shook her head. "So listen to me. I sound like an old lady already. They were hard times, what with Sam out of work and jobs as scarce as *goyim* in *shul*."

Rose rested her head in her hands. Sam was dead, what, twenty-five years? Here she was, a widow again, and she couldn't keep her dead husbands straight, may they rest in peace. What was she going to do? Go live with Manny, like he was asking every Sunday when they talked on the phone? Or, God forbid, visit him at his summer place? Every Sunday they had the same conversation.

"Mom, come spend the summer with us, in Vermont," he said.

"What would I do in Vermont all summer?" she'd reply.

"What will you do in Florida all summer?"

"I have a life here." Even Rose knew this was a feeble argument.

"Mom, ever since you moved to Florida you've done nothing but complain."

"Isadore wanted to live here," Rose said.

"Mo-om." Manny dragged two syllables into the word, like he was still a little boy and not a grown man.

"God rest his soul." She meant Isadore, not Manny.

"It's cool in Vermont in the summer," Manny persisted.

"Cool? It's cold, even in summer!"

"You can't stand the Miami heat come July. You've said so yourself. You become a prisoner to the air-conditioner."

"At my age, you're a prisoner wherever you are."

"In Vermont, you'll be with your grandkids!" She could hear the triumph in his voice, like he'd made trump.

"And is there a *shul* in Vermont?" she asked.

"Since when do you go to synagogue?"

"And a kosher butcher? What am I going to do up there, among the *goyim*?"

"What's this? Have you suddenly gone religious?"

"It's nice to have a choice," Rose said.

"You have a choice: swelter in Florida or come to Vermont. Jeannie will take care of you."

"I'm not such an old woman I need to be taken care of!"

"You know what I mean. You won't have to shop or cook. You can relax."

"Relax? You mean sit like a zombie. What am I going to do all day in this life you're subjecting me to?"

"You can read. There's a library. And you can listen to music, hear Rudolf Serkin play."

"Rudolf Serkin? In Vermont?"

"The Marlboro Music Festival. We'll get you tickets. Your favorite musicians play there: David Soyer. See? You won't even be the only Jew."

They repeated this argument, with variations, every Sunday. And every evening, Rose lit her candles. Thinking candles, she called them. After thirty-six nights of watching them vaporize into night-time thoughts, Rose purchased another box of seventy-two. And after those, another. She didn't travel north for *Pesach*. She stayed in Florida and thought.

One night in late spring, Rose lit two candles, no longer in mourning, but in an affirmation of life. She was only sixty-four years old! She watched the candles burn into their sockets, and before retiring, she plugged the next day's tapers into the remaining puddle of wax. Rose was halfway through her fourth box of candles when she surprised her son one Sunday morning, after they'd both had enough time to read the *Times*' Week in Review, so they could argue about the news. But they didn't argue that Sunday, because after Rose said hello, she said, "Manny, I'm coming to Vermont."

All of his life, Percy Mendell regarded New Year's Eve as opening night, the beginning of things, the magical midnight of the clock whose quarters were the seasons and whose minutes were the gift of days. After all, he'd been born at the midnight of the century, on December 31, 1899, and he'd lived his life in the broad daylight of the twentieth. But this New Year's Eve was different, and for the first time, Percy wondered if maybe the curtain wasn't starting to go down; if instead of the high noon of his manhood, he wasn't slipping into dusk. He'd turned sixty-four last night; in a year, he would have to retire.

Retirement itself was a twentieth-century concept; maybe even newer than that. His parents didn't so much retire as dwindle. When the town switched from rollers to snow-plows, his father gave up winter road work. In the spring, Arden Mendell showed John Ready how to use the grader. It was a couple of years before Arden gave up the roads altogether, but gradually, he just spent his spare time visiting at the maintenance shed and grinding blades and oiling machinery because he never could abide being idle.

As her eyesight faded, Percy's mother had stopped quilting. For a while, she crocheted, but she quickly saturated the house with doilies and lost interest. Nevertheless, Percy's folks never stopped working; they just farmed on an ever-decreasing scale until there was just one cow, a dozen hens, and a kitchen garden. But right up to the end, Arden Mendell split his own stovewood. Just took him longer to do it, that's all.

At sixty-four, Percy was healthier than his father had been at fifty. Not that his dad had been sickly. Not at all. Just that all those years of hard labor wore a man down, and Percy had opted out of the farm life, out of farming directly, by working for the Extension Service. For forty years, now, he'd been studying the science of agriculture and passing the information on to farmers to use for the betterment of their livestock, their cover crops, their livelihood. Lots of the new information brought relief to a farmer's aching limbs. How many manure trolleys had he helped install? There's a gob of back-breaking work saved right there. And the automatic milkers, stanchion feeding systems, electric wire for fencing instead of miles of barbed wire. Heck, farming wasn't anything at all like what his folks had endured. If he were a young man now, maybe he'd reconsider. Maybe if he had to make the choice now, he'd choose to take over the farm instead of going off to school. But that was all water under the bridge. Here he was, sixty-four, and his working life was coming to an end. What was he going to do?

He stood in front of the piano in the stillness of his dusted parlor as the dim light of New Year's Day crowded the windows, as if the grayness wanted to enter the house. Percy stood, listening intently to the silence of the house now that the record had ended. At last, the argument inside his head abated. His shoulders dropped, and he exhaled. Deliberately, he touched a key.

The sound wobbled, so he listened to the Goldberg Variations again, again amazed at those first few notes. That a single key could be depressed in such a way that the sound came out as round as a perfect breast. That first phrase, a tentative touch on a languid afternoon. The sadness of the perfection of it all—a kind of love-making he longed for the way he longed for the next note and the next and the next, until the initial theme broke into a hurry of music that was human delight itself, bright sunshine on a high pressure day, and that deep note in the bass throbbing, a whole parallel bassline of grass growing, fox stalking, the wind rippling through the hay while the treble sang in a voice of butterflies, dragonflies, and bees.

Did others hear music the way he did? Like the perfect ticking of an antique clock, like the view of the distant hills, the petals of trillium repeating themselves in the leaves, the propellers of the forsythia blossom, the structure of snow crystals, and the mechanical regularity of kernels on a corn cob. The stately delphinium and the plump pumpkin, Percy heard all these shapes in the sounds, miraculously scratched out of black plastic spinning into his front room with its quiet lace curtains and sedate, polished floor.

This boy Gould, a Canadian, he had a way with the piano, as if he were Bach's true heir despite the superfluity of offspring Bach sired. His playing opened a gate not just to the past, but to time itself, as if Bach had anticipated Einstein. Percy could hear the universe expanding in each variation, the music rippling out into the black universe the way the stars punctuated a clear night sky.

The record came to an end and the player arm automatically lifted itself and swung back to its cradle. Instead of turning the record, Percy stood in front of the upright. Just staring at it, he could hear perfect notes reverberate from the sound board, as if Glenn Gould were at the keyboard, filling the house with music. Ever since Addie died, he heard music all the time.

He had never been much of a talker to begin with. After telling his father he wouldn't carry on farming, what was left to say? There was nothing to discuss, and his father said no more about it. When his folks passed, Percy sold all but the house and twenty acres—some meadow, but mostly woodlot, for fuel.

His sister was married at the time, living away, and she blithely forfeited her claim to the real estate, claiming God would provide. Who knows what she was thinking? Certainly not that her husband, the Reverend Emery Fountain, would be struck down, without issue, after too much Sunday roast. So Addie returned to Orton to keep house for her brother.

At first, Percy enjoyed the companionship, and certainly the dusting, laundry, and meals which his sister provided, unasked. Before her return, he'd done well enough on his own, with the help of Mrs. Parsons, who came in Thursdays to mop. Meals were easy to come by. As the extension agent, he was a popular guest at the farms he visited, and it was rare for him not to be invited in for a hearty, farmhouse meal. With one of those tucked under his belt at noon, he easily filled in the holes of a mild hunger at either end of the day. He wasn't one of those men who needed a woman to pour cereal into a bowl for him, or boil his tea water. He was competent in providing for himself the things he liked to eat: eggs, hot cereal, toast, even pancakes on a Sunday; tuna sandwich, tomato soup, and chops or steak when he felt like bothering. After Addie returned, he dutifully sat down to supper if she fixed it, and fixed his own if she didn't. Without discussion, he ate what was set before him, and without being asked, he did the washing up.

Despite his own contentment, Addie lashed out, "What do you know about marriage? I was a part of something, for better or for worse. I was a *wife*!"

He stood still in the face of her rage. "I appreciate all you do here, Addie."

"What's a widow? Used up, like a leaf skittering across the road in the fall."

The poetry surprised Percy. He offered to build her her own house.

"I'd like that," she agreed. "But just a parlor, bedroom, and bath. There's no need for two kitchens."

On weekends, Percy built the addition, a mirror image of his own Cape, connected by a narrower, story-and-a-half corridor; the building looked like Siamese twins joined from shoulder to hip. Percy moved the piano into her parlor, so he wouldn't have to listen to her thumping hymns. In his parlor, he installed a modern phonograph with an automatic record changer that could accommodate long-playing records, allowing him to listen to a whole symphony with only one intermission to turn the stack over for the third and fourth movements.

It was an amicable arrangement. Addie's doilies and dolls didn't interfere with his records or books. When neighbors called, they sat on Addie's side; when farmers stopped by, Percy invited them into his. The kitchen, spacious enough to accommodate both a harvest table and a couch against the wall, was neutral territory, where the informal life of the house occurred. Nevertheless, they ended up dancing around one another in the kitchen, fixing eggs side by side, hers scrambled, his boiled according to his watch.

Addie had died back in November, and silence descended upon Percy anew. Now he stood in his quiet house, stroking the silent ivory. It was as if by raising the cover from the piano, he'd lifted the lid of a coffin, bringing his past back to life.

At nineteen, and the age of the century itself, Percy hadn't ever so much as laid a finger on an ivory key. The piano was Lila's province. It was she who could translate the intricacies of Chopin into thrumming sound, sound that spoke his otherwise inarticulate feelings. He'd walk the three miles to her parents' place summer evenings. Invariably, he'd hear her before the house came into view, and the music would reel him toward her like a fish on a line.

Her parents approved of his visits. "Lila, Percy's here," Mrs. Winthrop would sing over the dish suds. "Why don't you close up that piano now and set on the porch?" But Lila would play to the end, not breaking the sad song till the final chord faded like dusk into night.

"Good evening, Mrs. Winthrop, Mr. Winthrop," Percy tipped his cap at the pair.

"Have a seat, Percy. Lila will be out directly."

"Well, she oughtn't rush on my account. I don't mind to listen." Percy saw the look Mrs. Winthrop gave her husband. Mr. Winthrop shrugged his shoulders and returned to reading the evening paper, or *Scientific American*, if a new issue had just arrived, while Mrs. Winthrop skulked about her clean kitchen in a rattle of discontent.

But what Percy said was true. He enjoyed listening to Lila's music drift through the front room windows onto the porch, where the notes joined the thickening dusk. He didn't know what the music meant or who it was by or when it was written. But he did know that Lila told him her secrets through the music those summer evenings. And when she did finally stop playing and came to join him on the front step, he understood her gratitude that he had let her play.

Percy's legs tired from standing so long. The furnace kicked on as he made his way to the wing chair and sat, without bothering to turn on the lamp. The furniture, whose wooden edges framed the whole of his life, went fuzzy, and a shadow of Addie bent over some mending crossed the weak light from the hall, followed by the shadow of Lila.

"Lila," Percy's voice cracked from disuse. "Lila!" But the shadow disappeared. For the first time since Addie's death, Percy heard the silence that filled his ears. Years raced by, the frantic notes of the Scarlatti that Lila played one Christmas. Forty years of feelings shuttered away in disuse surfaced in the dim room. A dance. A walk holding hands. Almost a kiss. And that final, awful, scene of Lila tumbling from the car, falling off, as if to sleep, in a tangle of petticoats and tresses.

He sat into night, until finally, stiff from so long in one posture, he heaved himself out of the chair and crossed again to the piano. He lowered his face to sniff the keys. Only dust. Ashes to ashes. Then, with the measured eye of an orienteer, he determined middle C and recalled the one time Lila had him sit next to her at the piano, as she guided him up the major scale.

Now, more than forty years later, he made the journey himself, playing each of the eight notes as if it were a psalm in praise of a heart unlocked. Still standing, Percy continued down the scale using his forefinger only, playing only the white keys, until he reached the low A. The last octave was muddy, but nothing twanged. With his right index finger, Percy plodded his way from middle C up to the tinny C at the top of the keyboard. It wasn't badly out of tune, but he'd call Larry Larken in the morning just the same. Still standing, he sounded the first phrase of the Goldberg. Even imperfectly played, the notes stirred him. He closed the piano and walked away.

2 | in the garden

"Mom, come join us," Manny called from the porch door.

"Join you? Join you where? Where are you going at this hour?" Rose slid her glasses down her nose but didn't budge from the chair by the good light.

"Outside. To look at the moon."

"It's dark out!"

Jeannie entered the parlor. "It's a full moon. Come see."

"Moon gazing," Rose sighed as she pushed herself out of the upholstery's embrace and extinguished the lamp. "So dark," her voice rang in the empty room. Keeping one hand on the edge of the end table and the other on her pounding heart, she said again, "So dark," only this time it was more a statement of fact than fear. "They got to go outside at night?" She couldn't see three feet in front of her, and she didn't know the room yet. Moonlight entered through the flimsy white curtains. Sheers—nothing to keep people from peering in. But who was going to look? There wasn't so much as another house in sight, just looming trees. Rose shuffled forward, toward where the outline of the door was slightly less dark than the room.

"Ma, are you coming?" Manny hollered. A ping-pong ball of light bounced across the walls. "Ma?" Manny held a flashlight. "What are you in the dark for?"

"I turned out the light. What, I should waste electricity?"

"Okay, okay. Here. Take my arm."

"I can manage. I just can't see. I don't know the house yet." She placed her hand on his forearm and moved with more certainty. "What's so special we got to go outdoors in the dark?" she asked. The screen door squeaked.

"It's not dark. You can practically read by the moonlight. Now watch your step."

Rose wobbled. Jeannie stabilized the back of a lawn chair as Rose eased herself into it.

"My feet are damp," Rose said.

"It's just the dew." Jeannie arranged a shawl across Rose's shoulders. She and Manny pulled up lawn chairs on either side. Jeannie said, "It's the strawberry moon. I hope it doesn't frost."

"Frost?" Rose asked, "In June?"

"We usually go strawberry picking," Jeannie said. "A frost would ruin the whole crop."

Rose settled against the chair's plastic webbing and stared at the giant moon. The conversation of the trees telling their secrets and the static of summer insects rendered her blind. "What's that noise?" She clutched the aluminum arms of the chair.

"That's an owl. It lives nearby," Jeannie said.

The night noises filled up the pause.

"So this is what you do for entertainment in the country?" Rose said, sighing.

"Just relax, Mom." Manny was focusing the binoculars on the moon. "In our lifetime, we're going to see a man land there."

"And what's so good about that?" Rose wanted to know.

"Well, for one, if we get there first, it will keep the Russians from planting a nuclear warhead up there, aimed right at us."

"And you don't think we'll put a gun up there, aimed at Moscow?"

"No. I don't think we will." Manny kept looking through the binoculars. "Everything's so clear tonight. I can see Tycho. Look, it's the big crater at the bottom. It looks like a hole with light spilling out." Manny handed Rose the glasses.

"What do I want to dissect the moon for?" Rose passed the glasses to Jeannie. "I like the moon just as it is. A little mysterious, maybe." Rose's voice became dreamy. "As a little girl, my *baba*—my grandmother—told me never to sleep in the moonlight, it would make me crazy. I think she believed it. She didn't like to go out after dark, but that was impossible. In the Old Country, in winter, it was always dark. During the day, even." Rose remembered her grandmother wrapped head to foot in black, hardly letting the sun strike her skin, let alone the moon.

"In two weeks, when the moon is new, we'll have good star-gazing, maybe even see meteors," Jeannie said. "You can make a wish on a shooting star."

"So what's to wish for?" Rose asked. "I'm too old to marry again."

"Surely there are other things to wish for." Jeannie's words dissolved into the velvet night. When Rose didn't reply, Jeannie continued. "There's your own health, the welfare of your grandkids, the war on poverty, nuclear war—"

"I should wish for nuclear war?"

"We could all wish against it."

"It'll never happen," Manny's voice boomed out of the dark.

"How can you be so sure?" Jeannie shot back.

"The generals, they thrive on nuclear threat. As long as the Soviet Union keeps building weapons, American generals can ask for larger appropriations. But a nuclear war? It would be over in a week—and there'd be nothing left. No, there won't be any nuclear war."

"I'm glad you're so sure about it," Jeannie said. "But if that's the case, why can't we just stop the arms race?" Jeannie's voice had an edge. "Why can't we just get rid of the military and pour all the money that goes into uniforms and mess kits into schools and books and medicine for the poor?"

"You can't get rid of the military!" Manny shouted. "If you do, the Soviets will take over. No, it's a matter of deterrence. Deterrence works."

"It sounds like an international game of Chicken, if you ask me," Jeannie said.

"That's exactly what it is."

"Well, then we should change it," Jeannie slammed her fist against the arm of her chair.

"How? You can't change these things!" Manny sat immobile.

"Write letters! Organize!"

"Now you sound like Mom," Manny said.

"Me?" Rose cleared her throat.

"Yes, you! All the time, growing up, you and Dad talking about unions this and unions that. I'm amazed you were never brought up in front of McCarthy."

"Manny, that's not funny!" She glared at him, even in the dark.

"It was a joke."

"Only the complacent joke like that. You don't know what it's like to punch a clock, work in a factory. Maybe I shouldn't have encouraged you to be so smart. You should have seen what your father and I had to endure."

"All right, all right. Truce. I'm sorry," he said.

"I sit here and listen to you talk. You, my son! And me—a member of the International Ladies' Garment Workers' Union! So, you teachers, you got salaries and tenure, you're too comfortable to change the world."

"Mom, someone here has to take the opposing point of view. Otherwise we'd all agree all the time. What would there be to argue about?"

"Manny, you get to be my age, maybe you don't want to argue."

"Okay, so we won't argue."

The three sat in silence and retrained their gaze to the great dome of night careening above them. As they watched the moon gleam, Jeannie uncrossed her arms and dropped her shoulders, Manny uncrossed his legs and relaxed into his chair, and Rose exhaled stale air from the bottom of her lungs. The air here almost had a taste to it, a taste that reached far back, to the dimness of her own past. She sighed again, unable to see through the murk of so many intervening years.

The next morning, Rose sipped her coffee. "So, can you get a newspaper around here?"

"We'll pick it up later, when we go swimming."

Rose shrugged, swallowed the last gulp, and started to clear the table, but stopped short in front of the sink. "What? No dishwasher?"

"Ma, this is the country!" Manny explained.

"So, that means you can't have modern conveniences?"

"Listen to her! The woman of the *shtettle!*" her son teased.

"*Shtettle, schmettle.* I been here over fifty years. I did plenty of dishes in my life, not to worry. But you," she waved a spoon to take in the wholesome family before her, "You give up all your conveniences for the summer?" She shrugged and turned to the sink.

"Country house, country plumbing," Manny said, smacking his small paunch with satisfaction.

"It's an old house," Jeannie explained.

Rose started washing dishes under running water.

"Ma!" Manny's voice could stop traffic. "You can't just let the water run!"

"What? I'm not washing dishes right? I'm sixty-four years old and I don't know how to do dishes?"

"It's just the septic, Mom," Manny said, making an effort to speak calmly.

"What's the septic?" Rose had a hand on her hip.

"Instead of a sewer. There's no public sewer here. And no public water. The water comes from our own well. Listen. You can hear the pump turn on."

"So?"

"So, you can't just turn on the water like you got the whole New York water supply behind you, and you can't just flood the septic system. These things got to be cared for."

"So teach me. I can learn. When I was Wendy's age, I used to draw water from a well. Now, you got electricity. I'll be careful with the water."

Meanwhile, Jeannie pulled the plastic dishpan from under the sink and filled it with soapy water. "Manny worries about the pump and the septic, Mom. Don't worry about him. Just listen for the pump and try to remember not to let the water run. As soon as it turns off, we can put up a wash. And we only flush when necessary."

"So why did you buy such an old house?" Rose washed the dishes.

"It's only for the summer. For two months, we can manage." Jeannie dried and put the dishes away.

Rose shrugged. Who was she to tell her children how to live?

"The country's good for the kids. Better than riding bikes in the street," Jeannie said.

Rose removed her apron and hung it on a hook. "Now what?" she asked, surveying the tidy kitchen.

"Mom, do you want to work with me in the garden?"

"Rose, Jeannie. Please call me Rose."

"Rose, would you like to come out? I'm going to plant beans."

"What's wrong with the grocery store? Don't they sell beans, you have to grow them yourself?"

Manny stepped into the kitchen holding a broom, which he used to shield his wife from his mother. "Mo-om."

"Manny, you're a grown man. You can call me Rose too."

"What's with this Rose business? You're my mother. I've called you Mom all my life."

"Well, I want to be called Rose. That's my name. I want to be called by my name, not my title."

"So you'll still be my mother?"

"Of course. Once a mother always a mother. There's no going back."

"But I can't call you Ma anymore."

"I'd prefer to be called Rose."

"What has gotten in to you!"

"I'll tell you!" Rose stomped her foot and squeezed her arms across her chest. "I'm tired of titles. I'm no longer a wife. I just want to be me. Rose. Rose Mayer. That's all!"

Manny started sweeping the floor. "Fine!" he said, roughly moving the chairs out of his way while Jeannie steered Rose out of the kitchen.

Rose already pushed the handle before she remembered she

wasn't supposed to flush. "So, I made a mistake." The water chugged down the pipes. "Who's perfect?" she asked her reflection in the mirror above the sink. "Whoever heard of having a toilet and not flushing?" Rose swept a comb through her hair and applied a deep red lipstick before adjusting the great straw hat Jeannie had handed her. She clasped her purse shut, slid it into the crook of her elbow and made her way outside, down the uneven stone steps and around the house to the fenced garden.

Jeannie's head bobbed behind a screen of delicate ferns. A bird flitted by. Another lit upon a pole, its black eye regarding Rose with curiosity; Rose stared back with suspicion. In the distant heat, the lawn mower droned as comforting as traffic.

"That hat becomes you!" Jeannie stood up, rubbing her back and lifting a trug filled with asparagus spears. "We'll have these with dinner tonight." She held the basket out for inspection.

"You grew these?"

"Sure. Most have gone by," Jeannie said, waving her hands toward the delicate greenery where she'd been kneeling. "Asparagus is a spring crop. These are the last of them. They're delicious."

"They're expensive!"

"Not when you grow them yourself!" Jeannie shifted the trug over her forearm. "Come, let me show you the garden."

Rose hesitated. "I don't think I have the right shoes," she said. They both regarded her polished toes peeking from the open-toed pumps.

"Hmm." Jeannie considered. "You've never lived in the country, have you?"

"Just the Old Country, may it stay on the other side of the world."

"You're awfully formal for gardening. Do you have any slacks?"

"White ones."

"What about shorts?"

"Shorts? In Florida, women wear shorts."

"In Vermont, too. Shorts and sandals. That's what you want for the garden."

"I'll go change."

At least her legs were tan, thanks to all those days walking on the beach with Sadie, who was probably sweltering and *kvetching*, complaining, as usual. Rose was just reaching for the screen door when the phone rang.

"Hello?" she said into the receiver.

"Sally?" a gravelly voice inquired.

"No, this is the Rubin residence," Rose replied.

"Hello?" the gravelly voice asked again after a distinctive click.

"Irma?" It was a clear alto speaking now.

"This is the Rubin residence," Rose repeated. "I think you have the wrong number."

The alto spoke again. "This is a party line, Ma'am. Please hang up."

Manny stormed in. "Hang up, Mom. It wasn't our ring." He grabbed the receiver and said, "I'm very sorry, Mrs. Boyce. My mother didn't know about the phone. It won't happen again."

"It's quite all right, dear. I hope your family is all well?"

"Fine, thank you," Manny said, the politeness of his voice at odds with the scowl he directed toward his mother.

"And we'll see you at the Fourth of July?" the gravelly voice spoke. "This is Irma Bassett, and I do hope Mrs. Rubin will bring her lovely coffee cake to the Ladies' Aid Booth again."

"Oh, how do you do, Mrs. Bassett. I'll tell Jeannie. We're looking forward to the Fourth."

"Very good."

"Bye now." Manny cradled the phone.

Rose had an eyebrow raised. "So, the phone rings when your neighbors want to talk to each other?"

Manny exhaled. Heat radiated from his body. "Okay, Mom." He exhaled again.

"Rose."

"Rose." He didn't mean to snarl. "Rose," he said, trying to neutralize his tone. "Here, we have what's called a party line. There are four houses with this number."

"What kind of *meshuggeneh* system is that?"

Manny held up his hand like a cop. "Let me explain." He wiped his hand across his forehead and then down the side of his pants.

"You should use a handkerchief," Rose advised. "You're so hot. Maybe you need a drink." Rose had the cold water running before Manny could stop her. The water ran while she looked for a glass.

"The water! Don't let the water run!" Manny hurried to close the tap. "We keep a pitcher in the fridge, Mom. That way we don't have to turn on the water all the time." He handed her the plastic jug. "Here."

Rose poured a glassful and handed it to Manny. "Drink. You're overheated."

"I'm fine, Mom." He took the glass anyway.

"Call me Rose," she said. She sipped water she'd poured for herself. "Water is good for you. Keeps you healthy."

"Look, Rose." Manny placed his glass on the counter. "I'll call you Rose if you'll remember a few things."

Rose nodded.

"First. Careful with the water. Second. Don't answer the phone."

"But what if it's for me?"

"Who's going to call you?"

"You think I don't got friends?"

"Okay. Okay."

"I got friends in Florida. Friends in Brooklyn still. Friends from Brooklyn who moved to Jersey, like the Bricks. You remember them?"

"Sure. I remember. Anne and Pete."

"Their daughter, Julie, who you used to be so sweet on, but who married a gentile boy. Well, he died."

"Rose! Later! You'll tell me all the news later. I got to go finish the lawn. But please. The phone is for us if it rings one long and two short. Looong-short-short. That's our ring. Any other ring, don't answer. You got that?"

"What are the other rings?"

"All you need to know is loooong-short-short."

"Tell me the others, so I know."

"Okay. The Boyces, that's whose call you just interrupted, they're two long. That's looong-looong. Then there's Holmes down the road. They're short-short. And Palmers, folks from Boston who are mostly here on weekends. They're short-short-looong. You always know when they're up. The phone rings constantly."

"Okay, looong-short-short. That's us."

"That's right."

"Okay."

"Okay."

The screen door slapped shut behind Manny, leaving Rose staring out the door, into the whine of the lawnmower, which Manny resumed pushing around the house. Rose made her way back to the garden. How could a sixty-four-year-old woman not know how a telephone worked? What was she doing here, away from all her friends—and faucets you could open and toilets you could flush without someone shouting, "You're ahead of the pump!" or "It's country plumbing, for God's sake!"

At the garden gate, Rose remembered standing at the edge of

the playground, a towering ten-year-old among kindergartners who taunted her in a hateful language she had yet to learn.

"Greenhorn! Greenhorn!" they chanted as they jumped for her braids. "Dummy! Dummy!" they sang as they circled her, she standing stock-still, as if tied to a stake.

The teacher rescued her and walked her to her classroom. "This is the hook for your coat, Rose. Follow me, and I'll show you your desk." While the other children splashed paint on paper, Miss Reichsman taught Rose how to read and add, so that in only a few months, she moved up to first grade, and skipped to second by the end of her first year.

Despite the kindness not only of Miss Reichsman, but also Mrs. Young and Miss Holtz, recess was torture, and lunch worse, when the little girls teased her. "A big girl in baby class!" and mocked the accent that was still thick as her Old World shoes. "*Vat deed you brought for lunch, eh?*"

"Mom? Rose? Are you okay?" Jeannie pulled off her gardening gloves and put her hand on Rose's arm. Rose wiped tears from her cheeks.

"Oh. I'm a silly old woman, feeling sorry for myself." Rose tried to smile.

Jeannie put her arm across Rose's shoulder.

Rose wiped her face with the back of her hand, then checked her pockets. "I don't even have a Kleenex on me. What a mess!"

Jeannie pulled a rumpled hankie from her waistband. "Here. Use this." She waited before speaking. "Sometimes, we just need a good cry."

"No! No! No!" Rose shook her head. "It's not that. You know what I was thinking?" Before Jeannie could reply, Rose continued. "I was thinking about how when I first went to school I felt so out of place, didn't know how to play hopscotch or even how to dip a pen. And I'd looked forward to school all summer. So much confusion, coming to America. I thought, as soon as I go to school, I'll fit in." Rose looked up, tilting her head birdlike. "All because I dressed in the wrong clothes this morning, and I answered the phone when it rang, but it wasn't the right ring. How was I supposed to know? So here I am, an American citizen already, but here, in Vermont, I'm a greenhorn all over. Since I was a little girl, I've only lived in the city." Rose paused for breath. "So, *Bubeleh*, Sweetheart, how can I help? What do I know from weeds? All I ever grew was some nasturtium in a cheese box."

"Well." Jeannie threaded her arm through her mother-in-law's. "You buy your vegetables from a greengrocer, right?"

"Of course! Have you ever tasted vegetables from a tin can?" Rose grimaced.

"Right. So I bet you'll find a lot that's familiar. Here. Let me give you a tour."

Arm in arm, the two women walked down the central path. "Here are the early crops."

"That's spinach!" Rose pointed. "And that?"

"Leaf lettuce," Jeannie bragged. "Not that tasteless stuff from the store."

"That looks familiar." Rose pointed to feathery plants in a line on the ground.

"Those are carrot tops. And over there, beets."

"And onions?" Rose pointed. "And these?" Rose gestured toward several rows of thick, bumpy leaves emerging from hills of soil.

"Those are potatoes. Eating potatoes, as opposed to Vermont potatoes."

"So what's a Vermont potato?"

Jeannie bent over and picked up a spud-sized rock. "They multiply by magic. The more I improve the soil, the better my crop of rocks."

Both women laughed.

Jeannie walked Rose past the pea fence, the towers of pole beans, the neat columns of broccoli, cauliflower, and cabbage.

"What are the cans for?" Rose pointed to seedlings emerging from tin cans buried in the soil.

"To protect the plants from cut worm." Jeannie waved her hand over the plot. "We have the fence to keep out the deer, and I send Manny and Martin out here to pee, to stop the raccoons and rabbits and groundhogs," she sighed. "Sometimes, gardening is really a kind of warfare. We're constantly under siege. And the raccoons are the worst. Half this corn is for them."

"So many animals?" Rose peered into the trees.

Jeannie pointed out the hot-weather plants: tomatoes, green peppers, cucumbers, and summer squash.

"Isn't this a lot of food?" Rose asked.

"If I keep up with the weeds," Jeannie sighed. "If we get enough rain. If the animals don't get it. Or some withering wilt or beetle. I'll tell you, Rose, after keeping a garden, fifteen cents a pound for green beans is cheap, let me tell you."

The two were strolling back toward the gate.

"What are you going to do with so many tomatoes?" Rose asked.

"Every year I say I'm going to can them, but they come in just as we're getting ready to go home, so we eat as much as we can, and we bring some back with us, and I give Sally Boyce what's left. Her husband keeps an eye out on the place."

"So much work." Rose was shaking her head. "So much food." She clicked her tongue. "It's a shame to give it all away."

"If we had a freezer—" Jeannie didn't finish her thought. "Old-timers, like Sally, they don't believe in freezing. They can everything."

"Is that so hard?"

"It takes time," Jeannie said. "And it's hot work when I'd rather be swimming." She folded her arms across her chest and looked back at the garden taking root before her. "I don't know, Rose. I don't grow the food because I need to." The two women walked between the feathery leaves of asparagus plants. "I guess I just like to garden. Whatever food I get is a bonus."

Rose shrugged her shoulders. So much food, it should go to waste? How hard could it be to can vegetables?

Without Addie to grumble at the untidiness of starting plants indoors, Percy lined the windowsills with the business-half of egg cartons filled with dirt and seeds. Without Addie to scold, "And who do you think is going to put all that food up, I'd like to know?" Percy planted three varieties of tomatoes; sweet peppers *and* hot peppers; eggplant, which Addie never cared for; and cauliflower, broccoli, and cabbage, which she did. He also started leeks, because he'd been up to Poultney recently, where the Welsh quarrymen who came over to dress stone were dying off and the quarries closing and what else was he going to do in retirement but garden?

Percy sprayed water on the tiny knobs of green emerging from each egg-cup. Water droplets landed on the newspaper lining the windowsills, beaded up, then collapsed, bleeding into the print, just as each day's news blended into the next, all the same, all indistinct. Percy put down the sprayer and went to the piano.

Despite having done his share of work in fields and barns and machine shops on other people's farms over the years, his hands were those of a desk worker: smooth and fine and pliant, with clean nails trimmed close. He set them over the keys just as the photograph in *Beginning Piano* instructed, so that they curled down from the middle joint, the thumbs sharing middle C. The book advised placing a quarter on the back of each hand, forcing Percy to play with a painful deliberateness, to keep the coins from sliding to the floor. He was a strong man, used to splitting wood, tilling the garden with a spade, hauling hay bales and grain sacks and even shoveling manure on some farm visits. But none of it was as hard as keeping his hands still and playing a single note without the quarters slipping off his hands.

Percy kept at it, starting slowly and gradually gathering speed, until his arms shook and his shirt wilted with sweat. Neatly, he flipped the quarters into the air and caught them, then placed them on the double-wide space of B and middle C and pulled the cover over the keys.

It didn't seem likely he'd live long enough to learn to play. If he were really serious about learning, he'd have to take lessons. But who would teach him at his age?

No. He wouldn't think like that. It was no different from planting a garden. No different from opening up those envelopes filled with tiny seeds, each one holding the instructions for a new pumpkin or carrot. So he'd just think of himself as a giant beet cluster stuck in the ground to mature slowly. Or a parsnip, which didn't ripen until after the weather turned cold.

He wasn't so old, after all. With planning, he could turn this retirement into something good. After all, he wasn't being sent to the knacker's. No glue factory for this old dog. He wasn't dog meat. Maybe he'd get himself a dog. One of Mrs. Chaillot's border collies, and a small flock to keep the pasture clear. Or maybe he'd buy some day-old chicks and raise a few pullets. Awful good manure. His blueberries could use it. He could even raise a porker, if he knew what to do with all the meat. A single man was no match for a barrel of salt pork. A certain sadness overcame Percy at the thought of a barrel brimming with brine and no bairns of his own.

Percy'd had a chance to start a family. After Lila died, there was no end of young women put in his way. Like the time he'd helped out Nick Tassos with plans for his new greenhouse, and the Greek insisted Percy stay for dinner.

Nick handed Percy a tumbler of wine and gestured he should take a seat in the rocker. "Salut!" He lifted his glass and drank.

Percy sipped.

"So," Nick smacked his lips. "This is good, no?" He waved his arm across the farmyard, past the barn, the foundation for the greenhouse and the fields beyond.

"Very good," Percy agreed.

"I work hard." This was a statement, not a boast.

"You do," Percy agreed, lifted his glass and sipped. "Just running a farm is a lot of work. There are some operators, it's all they can manage. But you just do this on the side. You have the store!" The Tassos ran a market on Main Street, where they sold groceries along with their produce and the meat they raised right on their farm.

Nick nodded, moving his giant, dark head up and down. "But you see," he shook a finger at Percy. "I'm not like one of those operators got to find a market for my goods. I'm my own supplier. All the profits are mine. And," he leaned forward to speak confidentially, "I got a secret."

"What's that?"

"I make my own manpower!" Nick peered right into Percy's

face then exploded in knee-slapping laughter. He leaned back into his chair and swallowed more wine. "So how come you're not married, a college educated man like you? And not bad looking!"

"I was engaged," Percy confided. Piano music, like water rushing over stones, filled his ears.

"She left you?" Fierce light shone from Nick's deep set eyes.

"She died." Percy met Nick's stare.

"So you're broken hearted." Nick's face folded into deep creases. "I know, it hurts."

Percy remained silent.

"So," Nick said. "You know the cure?"

Percy looked at him blankly.

"The cure for your broken heart!"

Percy shook his head.

"You got to fall in love all over again. It's the only way to heal the human heart!" Nick stood up. "Come! I can tell dinner's about to be put on the table. You come eat with us. You look at my daughters. Maybe you like Eleanor. Maybe you like Christine. They're good girls. They make good wives. They'll make me American grandkids. Then I'll know I'm in this country to stay."

The food was as abundant and delicious as Eleanor and Christine were beautiful—and silent. Their dark eyes flashed between their father and Percy, then dropped to the tablecloth. The girls watched the floor as they carried dishes back and forth from the kitchen.

For weeks afterwards, Percy tried to decide between the two sisters. Which would he ask out? Where would they go? But he never decided. He never called. Nick would never let him take either girl out on a date, not until they were engaged to be married. And Percy couldn't face paying a call, sitting in the midst of that family hubbub. Not unless he was sure of his intentions. Not unless his intentions were to marry one of Nick's daughters.

Oppressed by memory, Percy stepped outside, where nascent leaves hung limp, like newborn fingers, their pale damp wrinkles reminding Percy of any number of calves he'd seen unfold upon delivery to the barn floor, any number of bean sprouts pushing up from the earth, thirsty for sun. And so, it happened yet again: another crop of maple leaves had emerged overnight. Locust, of course, would still be weeks in coming. But the ash, the birch, the oak, they'd all opened up and here he was to witness it once again.

He inhaled deeply, able to smell deeper than the odor of mud, which just weeks ago was intoxicating in its announcement of spring. Now, the bouquet was more complex with undertones of trampled grass, nearly ready for mowing. And daffodils bobbed on sprung stems, like overeager buttercups. The lilacs were ripening, not quite ready to spill their fragrance. That would come. But he, he'd made it to another spring. And all the promises of nature's explosion pleased him as he stood on the porch step.

But there was something sad about this season, too. For the first time, newborns, red and mewling, barely uncurled from their mothers, tugged at his loins. All these years of contented bachelor-hood, and suddenly, Percy missed children. His own children. He'd never had that thrill of palming an infant's head as he clucked at it. Never laid a swaddled mite out along his forearm and marveled at his own seed, the miracle of his own animal act. His own barren life.

Percy removed a spade from the shed, and set to work at the corner of the garden, turning up soil, breaking up the clods of winter. After just a few yards, he stopped to pull off his wool shirt, whose odor was all winter, and no longer right for the season.

The sun fell on his back as he dug fiercely, pushing his foot down on his shovel, stamping out questions he'd never asked before.

How come now, now that he was the age of a grandfather, did he start thinking about babies? Why not forty years ago, when he was a young man? After Lila died, why didn't he ever ask out Eleanor or Christine Tassos?

Percy finished tilling the plot he'd planted for the past dozen years, the small square patch Addie had confined him to. Why had he listened to her? Why did her scolding stop him from growing more vegetables, more flowers? He could have just given the surplus away. She didn't have to can it all. He'd never asked her to do anything in his life! Well, hardly.

Percy bent over his digging blade again and plunged it into the turf-bound soil. Why couldn't he double the size of his garden? Who said he had to save every bean he grew? So what if they all just hung on the vine till hell freezes over? He was going to grow whatever he wanted, harvest as much as he could. He would husband every seed and seedling. Come harvest—by the time it came to harvest—by then—he'd have figured out what he was going to do.

Percy washed at the sink, not the large, shallow enamel one that his mother had used, but the divided stainless steel one Addie had insisted on as part of the piecemeal renovations typical when one family lives long in an old house. This was one renovation Percy regretted.

"You can always make a large sink smaller by using a wash-pan," he'd argued. But Addie claimed a divided sink was what she wanted and all she wanted and it was the least a brother could do for the sister who fetches his meals and keeps house, after all.

So Percy installed the side-by-side stainless steel basins for his sister, and he was gentleman enough not to say anything when he saw her struggling to fill the canning kettle by dumping jarsful of water from the faucet, because the kettle was too big to sit in the sink.

The old sink was still out in the shed, and Percy had a mind to hang it back up, though it meant pulling out the cabinets he'd built. Undoing work—never mind it was a mistake in the first place—undoing work hurt.

Well, projects like that could wait until retirement. He scrubbed the garden dirt from under his nails and appraised the kitchen. He could lay down wall-to-wall in the parlor if he wanted, or get rid of the old horsehair sofa that gave you a backache just to look at, never mind sit on. He could go down to Emerson's and buy some comfortable upholstery, and he wouldn't have to argue with Addie about the color or price.

She'd never let him even finish saying, "Well, it ain't the world's most comfortable sofa!" No sooner than he'd start, Addie would interrupt, "But it's an antique!"

"I won't argue that with you, Addie," Percy would remain even-toned. "But it still ain't fit to sit on, heirloom or not."

Percy shook his head, still unable to sort out how Addie could dispose of a perfectly good kitchen sink and yet hold on to a torture rack of a couch, and in each instance support her decision with the same reason: "But it's an antique!"

Well, he couldn't make his sister out while she was living, what made him think it would be different now that she was dead? He strolled into her parlor, turned on the piano lamp, sat at the bench, hands poised, head bowed.

For three months, now, Percy had been working his way through *Beginning Piano*, learning not only the names of the notes, but also their kind: whole, half, quarter, eighth. He learned legato and staccato, pianissimo and forte, the figured bass and the singing, treble clef. In three months, Percy had learned everything *Beginning Piano* had to teach about the craft of playing music, everything but making music itself. It was like teaching someone the difference between a wood screw and a carriage bolt, a four-penny nail and a finishing brad, a ball-peen hammer and a Phillips-head driver, then taking them down to Putnam's and showing them clear pine, strapping, and two-by-fours, and expecting them to be able to frame out a house. Percy had been thorough, could play all the juvenile melodies exactly—or so he figured. How would he know if he was making a mistake? He wouldn't unless he tried playing music he knew, music he'd listened to, music that he wore under his skin, keeping time to the beating of his heart.

Percy folded back the cover of *Easy Classics for Piano* and stared at the first page. "Minuet" by Henry Purcell.

Holding the page open with his left hand, Percy plucked the notes with his right, humming out the melody, more mournful even than nightfall. Dusk had descended. It was long past supper. But Percy sat at the keyboard, willing himself to make music. He used Addie's hymnal to hold open the page and placed both hands on the keys. They were stiff from his day of digging. What if, now that he wanted to play the piano, he'd ruined his hands gardening? What if age and labor conspired to swell up his knuckles and stiffen his limbs? Well, he'd start wearing gloves in the garden. A vision of Lila pressing her hand into his bicep as she struggled over a stone wall on an autumn walk crossed his field of vision. And that hand, that hand that pressed against his coatsleeve, that hand that held the bouquet of flame red maple leaves he'd presented to her, that hand was gloved. Lila wore gloves year 'round. "I'm saving my hands for the piano," she told him. That was one of the enticements to listen to her play. She'd sit herself down at the instrument, adjust the position of the bench, then pull off her gloves. Watching the empty gloves on top of the piano only emphasized the ache of the music she made, the hollowness he felt, the hollowness that Lila filled with sound.

What were the chances he could ever, ever re-create that sound?

He laid his hands on the keys, and struck the first notes of the Purcell. Fire shot up his arms. His fingers scaled the melody, not even tripping over the G-sharp. He shifted his left hand to a new chord that made him want to weep, it was so sad. His hands flowed around the phrase, moved on.

Maybe you could give someone lumber and expect them to build a house.

His fingers found the keys within the narrow scope of this sorrowful tune. Without looking at the keyboard, Percy's fingers shifted from black to white. As if by instinct, he weighted one note, lifted his hand to lighten another. He was becoming the music, the black notes, the curved phrases, the white keys, the G-sharp. He played the way wind moves through trees, and when he was done, Percy rose stiffly and limped up to bed.

As he did nearly every day on his way home from work, Percy stopped in at Greenwood's to pick up his mail, the paper, milk and bread if he needed, and the news of the day. "Well, Barrett. How's business?"

"Not bad, Percy. Not bad. How's the farm business?" Barrett continued dusting soup tins with his feather wand.

"Could be better. Could be worse." Percy unfolded the *Phoenix* and settled on a high stool. The overhead fan droned. Flies buzzed. The sleigh bells strapped to the screen door jangled when Bill Holland swung into the store.

"Evening." He nodded to Percy.

"How are you, Bill?" Barrett boomed. "Been a while since we seen you."

"Aye." The whites of Bill's eyes, the only clean thing in his face, flashed from Percy to Barrett, then swept the store to see who else might be lurking behind the soap powder.

"What can I get you? Pack of Chesterfields?" Barrett slid the duster into his back pocket and ran his hands across the comfortable bulge of his belly held in check by the apron tied snugly around his middle. He slapped a pack of cigarettes on the counter and asked, "Anything else? The missus need milk?"

Bill headed for the back cooler and pulled out a bottle of Miller, stopping by the opener attached to the wall to flip off the cap. He tilted his head back and took a long swallow before swaggering back to the front counter, smacking the bottle down and picking up the pack.

Percy waited for Bill to light up before folding his paper. "You cut any hay yet?"

Bill waved the cloud of smoke out of his face, blew more out of the corner of his mouth and muttered, "Next week."

"Hope the weather holds." Percy laid the paper on the counter and folded his arms.

"He can't do nothing about the weather, Percy. You know that." Barrett rang up the charge for Bill's beer and smokes and pulled Bill's ledger card out of the accounts box. Even with his half-glasses settled low on his nose, Barrett held the card at arm's length to peer at the balance due. He shot a glance at Bill, cleared his throat, wrote down the day's charges and refiled the card with those of his other regulars.

"Tractor's broke," Bill explained.

"Sorry to hear it."

"Broken axle. Damn hole in Palmer's pasture."

"What the hell you mowing Palmer's for, before your own hay?"

Bill wiped his mouth on the back of his hand, then let his arm with the bottle hang loose at his side. To the floor he said, "Need the cash."

Barrett and Percy exchanged glances. Bill took another hard swallow of beer.

Percy spoke up, "Barrett, sir. Be a good man. I wouldn't mind one of those beers."

Barrett nodded and ambled down the aisle, straightening tins and jars and boxes along the way.

As soon as Barrett's back was turned, Percy asked, "Didn't you borrow seed money?"

Bill shook his head, still regarding the worn wood floor.

"It's not too late. You need help? Stop by the office tomorrow— or I'll come out to the farm."

Bill kept shaking his head. "It ain't no use, Percy. I still ain't paid off last year's. Bank wouldn't advance me more even if'n I asked."

Percy just nodded.

"Besides—" Bill raised his eyes, but his head hung low between his shoulders. "Better money mowing for the Palmers, doing handyman work."

Percy said nothing.

"They got friends is gonna rent the cottage for four weeks. Mabel's thinking about maybe taking in boarders. Weekends, you know. Lots of folks from out of state coming to Vermont for the summer."

Percy nodded.

Barrett returned with the beer. "Rubins are up, the folks who bought Pickerel's a couple, three years back. You know, the old farm next to the cemetery on Wheeler Hill. Have to say, appreciate their trade. Rubins always stop by."

Percy and Bill stared at the storekeeper leaning against his side of the counter.

Barrett straightened up. "Well, folks who drive—what is it? 200

miles?—for the summer probably don't think twice about driving over to the IGA in Waterchase or even all the way to the A&P."

"Aw, they probably shop here 'cause they think it's so quaint." Bill lit another cigarette.

"What does that matter as long as I get their business?" Barrett asked.

Bill emptied the smoke from his lungs. "Did you hear that folks from away bought Phillips's store over in Norwalk? But they ain't gonna run it like a regular store. They're gonna specialize in cheese and syrup and penny candy. Serve the tourist trade."

"Well, they better sell gas, then. 'Cause that's what these folks need more'n anything else. Gotta put gasoline in their automobiles." Barrett nodded in the direction of the front door. "Some weeks, I think it's selling gas that keeps me in the black, 'specially in winter, with all the skiers headed over to Mount Snow."

"Don't they never do any work down there? How come they got all this time to come vacation in Vermont?" Bill chugged the end of his beer. "Percy, you ever been on a vacation?" He shifted his glare from Percy to Barrett. "Have you, Barrett? Ever close up the store for two weeks and take off somewheres?" Both Percy and Barrett were shaking their heads. "Where do they get the money? That's want I want to know. Are they all filthy rich Jews?" Bill launched himself down the aisle to grab another bottle from the cooler.

"More likely, they're FDR Democrats," Percy called after him. "Don't understand the first thing about farming." Percy shook his head. "Favor industry—as if workers didn't have to eat! As if the production of food didn't come first!"

"Hear! Hear!" Bill raised his beer in a toast.

"But you're just playing into their hands by folding, Bill," Percy said. "Don't do it! As soon as we return the Republicans to government, we'll put some common sense into all these regulations that don't take into account how burdensome they are on a small operator. We don't all farm a flat square mile, like they do in Iowa. And out there, it's not the farmers who own the places. They're just the hired help, working for some giant corporation who's running on some kind of government subsidy. It just don't make sense, that's all."

"Well, I can't wait, Percy. I got bills to pay." Bill nodded to the shopkeeper, holding his bottle aloft. "Put another on my tab, Barrett. So long." As he reached for the door, he turned back. "Looks like customers. Out-of-state plates." Bill stepped aside, holding the screen door open while a girl and boy rushed past him to the candy counter.

Jeannie Rubin smiled, "Thank you," as she stepped in, then greeted Mr. Greenwood. Just as Bill was about to let go of the door, her husband and a white haired woman started up the steps. Bill backed up, holding the screen door wide, until they were all safely across the threshold.

The older woman swept past Bill with a certain elegance. "Hello, Mr. Greenberg. Did you get any sour cream yet?"

"No, Mrs. Mayer. How are you today?" Barrett lifted his eyebrows above the woman's head and nodded to Bill with a shrug.

Bill raised his chin to Percy. "Maybe shopkeepers is more important than farmers, Percy. Maybe you and FDR are mistook."

Rose turned to Bill, who nodded and ducked out the door, then smiled at Percy. "FDR mistaken? How can that be?"

Barrett unholstered his duster and busied himself around the spotless shelves, biting the corners of his smile.

Rose stuck her chin in the air. "FDR was the greatest president who ever lived! Better than George Washington, even!"

"Ma!" Manny interrupted, trying to steer Rose by the elbow to the back of the store.

She shrugged him off. "Don't you 'Ma' me! It's a free country! I have a right to say what I think! And I think Franklin Delano Roosevelt got us out of the Depression, and helped save the world."

"Ma," Manny whispered tersely. "Not everyone agrees."

"So? They don't agree, they can speak up for themselves." She looked Percy up and down on the high stool. "Well? Do you disagree?"

Percy stood and cleared his throat. Barrett stilled his duster. "Well, Ma'am, I agree that Roosevelt was president during some tough times. Times so tough, maybe they would have got better no matter who was in the White House. And maybe, in the meantime, we wouldn't have such a giant federal government stepping all over states' toes, and raising taxes beyond what an ordinary citizen can bear, and making folks so dependent on federal programs that they've just about forgot how to look after themselves." Percy coughed again, nodded ever so slightly to Rose, picked up his paper and quietly said, "Good evening," as he made his way out of the store.

Back home, Percy pulled on his gardening gloves and carried the hoe out to the garden without even stopping at the house. He hoed between the rows of carrots and potatoes, beets, cauliflower, broccoli, and Brussels sprouts, thinking of what he should have said to that woman. FDR may have pulled the country out of the Depression, but he pretty much squashed the right to free speech and a whole bunch of other civil liberties while he was at it. "Making the world safe for Democracy" while undermining the very democracy that showed the world what it was!

Percy scraped the soil, felling the weeds that sprouted in the two days since he'd hoed last. Seemed like at the least opportunity, a weed would take root. At the least opportunity, a president would become dictator. How else to explain four terms in office? It wasn't right. But maybe it was nature. Nature was always in tension between opportunity and design, always sending up new shoots to suck the nutrients from the soil and rob his plants of sunlight and water. Was he in conflict with Nature, then, by trying to make a garden grow? Nature always filled a void. Human nature was different. Human nature could nurture the good plants and weed out the bad. That's why he hoed: because that's how you kept a garden tidy, how you increased yield, how you unwound at the end of the day. Just breathing in time to the scratch, scratch, scratch of the hoe calmed him after a day of other people's problems: the new silage pit over to White's Dairy; poor germination in Otis's corn, maybe misapplied fertilizer, the soil test would explain. Bill Holland giving up wasn't a big surprise, but having a lady from away lecture him on FDR in Barrett's store—well that was maybe a bit rich.

Percy was in the corn patch when John Ready's old Chevy rattled to a halt in the yard. Percy kept hoeing between the rising blades of corn while John hoisted himself out of the truck and lumbered across the lawn. The big man stopped at the edge of the garden, folded his arms across his barrel chest and maintained a wide stance while working over a plug of tobacco.

Percy nodded.

John squirted tobacco juice onto the lawn.

At the end of the row, Percy shouldered the hoe and ambled toward his visitor, who nodded at the corn, "*Knee high by the Fourth of July!* Corn looks good."

Percy leaned on the hoe and regarded the garden. "It's coming along."

"Ain't that a bit much for a single man by hisself?" John's nod took in the whole spread this time, from the pea fence to the bean towers, from the corn patch to the potato hills, from the soil–filled tires sprouting cucumber vines to the row of sunflowers coming up along the edge nearest the house.

Percy shrugged.

"What are you going to do with it all, pal?" John spat again.

Percy toed the dirt. "Just grow it, I guess."

John squinted. "What do you mean, 'just grow it.' You just grow vegetables and you end up with crops! What you got there, a dozen tomato plants?" John waved toward the rows of tomatoes that Percy had transplanted at the beginning of June and which were now filling out.

"Best be staking them," Percy muttered. To John he confessed, "Two dozen, to be precise."

"Two dozen tomatoes!" John lifted his hat and stroked his bristled head with his large paw of a palm. He replaced his cap and whistled. "You ever hear of old ladies who hoard cats? You know, they start off with a couple, then they adopt another, three more. Then folks start dropping their kittens off at her place, and she starts feeding all the strays and they start breeding like rabbits and afore you know it she's got a hunnerd cats on the property and the house smells like piss and even her clothes don't smell good, but she's so used to it she can't tell no more. Until finally, some busybody calls the authorities and the town health officer pays her a visit and closes her down, hauls off six dozen cats to the pound."

Percy continued leaning against the hoe, studying the ground. When John paused, he looked up with raised eyebrows. "So?"

"Why, man, that's what's happening to you here with your tomatoes! You're gonna have to set up a farm stand and sell 'em by the side of the road!"

Percy just nodded while John wheezed at his own joke. John wiped his eyes on his sleeves, his belly bouncing as he repeated,

"Percy Mendell selling tomatoes at the side of the road!" Finally, John coughed and regained composure. "No offense meant," he reached out to pat Percy on the shoulder.

"None taken," Percy assured him. "I just like to garden."

The two stood in silence a few moments, each looking out past the meadow, into the woods beyond. Percy broke the silence first. "Long days, end of June."

John nodded.

Percy hoisted the hoe to his shoulder and started walking back to the shed. John followed in his rolling, stiff-hipped gait. He waited for Percy to shelve the gardening gloves and latch the shed door. Together, they walked to a spot halfway between the porch and John's truck.

"Fourth of July's this Saturday," John stated. "The Committee asked me to ask you if you'd be a judge again this year. And the emcee."

"'Course," Percy nodded. "Pleased to."

"Parade starts at nine. See you about eight-thirty then?"

"Sure thing."

"Well, best be moving along. Fire meeting tonight."

"Say hello to the boys for me."

"Sure will."

John heaved himself back into his truck and was leaning out the driver's side window. "So long, Percy."

"Thanks, John. Thanks for stopping by."

The truck roared into gear and rattled away, John's beefy arm waving out the window.

3 | fourth of july

They were out of the woods and driving on pavement, where the open landscape was almost as baffling to Rose as the forested one: vast empty spaces strung together by telephone wires connecting the occasional farmhouse. Rose didn't exhale fully until they came to the village with its collection of white buildings clustered alongside the road.

The crowd was thickest near the intersection that marked the town center: Town Hall, Greenwood's Store, the steepled church, and the elementary school. The fire house, the parsonage, and Grange all extended the village down the road before the civic buildings gave way to village homes, each decorated with flags and tricolored bunting. Petunia and geraniums added festive color in window boxes of houses with dark green shutters and red painted doors.

Rose held Wendy's hand as they walked behind Manny and Jeannie, who were waving and saying hello to people left and right, as if they were the parade and all these people had lined the street to see them.

"Do you know all these people?" Rose asked as they squeezed

into place near the Town Hall.

"To say hello to," Manny said.

"You say hello to just anybody? Even people you don't know?"

"It's a country thing," Manny said. "You say hello to everyone."

"And we do know a lot of these people. Who they are, anyway," Jeannie said, placing a hand on Rose's shoulder and turning her toward the town hall. "Those people on the porch," she explained, "They're the judges for the parade. Mr. Boyce is the man in the plaid shirt. He and Sally live just up the road. He mows our field."

Rose nodded. She'd heard of the Boyces.

"The man next to him, that's John Ready. He works for the town. Foreman of the road crew, I think. He's also fire chief."

"Two jobs?" Rose shrugged.

Jeannie continued. "I'm not sure who the man with the white hair is."

"That's the man from the store who doesn't like FDR." Rose frowned.

"Well, that's not surprising for a Vermonter," Manny said. "It's a Republican state."

Rose just shook her head. This is where her son wanted to spend his summers, who was she to argue?

A woman wearing a hat, gloves, and tailored dress joined the knot of judges. "That's Mildred Aitcheson," Jeannie's voice hardened. "She's the state rep from Orton."

"A woman?" Unmistakable approval broke into Rose's voice.

"A woman," Jeannie frowned. "A woman who opposes the state budget because she thinks towns should be in control of everything, like education, from funding to curriculum. She's a woman who wants to keep the town farm, a medieval system of caring for the poor by enslaving them. Her idea of a compromise was to support a sales tax instead of the income tax. She may dress like a woman, but she thinks like a man: Punish the poor, under-educate the children, put the old folk out to freeze."

Rose shook her head in disapproval. "I guess you don't like her much."

"There's not much to like!"

"Not much to like about what?" Manny asked, rejoining their conversation.

"Mildred Aitcheson!" Jeannie fumed.

"Lower your voice!" Manny warned. "Remember the majority of these people voted for her."

"That's what I don't understand," Jeannie shook her head. "They all seem so nice—until you hear their politics!"

Shaking her head, Rose muttered, "He's probably against labor unions and Social Security and the WPA."

"Who are you talking about?" Jeannie asked, but before Rose could answer, Percy stepped up to the mic.

"It's starting!" Wendy jumped as the crowd pushed back to make room for the sheriff's car, polished to a high shine. Orton's own Abel Towne, former state senator and the parade's grand marshal, followed.

The crowd applauded. "You're looking good, Abel," crackled from the speaker sitting atop a stepladder on the town hall porch.

Abel turned to the review stand and tipped his straw boater. "How do, Percy!"

A dozen veterans of the Great War marched behind Abel, visibly sweating in their woolen uniforms. Male spectators bared their heads as the standard bearer passed in front of them with the Stars and Stripes slung in a leather harness. Rose placed her hand over her heart. Even though she disapproved of warfare, she had World War I to thank for getting Sam out of Europe.

Sam's parents refused to leave, even though all his older sisters and brothers were long gone, mostly to America, one to Argentina, and another only as far as Antwerp. Becky, his favorite, was settled in Philadelphia, and often wrote, urging Sam to come; he could work in their grocery. If he wanted to go to New York, she'd make sure Lotty took him in; after all, it was a sister's duty. Isaac, in Buenos Aires, worked too hard to write, but Sam knew he could go there, go into banking. Julius sent money from Antwerp; the offer to join him in the diamond trade stood firm. But Sam stayed because if he left, who would look after their parents? They were rooted in the mud of Galacia, waiting only to be buried there. When they were tucked into the cemetery next to their kin, then he would leave. Someone had to see to that.

But Sam's plans changed in 1914. Even his parents agreed he had to leave, if he still could. Twice, en route from Lvov to Antwerp, he was stopped at the German border. The third time, the border guard recognized him and said that he would personally escort him back to Lvov that afternoon. Even though his teachers had thought Sammy was stupid because, as a natural lefty, his right-handed cursive was poor, Sam was no dummy. He bought the guard lunch. They ate well, drank beer, laughed, smoked after the meal. Sam excused himself to use the toilet; the guard nodded, and Sam slipped onto the train. In Antwerp, Julius tried to talk him into learning how to cut diamonds, but Sam decided it was time to go to America. Julius should come, too.

"America's barbaric!" Julius taunted. "Stay here. Europe is the civilized place to be."

Sam shook his head. Julius sported a round belly beneath his tailored broadcloth. His hands were clean; he had a fat wife and plump daughters. "I'm young," Sam said. "Europe is old." With Julius's blessing, Sam sailed.

The high school marching band was just finishing "America

the Beautiful" when Rose reentered the present. The bass drum thumped inside Rose's chest and the snares made her knees flutter.

"The clown!" Wendy squealed as she dropped Rose's hand and scrambled along the ground, picking up as many cellophane wrapped sweets as she could grab before other children snatched them. "Look, Grandma! Look at how much candy I found!"

"Candy?" Rose slapped it out of Wendy's hand. "You can't eat candy off the street!"

"Mom," Manny interfered. "It's okay, Mom."

Wendy scootched down to retrieve what had fallen.

"What do you mean, it's okay? Okay to eat candy thrown in the gutter? Since when is it okay to eat candy from strangers? Tell me, has the world become such a safe place?" She turned from Manny to Wendy. "Give it here. I'll buy you candy. At Greenberg's store, whatever you want."

Wendy appealed to her father while hugging her loot to her chest.

"Greenwood's, Mom. It's Greenwood's Store."

"Greenberg, Greenwood. I'll buy her candy at the store. My granddaughter, she doesn't have to eat candy off the ground. What *mishegoss*! Craziness!"

Wendy stepped into the protection of her mother's flank.

"You're going to let her eat that?" Rose glared at Jeannie.

"It's okay, Rose. Really."

"It's okay she should be poisoned? Your own daughter?"

"Believe me, Rose," Jeannie said, her hands resting on Wendy's shoulders. "The clown's the minister's son. They're not out to poison their own flock."

"Stop fighting, ladies. Here come the fire trucks!"

The whole crowd stepped back to let the road-hogging machines rumble by. The white eye of the sun bounced off the gleaming hood of the first engine.

"Orton Volunteer Fire Department," Rose read the gold lettering. "What's that mean, 'Volunteer Fire Department?'"

"Men volunteer," Manny answered.

"Men volunteer to do what?" Rose wanted to know.

"To put out the fires!" Manny reined in his voice. "They're not paid. They do it as a public service." He smiled and waved at a familiar face riding the running board of the next truck.

"Orton Center, Volunteer Brigade," Rose read on the door. The driver sounded the siren and flashed the lights as it passed the review stand.

"So many fire trucks," Rose noted, reading the door panel of the third to drive by. "Norwalk, Pumper One." She turned to Manny. "In Norwalk, are they all volunteers?"

"Yes, Ma. They're all volunteers. All these small towns depend on volunteers."

"So what happens if there's a fire?"

"The volunteers rush to the station, start up the truck and do their best to put the fire out."

"Are they successful?"

"I guess so. Some of the time, anyway. There are an awful lot of old buildings still standing."

"Here comes another. Waterchase, this one." It was bigger and newer than the rest, and was followed by a low gray hearse that had "Ambulance" written backwards across the hood. "Windham Valley Hospital," Rose read the red writing along the side. "Are they crazy? They think a sick person is going to get into a hearse?"

"Ma! Calm down! It's just a small hospital. The Funeral Home donated its old hearse, okay? You should want sick people to ride in the back of a truck?" Manny rolled his eyes. "Look! Here comes the Norwalk Coronet Band."

The marchers, in snappy red jackets, broke into a Sousa march that had everyone within earshot forget the mounting heat, unless they were watching a middle-aged trumpeter whose face was as red as his coat and who looked as if he would as soon explode as hit the next note. Loud applause followed the band's performance, followed by the bandleader's shrill whistle instructing the musicians to turn smartly and march on.

Two dozen men, about Manny's age, marched by in their Eisenhower jackets.

"Manny," his mother said, tugging at his elbow. "You could have marched!"

He nudged her away.

"Well, you could have!" Rose insisted.

"You weren't so keen on me joining the army."

"Well, what did you expect? When a woman has only one son, what? She should be glad to send him off to war?"

"Fine, Ma. It's okay. Just don't make me out to be a hero, or pretend it was easy times, okay?"

Rose nodded, wiping a tear stinging her eye.

It was after Sam was dead four years already. They were just getting back on their feet, coming out of the Depression. And what happens? Manny leaves college to enlist.

"You couldn't wait to be drafted?" She shouted when he came home to tell her. "What? I've been working for the army all these years, raising a soldier?"

Manny didn't say anything until the flood of her anger ebbed. Then, standing with military straightness, he said, "Ma, it's the right thing to do."

She closed the gap between them and hugged him around the waist. "You've done the right thing, Manny. I'm proud of you, son." And she cried into his shirt.

He had written her from basic training, somewhere in the humid South. In one of his letters he mentioned a girl back in Brooklyn, Jeannie, who he planned to marry—if he came back.

That was a low blow, and Rose sat down hard on a kitchen chair after reading it. But what could she expect? That he'd be a mama's boy all his life? What was she thinking? That Manny would take Sam's place?

"Get a hold of yourself, Raizel!" Her words fell flat in the empty apartment. Shaking her head back and forth, the letter crumpled in her fist, she muttered, "Rose Rubin, what are you going to do with your life?"

The first thing she did was go the the Red Cross, where she donated blood and picked up a bag of cotton thread. Back home, she knit bandages non-stop, praying at the end of each row that her Manny would be spared injury, but bargaining with God for an injury over death, nevertheless.

When the telegram came saying he'd been wounded, she'd feared all kinds of *tsuris*. A lost limb, a lost face, lost manhood, a brain injury, God forbid. She worried herself until her kitchen, ordinarily clean, was spotless. She probably would have scrubbed the paint off the walls if one day, two weeks later, the doorbell hadn't rung. She peeked through the spy hole and saw a stunning young woman.

"Yes?" she opened the door.

"I'm Jeannie Oxner," the young woman said. "Manny's fiancée."

Rose threw her arms around the girl and cried into her shoulder "Come in! Come in!" She pulled her into the apartment, then held her at arm's length. "You're a beauty! And you really love my son?"

Jeannie's dimples punctuated her face as she nodded and her

black curls bobbed. But her smile fell as the older woman shut the door and said, "So you know what happened? I got a telegram saying he's been shot."

"I know. I know, Mrs. Rubin. But it's really good news."

"He's wounded and it's good news? How's that?"

Jeannie pulled a letter from her handbag. In Manny's handwriting. It was like a stab in the heart, him writing to his fiancée instead of his mother. Jeannie held the letter out for Rose to read, explaining, "It's only a bullet wound to the arm. It means he'll be out of the trenches, away from the front. He'll be safe for a while."

Rose fell on the girl again, then straightened up. "Come. Come and have a glass of tea."

Rose didn't catch up to the parade until the new town plow, several tractors, and a troop of Boy Scouts had passed by.

"Ladies and gentlemen," the P.A. rasped. "The Honorable Jonathan Squires! Barney Johnson! Wallace Cook!" Polite applause greeted each of the political hopefuls. "I'm sure each of them would be glad to talk to you after the parade, so don't be shy. Introduce yourselves and give 'em a piece of your mind. Better yet, invite them to the pie toss on the side lawn next to the fire house at three o'clock this afternoon."

The three politicos shook their heads and waved toward the review stand. "That Percy! Now why don't he run for office?" Wallace Cook asked the nearest group of spectators.

As far as Rose could tell, these three looked pretty much like politicians anywhere, except they seemed to know everyone's name when they leaned into the crowd to shake hands. She'd listened to speeches, but she'd never touched an elected offical, not even a union boss.

"There's Marty!" Wendy pointed to her brother peddling at a careful pace so that the playing card he'd clothespinned to the frame of his bike fluttered against the spokes in a satisfying staccato. The "ching–ching" of bicycle bells alternated with the honk of rubber–bulbed horns as the cluster of decorated bikes ended the parade.

Just as the walls of people lining the route were about to collapse into the roadway behind the cyclists, Percy's voice boomed over the speaker. "Whoa! Whoa there, folks! The parade ain't over yet. Keep your places please!"

"What's going on?" Rose stepped back to the edge of the pavement.

"We have some prizes for the marchers, and we'll be giving them out as the parade passes back." Percy covered the mic with his hand while the judges consulted a moment. Then he leaned back to the microphone. "Mildred here is going to present the ribbons."

"What? We're going to see the parade again?"

"While we're waiting for the parade to turn around," Percy addressed the crowd, "I've been asked to remind you that the Annual Orton Fourth of July Street Fair will get underway immediately after the parade! There's a white elephant booth; a Christmas booth; Helene's Pantry for all your fancy jams and fine relishes; books for sale at the library; and a bake sale at the church. Chicken barbecue will start serving at noon. That's half a chicken, cole slaw, potato salad, pickle, roll and butter, hot coffee, and a slice of watermelon, all for a dollar and a half. Can't beat that! And don't forget, pie throwing." A commotion of voices called to Percy. "Hold on a minute." He turned away to consult, then picked up the mic. "Sorry about that," he straightened up. "My mistake. It's a pie-eating contest, going to happen right here, between the town hall and the fire house at three o'clock this afternoon. Be sure to sign up!" Percy peered up the street. "For the kids, there's a bean-bag toss, a fishing pond, and a dart throw. For you gamblers, there's bingo upstairs at the fire house, starting as soon as the parade is over. Finally, keep your strength up. Tonight at seven, square dance at Town Hall with the Sap Boilers providing the music. Larry Larken will call.

"Well, looks like the parade is just about to start back, folks. Step back, and let's see what we've got this year for best fire truck!"

As the awards droned on, the crowd buzzed, turning to applaud now and then, and remaining politely in place until the kids on their bikes finally brought up the rear.

"It's as hot as Florida," Rose dabbed her forehead with a hankie. "Good thing I wore my hat." She pulled the straw bonnet from her head and fanned herself.

"Let's go find some shade," Jeannie suggested, as they were swept along by the stream of pedestrians flowing toward the games and handcrafts set up on the side lawns around the village.

"Good morning, ladies," a tall, angular woman greeted them. "Mrs. Rubin, I can't tell you how disappointed I was this morning. Even though I was here quite early, your cake was already sold. I'd hoped so much to be the one to get it, too."

"That's very kind of you to say so, Mrs. Robinson. If you like, I'll make another," Jeannie offered.

"Would you? That would be so kind! I'll make a donation to the church, just as if I bought it here today."

"You'll have to wait until I can get down to Waterchase to buy sour cream. Mr. Greenwood doesn't carry it."

"He doesn't? Well, I'll have to talk to him about that. He's my brother-in-law, you know."

"I didn't know," Jeannie said, shaking her head. "My mother-in-law," Jeannie turned to Rose, "has already pestered Mr. Greenwood for sour cream."

"How do you do. I'm Mabel Robinson." Mabel nodded at Rose with an air of approval.

"Rose Mayer." Rose nodded back.

"Don't worry about Barrett." Mabel looked at both women. "It takes a fair bit of nagging to get him to do anything different from what he's done before. But men are like that." Mabel shrugged. "I should know." She leaned toward Rose. "I've been married to three, and mother to four." She continued in a half-whisper, leaning forward from her waist. "The reason men make such a fuss over women changing their minds all the time is, they never do, even when they're wrong! Can't never admit they've made a mistake."

Rose chuckled.

"Ah, I see you agree! Well, Mrs. Rubin, Mrs. Mayer," she nodded to each of them. "You enjoy yourselves, and I'll talk to Barrett about stocking sour cream in that store of his."

As soon as they were a safe distance away Rose said, "I never expected her to be so opinionated! She looks so straight-laced!"

"Vermont is full of surprises, Rose. Not least of which is who is related to whom, and just about everyone is—except us. So you really do have to be careful what you say."

"Where's Wendy?" Rose clutched her bag and looked around.

"With Manny, and it will be a toss-up who's having the most fun. Shall we go see the needle crafts?"

They walked into the Evening Star Grange. Jeannie stopped to chat with a cluster of women, so Rose wandered from table to table, fingering the crafts on display: the embroidered linen table runners, the quilted patchwork, the knitted sweaters and crocheted baby blankets, the homemade dresses and skirts. Memories tugged at her heart like a knotted thread. She acknowledged the needle-women's eyes upon her as she admired a buttonhole or inspected a seam. She nodded and mumbled, "Nice work," but in truth, Rose squinted in the poor light of Rev Asche's workshop, where for two years she'd plied her needle from Sunday morning till Friday dusk.

She'd wanted to continue at school. Her teachers had encouraged her. "Rose, you're smart Rose. Go to high school. Make something of yourself!" Mr. Sullivan even came to speak to her parents, but her mother shrank into the kitchen, and her father refused to acknowledge the Irishman standing by the door.

Caught between her father and her teacher in the stuffy front room, Rose translated her father's words. "He says," Rose said, meeting Mr. Sullivan's sunny blue eyes, "He says the family needs my wages more than the world needs an overeducated woman." Rose blushed and studied the floor.

Mr. Sullivan persisted, speaking directly to Mr. Markowitz. "With a high school education, your daughter will be able to get a better job, as a secretary or a bookkeeper." The teacher continued in the face of the father's implacable passivity. "In America, high school is free!"

Rose stood mute. Why translate? Her father had said no. Nothing Jim Sullivan could say would change his mind. "Thank you, Mr. Sullivan." Why wouldn't he just leave? "My father thinks it's best for me to work until I marry." She thought her cheeks would burst into flame.

Mr. Sullivan first shook his rusty-haired head, as if to contradict what he was hearing, and then he nodded. He understood. "There's always night school, Rose." He spoke confidentially in the doorway.

"And there's always—how do you say?" Rose hesitated for the English, "The school of knocks?" She tapped her fist lightly against her skull.

Mr. Sullivan laughed, which made him look younger, less careworn.

"School of Hard Knocks," he told her. "And everyone goes to that school, even when they're educated!"

They stood an awkward moment longer. Rose saw that his shoes needed polish. Her head started to ache from his steady gaze. "Well, good-bye, Mr. Sullivan." She shook her head with a hasty glance at her father, and the teacher winced, pocketing his hand-shake. He nodded curtly toward the bearded man shrouded in his Old World ways. Then he was gone.

At fourteen, Rose left school. No amount of begging could change her father's mind. Her mother, too, said, "*Sheine*, my beauty, we need the money. You go to work, double the family's income."

She worked for a *landsman*, Rev Asche, who'd been nothing in Zolochev but a tailor, the butt of all jokes. Here, he employed four girls to work in the front room of his tenement flat, the same room his four sons slept in at night.

The girls sewed in silence while Mr. Asche cut the fine wool and fit the jackets to the customers who called. Mrs. Asche toiled in the kitchen, not three yards from where the girls stitched, stitched, stitched, teasing their hunger with the smells of her cooking, the aromas heartier than the midday meal she served them of bread and meager soup. Like the end of the thread they pulled through the cloth, the girls' stomachs were knotted with hunger and some-thing more—a craving for life.

The days of enforced quiet—Mr. Asche raising his eyes over his spectacles to silence even a sneeze—drained the girls of their voic-es, so that when they finally gained the street at the end of their day, they were too weary for more than the briefest "Good day, I'll see you tomorrow," or "*Gut Shabbes*," before a blessed day of rest.

It was this day of rest that provoked Rose's father. Rose figured if she couldn't go to school, she could at least get a factory job with better hours, better wages, and time off to go to the movies or concerts at the Settlement House. She didn't have to slave away in the Rev Asche's workshop for so little life, so little pay. Not in America. So she found herself a job at a shirtwaist factory, Monday to Saturday, 8 to 5.

"You will not work on *Shabbes*!" Papa had roared.

Rose stood silent, her head full of argument. If she had to go to work, if the family really needed the money, then how could he complain? This job paid twice as much to start with, and there was room for advancement.

"No daughter of mine is going to work on the Sabbath!" He shouted at her obstinate quiet.

She waited for the wash of his words to drain away. They stood facing one another, his trembling lips glossy with spittle in the center of his black beard; her fingers knotted together, so as not to betray her fear. She cocked her head to the side as she looked up at him, like a street urchin sizing up a man whose pockets she might pick.

On Monday, she started her new job, thrilled by the rows upon rows of coworkers at machines on either side of the workroom. By Tuesday lunch time, she had new friends. By Wednesday, she'd been asked to join the union, and by sundown Saturday, she had a fat pay envelope in her hands.

She handed the money to her mother, who removed a small sum and pressed it into Rose's hand. "For your pleasures," her mother said. They heard the door from the street open and shut. "Hide it," her mother urged, quickly tucking the envelope into her apron. Footsteps could be heard climbing the stairs. "Your father is back! It's time for the *havdalah*!" Rose joined her mother and sister at the table, where a braided candle stood next to a glass filled with wine.

Her father opened the door, touched his fingers to his lips and then to the *mezuzah* before crossing the threshold. In that simple gesture, Rose saw that her father loved God more than he loved her. That scroll that he kissed every time he entered the house was proof. He could forget to kiss her, his own flesh and blood, but not the words written on the parchment inside the little case nailed to the door jamb: *O Israel! The Lord our God is One!* He would sooner let his daughter rot in ignorance than forget to love the Ruler of the Universe. To serve Him with all his heart and with all his soul. To inscribe these words upon the doorposts of his house.

Her father's eyes glanced past her as he nodded to her mother and sister. He stood at the table and lit the double candle. As if warming his hands in the flame, Papa bid farewell to Queen Sabbath, to the end of rest and to the beginning of work, just the way God separated the darkness from the light. He lifted the wine to his lips and chanted his prayer to the Lord of the Universe and handed the glass to his wife. Before Hannah could pass the goblet to Rose, as was the custom, Papa took it back and handed it to Lena, Rose's younger sister. He reclaimed it again and raised it high, his eyes lifted to the ceiling. He boomed, "God created the Heaven and the Earth. God gave us the Ten Commandments. God commanded that we keep the Sabbath. Only those who keep God's day of rest can bid it farewell." He downed the remaining wine in a noisy gulp, placed the empty cup on the table, and retreated to his chair.

"Aaron!" Hannah followed after him, pulling Rose's pay envelope from her waistband. "Look what our Rosela has brought home!"

Aaron waved her away with the back of his hand.

"It's twice as much as she earned at Rev Asche's," she said, setting her jaw.

Aaron said nothing.

"You want to push her away, too? You want all your children to leave you?" Tears crept into her voice.

"I want my children to obey Torah!"

"It's a new world, Aaron. There are new ways of doing things." Hannah's voice trailed off as her shoulders sagged.

"What are you talking about?" Aaron sneered. "It is written, *Observe the Sabbath*. It doesn't say, *Observe the Sabbath when it's convenient*. It is also written, *Honor thy Father and Mother*. Does she do that? Did I ask her to work in a factory? No! I forbade it! And what did she do? Does she honor her father?"

"She gave us her earnings, Aaron. She's working because you said she couldn't go to school." Hannah shook her head sadly.

"Some *goldeneh medina*!" Aaron spat. "Golden country? It's a country that worships gold!"

"You got another way to buy groceries?"

"I don't care. My daughter will not work on *Shabbes*!"

"I can't stop her. You'll have to tell her yourself."

"I will not. I will not talk to a girl who disobeys her father. I will not talk to a Jew who breaks the Holy Day of Rest!"

And he didn't. He didn't speak to Rose again for almost two years. In the space of five-hundred square feet, they lived parallel to each other, without touching. At the table, they eavesdropped on one another, but spoke aloud only to Hannah or Lena.

Against the backdrop of her father's silence, Rose heard the music of the dance hall, the clamor of the street, the organ in the movie houses. Even the hum of the machines at the factory trilled merrily in her ear, singing the cacophony of her yearning. With her friends Lilly and Esther, she went to the movies, she window-shopped on Grand Street, she bought factory-made clothes on Orchard. With Lilly and Esther, she discovered the pleasures of dancing and meeting young men, though they only told their parents about the movies. Even her mother would object to Rose's dancing with strangers, some of them not even Jewish.

Her parents kept talking about her marriage, but she didn't think they had anyone in mind. Besides, until Lena could start working, they couldn't afford to lose Rose's income. As long as she could keep Lena in school, Rose could dream of love while her parents dreamt of a groom with *yichus*. Prestige. What was it? In the Old Country, it was learning. In the new, it was money. So would her parents find her an engineer from Columbia? What Jewish boy ever went to a *goyishe* university? What graduate of *cheder* ever learned anything useful for living in the *goldeneh medina*? It was a paradox, a puzzle that couldn't be solved.

So Rose, she went out and had fun, even learned a little something. She signed up for classes at the Settlement House. First, she just wanted to speak better, lose her accent and sound American. Miss Kahn encouraged her to attend a literature class. Reading *Leaves of Grass,* Rose fell in love with the language. Miss Kahn lent her carefully chosen stories, then made herself available for discussion. She invited Rose to join a series of classes, but Lilly and Esther wouldn't come. Rose tried to content herself at the dance hall, but she found herself returning to the well-lit parlor of the Settlement, where she could read until late at night.

It was at the Settlement House that Rose heard her first quartet, which pulled the strings of her heart so taut she lost her breath and had to loosen the collar of her blouse. Her blood rose with the violin's song, and she felt faint until the deep voice of the cello sounded and steadied her.

Music filled her father's silence and gave Rose both solace and courage. Because she was skilled, the forewoman gave Rose first buttonholes and then finish work, but soon the novelty of even these tasks wore off, and the raises that accompanied the promotions weren't enough to conquer the boredom. Not even the socializing counterbalanced the repetitive drudgery of factory sewing. Rose found a better job.

Mrs. Mercedes taught Rose fine millinery at her hat shop on Fifth Avenue. First, Rose followed Mrs. Mercedes's instructions, trimming and tucking, sewing invisible stitches, pleating slick silk and creamy wool. Next, Mrs. Mercedes gave Rose fashion magazines and a pencil and paper. "Design a hat!" she said. Rose, whose handwriting was loose and loopy from lack of practice, couldn't sketch anything remotely resembling a hat, and chin at a tilt, told her boss, "I can't draw it, but I can make you the hat I see in my mind."

Mrs. Mercedes raised her penciled eyebrows.

Rose was sure she was going to be fired.

"Okay. Show me what you can do!"

Rose's hands trembled at first, but as she tacked jet beads to the side of her creation, her needle obeyed her ideas, and in less than an hour she was able to present the image of her eye to her employer.

Mrs. Mercedes regarded the hat and then the girl. "Maybe you can't draw," she finally said, "but you certainly know how to design a hat."

Rose sighed as she moved along from one table to the next, pausing in the present in front of a display of quilts. Out of habit, Rose touched the work, running her fingers over the waves of colored patchwork that spelled out the design. Without thinking, she turned over a corner to the back side of solid white and made a sharp, involuntary noise.

The woman behind the table looked up.

"This work is exquisite," Rose said, holding the quilt's corner so that she could admire the pattern of tiny, even, white stitches against the white cotton backing.

"It's called 'Tree of Life,'" the woman said, unfurling the quilt so that Rose could admire the pattern of stitch work on the white ground. "It's frequently paired with this pattern on the other side." She flipped a corner over to the front of bright fabrics pieced together. "This pattern is called 'Dawn,'" she explained. "It's just two-inch squares, but what makes it interesting is the arrangement of the colors, from dark to light, so that at a distance it looks like morning light breaking through the night."

Now Rose was inspecting the binding of the front and back. "It's beautiful," she said.

"I can tell you sew," the woman said. "You can always tell when someone is a sewer by how they admire the work." She smiled at Rose.

Rose nodded.

"Would you like to join us?"

Rose tilted her head, not quite understanding.

"We have a quilting club. Meets every Tuesday. Right now we're working on a quilt for Anna Mae's daughter, who's getting married in September. It's a Double Wedding Ring."

"You mean this is the work of a committee?"

The woman laughed. "Well, not exactly. Everyone does her own piecework, you see. But the quilting is done on a quilting frame. Half a dozen of us sit around the quilt and stitch the pattern on the back side. We meet here—the Orton Grange—Tuesdays at seven. Come watch."

Rose took a small step backwards, not understanding.

"Oh, I'm sorry," the friendly woman apologized. "I'm Irma. Irma Basset." She smiled. "I know you're staying with the Rubins. Mr. Rubin's mother, I think?"

Rose nodded. "Rose Mayer," she said. "How did you know who I was?"

Irma laughed. "This is a small town!"

Rose straightened her skirt, checking her hem that her slip wasn't showing. There wasn't anything that would escape notice here.

"Will you join us?"

Rose liked Irma's deep rumble of a voice. Was she the woman on the phone? Rose felt her cheeks flush. "Maybe to watch." Rose frowned. 'But I'll have to see—see what the family is up to."

"Mrs. Rubin is welcome, too."

Rose shook her head. "She gardens."

The two ladies exchanged a look of comprehension.

"I have to go find her. Nice meeting you." Rose turned to leave.

"I hope we'll see you at the quilting bee!"

Rose drifted toward the door, only vaguely aware of well-executed crewel embroidery, and a chair elegantly upholstered in needlepoint.

"Now what?" Rose blinked in the bright sun where the whole family was waiting.

"Home for lunch," Jeannie said.

"We're going?" Rose asked.

"We've been here all morning," Manny said.

"Do you want to stay longer?" Jeannie asked.

"You could come back and pick me up maybe?"

"Ma, you'll get tired," Manny said.

"What do you think I am?" Rose asked. "An old woman?"

"Okay, okay." Manny stood up and looked at his watch. "We'll be back at three. We'll meet you by the steps to town hall."

"Can I stay with Grandma?" Wendy asked.

"No, honey," Jeannie took Wendy's hand. "You have to rest before swimming."

"But I'm not tired!"

"Do you want to go to the square dance later?" Jeannie asked.

Wendy stuck the end of her pigtail in her mouth and started dragging her feet behind Manny as they made their way to the car.

Rose felt a weight drop from her shoulders as they filed out of sight. It was probably the first time she'd been left alone, and she'd been in Vermont, what? ten days already. *Gevalt!*

Rose looked for the Orton Public Library, expecting one of Andrew Carnegie's brick edifices to rise alongside the road, but all she saw were white clapboarded buildings with green shutters. She finally had to ask where the library might be, only to discover it occupied a single room inside the town hall.

A welcome draft of cool air embraced her as she entered the semi-dusk of the public building. On the right-hand side of the hall was a door leading to a large room with two floor-to-ceiling windows and walls lined with books. On the oak table in the center of the lofty room were long rows of books laid out so that their spines were facing up. A sign in a spidery hand read, "All books, ten cents."

A couple of women were leafing through the discarded magazines stacked at one end of the table, comparing recipes and knitting patterns they'd each discovered. A few youths filed through a tall stack of *National Geographics*, tittering at the photos of bare-breasted natives. Only a single man was examining the used books for sale.

Him.

Well, it was a free country! Rose marched to the opposite side of the table and started searching through the hardcovers. "These are good books!" she blurted as she tucked one under her arm, just as if she were at Loehman's and had found a Chanel suit stuck in among the off-the-rack knock-offs.

The man from the microphone, across the table from her, looked up and smiled. "What did you find?"

"This was a best seller!" Rose's eyes sparkled as she tilted the cover for the gentleman to see the title. "*The Making of the President, 1960.*"

Percy shook his head and frowned. "Democrats won that one!"

Rose stepped back and snapped, "I suppose you think the Republicans do a better job running the country?"

"Well they don't go meddling with folks' lives, that's for sure!"

"And what do you think would happen if **LBJ** hadn't signed that Civil Rights Act yesterday? You think Alabama was ever going to cross its Jim Crow laws off the books by itself? Or eliminate the poll tax?" Rose's voice started to rise and the quiet library became silent.

"It's the principle of the thing," Percy spoke quietly. "People ought to be allowed to govern themselves. Just give folks enough time; they'll do the right thing, eventually."

"*Eventually* is too long a time if you're a colored person," Rose spat a hoarse whisper back.

"We don't have any coloreds here," Percy straightened up. "I don't have any quarrel with them, either."

"What's your grudge then?" Rose lifted her chin in the air. "You think the rich are going to look after the poor out of the goodness of their hearts?" she sneered.

"In Vermont, we pride ourselves on looking after each other. We take care of ourselves." Percy shook his head. "What right has the federal government to tell us how to live?" he asked calmly.

"What do you mean?" Rose lowered her chin a fraction.

"Reapportionment," Percy stated.

"What's that?" Rose asked.

"It's how we elect our legislature. And it's worked just fine."

Percy placed his fingertips on the edge of the table and leaned forward. "What right do the folks in Washington have to come in and tell us to fix what ain't broke? It just flies in the face of logic—and it destroys local control."

"Well, how do you elect your legislature?" Rose asked, hugging her book in her crossed arms and shifting her weight to one hip.

"One town, one vote." Percy tapped the table with each word.

"Are you saying that Orton, this—this—" Ruth gestured to the one-room library, "This tiny village gets the same representation as—" she looked at Percy. "What's the biggest city in the state?"

"Burlington. Then Barre. Then Rutland."

"And all the people in Burlington have one representative in state government?"

"In the House, yes." Percy folded his arms across his chest and nodded.

"And that woman, Mildred I think her name is, represents all the people from Orton?"

"That's right," Percy nodded.

"And how many people live in Burlington?"

"Twenty-odd thousand. Close to thirty."

"And Orton?"

"About 290."

"Two hundred and ninety?"

"That's right."

"And you think that's fair?"

"Well, it's mostly foreigners up there."

"Foreigners?" Rose squeaked.

"Catholics, mostly. Factory workers. Folks who want unions and wage guarantees."

Rose had a hand on her hip. "And what's wrong with that?"

"People should be paid for good, hard, work, not guaranteed a wage, regardless."

"It's clear you've never worked in a factory," Rose sneered.

Percy straightened. "You can't get any more democratic than Town Meeting: One man, one vote."

"The world is bigger than this little village!" Rose spat her words in a hoarse whisper. "And it's changing all the time." Rose turned on her heel.

Percy muttered, "Change isn't always for the best."

When the family entered the Orton Town Hall that evening, the room was cleared for dancing, with only a refreshment table at one end, and wooden chairs lined up against the wall. Rose returned the nods that greeted the family. She already recognized many of those present, even if she didn't know who they were.

Almost as soon as they arrived, a fat man in a plaid shirt and red suspenders tapped the live mic, stilling the crowd to attention. He nodded and the band started playing. "Find your partners, form your squares!" His sharp tenor rose above the music that was setting toes tapping across the wooden floor.

"You go," Rose urged her kids. They paired off, Jeannie and Martin, Manny and Wendy, and joined one of the squares in the middle of the throng.

"I'm Larry Larken," the fat man said, tipping an imaginary hat, "and we're the Sap Boilers. We expect to have you hopping in no time. Now bow to your partner." The crowd in the center of the room bobbed. "And bow to your corner." This movement wasn't quite so neatly executed. "Your corner is the gent to your right if you're a lady, and the lady to your left if you're a gent." The caller's words came out in a singsong patter, its high pitch sailing over the fiddle behind him. "We'll take it easy, so don't get queasy. Listen up and I'll walk you through. Listen close for what to do.

Just follow what I say and the squares will swirl and sway. But first there're a few terms you ought to know, so we'll take this dance nice and slow." Larry stepped back, and the band picked up for a bit. Then Larry started calling in earnest and the dancing began.

Rose worked her way to a seat at the side of the room. In her prime, she'd never sat out a dance. At the New Yorker, she and Esther and Lilly hardly stepped inside the doorway before men were paying for their dances, offering to treat them to a soda. But you had to be careful: a fellow treated you to a soda, he thought he owned you, thought only he could dance with you that night. And if he treated you two nights in a row, why, you were practically engaged! Lilly learned that the hard way, with that boy—Avram Schuyler—following her home, trying to kiss her, introducing himself to her mother in the market. *Oy!* Rose shook her head. They had to switch to the Hester Street Hall after that. Lilly learned her lesson, too. No more sodas!

The dancers bobbed up and down as they worked the figures around their squares, white heads as well as brown ones. Was she the only old lady sitting out? A pair of new mothers cradled their infants nearby, and a few men stood by the doorway, leaning back on their heels, arms folded across their chests. Some of the women Rose recognized from the street fair were ladling out punch and selling refreshments, but she looked like the only wallflower in the whole place.

Well, what did she expect from widowhood? And that man from the library, even if he were here—and she didn't see him—she wouldn't dance with him! Rose placed her hands on her cheeks to cool them. She never was one to curb her tongue! By now, everyone in Orton and all the way over to Waterchase probably knew that Rose Mayer was a loud-mouthed Democrat. She folded her arms across her chest. Well, she was what she was. She wasn't going to pretend any different.

"Would you like to join the next dance?" A dapper fellow in a pressed shirt bowed to Rose.

Rose blushed, afraid maybe he'd overheard her noisy thoughts. "I've never done this kind of dancing," she said. Just then Marty and Jeannie waved to her as they swung around.

"Your grandson has caught on. It's really quite easy," he assured her. "I'd be glad to show you how."

"How did you know that's my grandson?"

"My name is Wilson Nye. I believe you're Rose Mayer, Manny Rubin's mother?"

Rose shook her head. "It's a little spooky, the way everyone knows everyone around here, like you're all friends of J. Edgar Hoover or something."

Wilson chuckled. "I guess it might seem a bit forward to you city folk. But Irma Bassett told me she'd met you. And Percy Mendell. You're a real celebrity around here."

"Percy Mendell?" Rose stood tall. "White haired? Made the announcements at the parade earlier?"

"That's Percy," Wilson nodded and looked away. "Said you're a Red—a genuine hot-headed communist in our midst!"

"That's an absolute lie!" Rose stamped her foot. "I'm not a communist, I'm a Democrat!"

Wilson smiled.

Rose softened her voice. "From my conversation with this Percy Mendell, I figure that's pretty radical for Vermont."

"Oh, I don't know about that," Wilson rocked back on his heels. "Governor's a Democrat."

"The governor of Vermont?"

"Phil Hoff," Wilson stated. "First one in a hundred-odd years."

"Well, you're making progress," Rose smiled.

Wilson bowed slightly at the waist.

"I was beginning to think all of Vermont thinks the way this Percy Mendell does."

"All think like Percy?" Wilson straightened his tie. "Goodness, no. Percy believes in 'Better living through agriculture' and all that. No. Not every Vermonter's a farmer, not by a long shot."

"Is he a farmer?"

"Percy? No, he don't farm. He just tells those who do farm how to do it better."

"And what do you do, Mr. Nye?"

"Wilson, please."

Rose batted her eyes.

"Me?" He shrugged. "I'm in real estate. Don't happen you want to buy a place of your own now, do you?"

Rose shook her head no. Maybe there was such a thing as a liberal Vermonter. She smiled. Aside from his mustache, Wilson had a pleasant face, tanned but not burned by the sun. No wedding ring. His hands told a history of past work, but they had the smooth cleanliness of recent ease, and his shoes were polished and clean.

"I understand you're from Florida," he said.

Rose nodded.

"How do you like it there?"

"I only lived in Florida a few years," Rose sighed. Everything was different, now she was a widow. "I'm really a New Yorker. I've lived all my life in the City."

"So what do you think of our country ways?" The music stopped.

"They take a little getting used to." Rose joined the applause.

Wilson nodded as he guided Rose onto the dance floor.

"Even this music is different," Rose said.

"And what kind of music do you listen to?"

Rose glowed. "Classical. You know, like at the Marlboro Music Festival. I'm hoping to get there one of these weekends."

Wilson stiffened. "You won't find any Vermonters there."

Rose curtsied as the caller instructed. "No?" Rose raised her eyebrows at her partner's sudden chill.

"Strictly out-of-state," he said.

Fiddle music filled the air. Rose shrugged, "Show me how this dance goes!"

Rose caught the rhythm and the figures, and Wilson relaxed as he took her on a promenade around the world. As they circled, women said "Hi," and their partners nodded to them in acquaintance. When the dance ended, Rose said, "I never expected to have so much fun in Vermont!"

"You're a good dancer," Wilson assured her. "And a quick learner."

"You're a good teacher. I forgot how much I enjoy to dance!" Rose laughed. "Or I did as a young girl."

"I'm sure you're still a girl at heart."

Rose hoped the heat in her cheeks was only from the exercise. "Thank you," she mumbled.

"Are you game for another?" Wilson offered his arm.

Rose shrugged, "Why not?" and led the way.

4 | marlboro music

This was the one barn Percy had ever been in without feeling at home. Strictly speaking, it wasn't a barn but an auditorium, built two years earlier as a performance space for the Marlboro Music Festival. The outside of the building claimed some pretension at contemporary architecture, with its narrow windows under the roof and low silhouette along the side of a hill. But inside, it was a barn. Only a barn enclosed such vast empty space, and only a barn could be excused an interior so unfinished. The laminated arches supporting the roof gave the place its only sense of decor; they also superseded any rafters that would have supported a hayloft if this were a real barn, for cattle.

These arches lifted the roof high above the chatter and the heat as the audience of out–of–towners settled down for the afternoon concert. After a half-dozen years of attending the Festival, Percy recognized many of the musicians in the crowd. He even recognized some of the concert–goers, the same faces year after year. The women with their astonishing lipstick and earrings, their sense of fashion, even in their casual attire, confirmed Percy's vague notion of exoticism lurking just south of the Vermont border. Even the several men who didn't wear neckties seemed better dressed than a local man similarly informal.

Marlboro was only about twenty miles from Orton, but about as far away from Vermont as Percy had ever been in his life. The English spoken here was often accented with Europe; sometimes the language wasn't even English, but Russian or German, he guessed, depending on who was speaking. The speakers had names like Rudolf and Pablo, Mischa, Sascha, Florica, Felix, Pina, Pierre, Endel, and Boris. Percy didn't even know how to pronounce Miec-zyslaw, but he recognized the man's touch at the piano, which is why he came at least once every year.

Maybe next year he'd buy season tickets, become a subscriber like the out-of-towners. With a pass, he could attend open re-hearsals and the informal Wednesday night concerts. That would give some structure to retirement and a summer that otherwise looked formless, without employment. Applause erupted as Pablo Casals made his way to the podium. If only Percy'd been a mu-sician, he wouldn't have to retire at sixty-five. Casals was in his nineties and still hard at work. The house settled down as the old man raised his baton for the Brandenburg No. 4.

With just three orchestral chords adorned by two flutes and three more chords before the violin's flight above the orchestra, the vast barn became a well-furnished palace finished in parquet and gold leaf. Filigree rose from Alexander Schneider's violin and light bounced off crystal chandeliers as Ornulf Gulbransen and Nancy Dalley piped their flutes. Underneath the melody ran the under-current of the orchestra, like electricity flowing through Percy's veins. The music circulated inside him like the fire of hard liquor, but instead of numbing him, the music danced to his fingertips until he thought his skin would peel off. The solo violin sang to his heart, and the flute duet soothed it, tugging back and forth from passion to balm, with the stream of the orchestra like water tumbling down a brook, pulling the all of him through the woods, across pastures, over rapids into an ever deeper flow over sunken boulders into eddies, downstream and downstream, Bruce Brook to the West and the West into the stately Connecticut.

Andante. The deep cello and sad song of slow-moving water streaming south with the inevitability of gravity stopped Percy's heart from beating. Now he was in a marsh on a late autumn day, watching the last of the geese take flight, leaving him to another winter, alone. The same instruments that were all heat and light only moments ago were now singing dark November. Was it the November of his life? Was this the music of his passage into retirement? The happy stream of his life joining the giant slow river of all who'd gone before, joining the great progression of ancestors into the world of prior lives? What else could such sad chords intone? And the flute singing a plaintive solo against the ocean of strings—was that a last cry before death?

Presto. The ocean was life and light, tide and waves, great currents drawing him back into the happiness of breathing green air in the sun of summer. Insects rubbing their wings together in the satisfaction of sex, the wind rippling across a hayfield, corn tassels, plump tomatoes ripening on the vine. All this was ahead of him, the bounty of life. Fish swimming in the sea. The leviathan that was music sounding and taking him for a wild ride.

Applause erupted—nothing polite about it—as exuberant as the music just ended. It was always like this, and it always surprised Percy, who expected these city folk to be polite—cooler, even, than New England.

The hall filled with the combined noise of animated conversation and released restlessness. Percy needed air. He needed the reassurance of the grass and the trees that he belonged here, even if he knew no one. But as he was crossing the lobby, he saw her: the woman from the library. She looked like one of them, with her jet earrings that echoed the print of her summer dress, cinched at the waist with a belt. She even had an out-of-state figure, and she was the mother of a middle-aged man.

He nodded to her.

She smiled back.

"Hello," Percy said, approaching. "How nice to see you."

She tilted her head like a bird. "You don't have to be polite with me!"

"Pardon me?"

"I'm the Democrat, remember?"

"Yes, you bought the Theodore White book."

"So you don't have to pretend to be friendly. I'm not offended."

"Maybe when you live in a big city you can afford to befriend only those who hold the same opinions, but you can't do that in Vermont, not unless you don't mind being lonely! Goodness, do you think we all agree with each other all the time? Wait until you come to Town Meeting!"

"But you told Wilson Nye I was a communist!"

"What?" Percy went stiff. "I haven't spoken to Wilson Nye outside of town business in nearly forty years!"

Rose narrowed her eyes. "He said Vermonters didn't come to these concerts."

Percy hesitated. "Well, I'm here."

They faced each other in awkward silence.

Percy cleared his throat. "It's not always easy to buy tickets."

"So I was told." She fanned herself with her program.

"If you can't get a ticket, you can always sit outside," Percy nodded to the bank alongside the hall where some families had spread blankets.

They continued to face each other, not speaking, until Rose asked, "What did you think of the Brandenburg?"

Percy exhaled. "I don't think I have words to say," he frowned.

"I liked the way they played it," Rose said, "with lots of verve! So often, you hear insipid renditions, like the musicians all have strict metronomes where their hearts are supposed to be."

"Do you go to many concerts?"

"Not so many in Florida, but when I lived in New York, all the time. I subscribed to the Peoples' Symphony Concerts." Rose looked at him slyly. "It's a series for workers who can't afford up-town prices."

A new shaft of light illuminated Percy's vague picture of urban life.

"This audience," Rose indicated the crowd milling around the lobby, "it behaves a little bit like at Peoples' Symphony."

"How's that?" Percy asked.

"Opinionated," Rose said. "And enthusiastic!"

Not only were there concerts to choose from, but subcultures among audiences. Maybe city life had more to offer than Percy'd imagined.

"What about you? Do you go to many concerts?" Rose asked.

"Mostly, I listen to records."

"Records!" Rose wrinkled her nose as if the word had a stench. "It's not the same." She shook her head. "You hear the same thing over and over. No variation. No spontaneity." Her voice was filled with regret.

"I never thought of it like that before," Percy said, looking past Rose at some distant location visible only to himself. "But I see what you mean." He shifted and looked at her. "Maybe that's why I've started buying duplicates. Music I already own, but recorded by different artists. I've listened to Toscanini conducting the NBC

Orchestra's Beethoven symphonies for years, but I've just bought Herbert von Karajan conducting the Eroica with Philadelphia." He looked at Rose for approval.

She had her hand over her heart. "Toscanini! We used to go down to NBC and listen to the broadcasts—live!" She shook her head at the memory, then looked at Percy with sharp eyes. "Have you ever heard an orchestra play Beethoven live?"

Percy folded his hands across his chest. "No, I can't say that I've had that pleasure."

"Pleasure? Agony! It's so—so much sound! You can feel it!" Rose pounded her fist against her chest. "It goes right through you, music like that." She threw her head back and closed her eyes as she shook her head.

Percy glanced around to see if this woman was attracting attention, but the crowd ignored her in the buzz and hum of its own conversations, some as emphatic and accompanied by similarly noisy gestures.

Rose faced Percy again. "Recordings?" she said, shrugging. "It's the sound captured by a mechanical ear. It may sound like music," she said, tapping her chest, "but it has no heart."

"It's better than nothing," Percy said. "Listening to recordings has afforded me great pleasure."

"And why not?" Rose's attention wandered around the lobby, which was starting to empty as people made their way back into the auditorium. She turned to Percy. "Well, time for the triple concerto."

"I hope you enjoy it." Percy hesitated for her to precede him into the hall.

Three pianos now occupied the front of the stage. The audience hushed, then erupted into foot-stamping as Mieczyslaw Horszowski and Rudolf and Peter Serkin, father and son, bowed.

Casals approached the podium, the crowd settled, and, with the stroke of the baton, the music of Bach's Concerto in C Major for Three Pianos was set into motion.

Metronomes where their hearts should be, Percy mused. All these years, his records had given him so much solace, and here, in an instant of casual conversation, the veracity of listening to that mechanically reproduced music was thrown into doubt.

Well, he'd enjoyed it. And he still would! But he would try to attend more live performances, too. There was something inexplicably wonderful about hearing the sound as it escaped the bow. Like the difference between vine ripened tomatoes and store-bought. The music soared and Lila's fragrance wafted into the room. Percy's heart beat behind his knees, his loins throbbed, his face flushed. He fanned himself with his program. The music washed over him the way water did when he stood under the spillway down at the cedar crib dam.

If he did buy season tickets, he would try to get a seat on the left of the house, so he could watch the pianist at work. He was too far back to see any of the keyboards today. Just the backs of heads of the listeners ahead of him. Hers, a white mane to the middle of her neck, four rows ahead, on the right. Tanned skin. Straight shoulders. And all the music she'd ever listened to wound up inside her head. Live music. The intimate voices of chamber music, and the sonic boom of an orchestra. Maybe that's what's given her the force of her convictions. How many women did Percy know who spoke up the way she did? No, he wasn't talking about Mildred Aitcheson ranting about state business, or Mabel Robinson slandering her friends under the guise of important local news. What men did he know, for that matter? Folks always talked about the weather, and maybe snuck in an opinion about something else by the way. But for someone to just come out and say something direct to your face? Well, that was rare.

The pianos intruded. The Serkin boy was just a teen. Imagine being able to play like that! At that age! Imagine having a father who could teach you!

Well, his father taught him. Not piano, but planting and fishing, hunting and husbandry. Showed him, really. "Here's how you sharpen an ax," his pa demonstrated. "And here's how you split wood." His father's great shoulders rose upwards, his arms elongated by the ax handle so that the ax head was in the middle of the blue sky before falling, like a meteor, cracking through an up-ended log on its fall back to earth. "Now you try it."

Percy was maybe six, and even the two-pound ax was hard to lift, never mind his father's fiver. He raised his arms till he felt the late September air kiss his tummy as his shirt rose with his shoulders. When the ax reached the top of the arc, he changed momentum and the ax fell into the wood, sticking there.

"Practice, Son. Practice. You'll get it with practice," his old man told him as he filed through the wood pile for the straight-grained sections of ash and birch, wood that was easy for a beginner to split. "You start with this. As you get stronger, you can move on to maple and oak. When you're ready, I'll show you how to break knots and cross-grains with the maul."

What would it have been like to have had a father who took you in his lap at the keyboard and showed you how to play scales? What would it have been like to have a father who said, "Practice, Son. Practice," and for him to mean practice a skill that has no practical application, that can't be used to heat your home or fill your belly, but which feeds your soul?

Percy headed for the out-of-doors before the applause died away. He needed air and maybe even the heat of the sun to scour the feelings that unsettled him. All these years of service, promoting agriculture, spreading the word of science to improve farming, bridging the gap between the horticulturists and the farm operators—all for what? Why did regret rear up now? He kicked the ground and ambled away from the people pouring out the doors, inhaling deeply of the summer afternoon.

Weren't you supposed to feel good at the end of your life? Happy to have made the world a little bit better? Maybe only men who had children felt that. In all these years, he'd never yearned for children the way he did now, now that it was too late. He stood with his hands in his pockets, rocking back on his heels as his eyes followed the horizon to where the ridgeline folded into the earth, creating the bowl that embraced the buildings of the small college. It was a long view, and it tired him. The distant horizon gave him no more pleasure than the music had. He turned and walked back toward the crowd.

Sitting on a boulder beside the auditorium was her solitary figure.

He ambled toward her. She was reading a newspaper, folded into manageable fourths, half-glasses balanced at the end of her nose. She didn't look anywhere near sixty, but Manny Rubin must be in his forties; she had to be. She was better looking than women half her age. He squared his necktie and pushed his shoulders back. She looked up.

"The Republican convention starts in San Francisco," she blurted as he approached. Before he could reply, she said, "A Goldwater nomination will be a disaster!" Rose shook her head at the paper, then fixed her eye on Percy and challenged him. "He's a John Bircher—the worst kind of racist, an extremist of the very worst sort. Goldwater is worse than McCarthy!"

"I quite agree."

Rose's brow furrowed. "Well, you're a Republican. Why don't

you do something to stop it!"

Percy smiled. "Me, personally?"

"Who else? It's your duty! That's how democracy works!"

"And what do you suggest?"

"Send telegrams to all the delegates!"

"And what should I wire them? To nominate Nelson Rockefeller or Governor Scranton instead?"

Her face clouded over. "If Goldwater gets the nomination, the party will back him."

"The party leadership will, but the rank and file? I wouldn't be so sure." Percy rocked back on his heels.

Rose eyed him. "You know something?"

Percy raised his brows.

"What is it? Tell me! What do you know?"

"Well," Percy said, clearing his throat and leaning toward Rose's ear. "I have it on good authority that a delegate from a certain rural state in the northeast is going to nominate a certain senator from Maine—"

"Margaret Chase Smith?" Rose interrupted. "A Vermont Republican is going to nominate a woman for president?"

Percy chuckled.

"You're pulling my leg!"

"We'll see," Percy said. "It was Vermont's own Flanders who initiated McCarthy's censure in the Senate. And Senator Aiken backed Mrs. Smith's 'Declaration of Conscience' against him."

Rose's face was all confusion.

"Better get back." The last of the audience was entering the building. "They're about to start."

The Third Brandenburg had never sounded so triumphant. Percy had to stop himself from slapping his knee! He could hardly wait for Wednesday, when Aiken would nominate Smith on the first ballot. Six of the Vermont delegates were going to support her. Not that she'd win, but it registered a protest against Goldwater. Though why it was just a protest, Percy didn't exactly understand. Margaret Chase Smith had a good record in the Senate, and he, for one, didn't see why being a woman had anything to do with it or why she couldn't be president as well as any man. Better than most.

Wouldn't that surprise Manny Rubin's mother? Astonish her! Percy touched his cheeks, sore from grinning. His heart pumped with the elegant regularity of the concerto, like an intricate time-piece clicking away while his spirits soared with the brass up against the rafters.

He could hardly wait till Wednesday. Meanwhile, he'd have to find out Manny Rubin's mother's name.

The beans were upon him. Addie had complained yearly about the bean glut, forbidding Percy to plant more than a short row, insisting that she would neither can nor freeze food when she could just as easily go down to Childs' IGA and pick up Del Monte off the shelf, or the new Birdseye from the freezer department. Frozen, the beans were supposed to be healthier. More vitamins. For all her arguments, Addie had never been able to convince Percy that frozen tasted better than home canned. So he took himself down to Erskine's and invested in a spanking new pressure canner.

Every evening during the last week of July, Percy picked beans before supper and canned them after. It was a gob of work, he conceded as he finally wiped down the kitchen near ten o'clock, keeping his ear cocked for the "pop-pop" of the two-part lids sealing as they cooled. Fatigue worked up his legs; his back ached with new appreciation for kitchen labor. But he had the growing regiment of quart jars assembled on the counter, quarts of canned beans standing with their sloped shoulders in rigid formation as if they were going to march through the winter blazing the flavor of summer. Percy couldn't articulate his satisfaction as he added another half-dozen jars to the line-up each evening. It was like listening to good music.

But Percy hadn't done much of that, either, not since the concert at Marlboro. For one, it was the busy time at work. Nothing like July to keep a farmer hopping, and Percy hopped right along with every operator in the county who wanted the information about the new pesticides Percy'd tried to tell them about back in January, when they had the time to study but didn't have the problem staring at them in the field. Human nature, it was, to learn what you needed to know only when you needed to know it, and not a moment sooner.

He rubbed the back of his neck and stood indecisive by the kitchen sink. Percy hadn't played a single record since Rose Mayer said recorded music was mechanical and heartless. He spread his hands out and regarded them. He hadn't played the piano, either. His fingers were stiff from the garden, and there just wasn't time for everything. Percy now understood what Addie had been complaining about all those years, but he'd only asked her to do the kitchen work, not the garden chores as well. He was doing both. No wonder he was tired.

Percy shut off the light and limped into the parlor, too tired to place a record on the turntable but too unsettled to go to bed. He'd have to get over to Marlboro again. Maybe he'd stop by the Rubins and see if Mrs. Mayer wanted a lift.

But when he stopped by the Rubin's the following evening, who was visiting in the front room but Wilson Nye.

"Well, hello, Percy!" Wilson stood. "I didn't know you were keeping company with Rose, here."

"Hello, Wilson," Percy nodded, ignoring Wilson's outstretched hand. "Hello, Mrs. Mayer."

"Sit down, please."

Percy grimaced. Wilson was comfortably reseated in an overstuffed chair. "I'd heard you were going to drive back cross-country, after the convention," he said.

"You were in San Francisco?" Rose, still standing, smiled at Wilson.

Wilson beamed. "Plans change," he shrugged.

Percy remained standing.

"Wilson was just telling me about trying to unseat Mrs. Aitcheson this fall," Rose said, turning toward Percy, her chin tilted.

"Is that so?" Percy folded his arms across his chest. "Are you going to challenge her in a primary?"

"Naw!" Wilson slapped his knee.

"You're going to run as a Democrat?" Percy tried to keep his voice flat.

Wilson turned to Rose. "He's a real joker, Percy is." To Percy he said, "I'm going to run as an Independent, like your friend Senator Aiken. Since the convention, anyways."

Percy said nothing.

"I'm not stepping on your toes, now, am I?" Wilson was leaning back in the armchair, his head rested against the cushion. "I know Abel Towne's been trying to get you to run for office ever since he retired." Wilson faced Rose. "Percy, here. He's a real celebrity around the county. Well known. Well liked. Well respected." Wilson shrugged. "He'd be tough to beat."

"Are you thinking of running?" Rose asked.

Percy shook his head. "Oh, I've thought about it all right. But Mildred Aitcheson is doing a fine job. Besides, I wouldn't want politics to get in the way of my work. Working with farmers, you know."

"He already talks like a politician, don't he?" Wilson laughed.

Percy's voice tightened. "But that may change when I retire, you know."

"Retire?" Wilson slapped his thigh. "Why you old son-of-a-gun!" Wilson slapped his thigh again. To Rose he said, "That Percy, he always did play his cards close to his chest."

"I've never made a secret of it, Wilson. Don't know why you should be so surprised. I'll be turning sixty-five come winter. I've been a year older than you when we were boys, and I'm still a year older." Percy nodded to Rose. "Good evening, Mrs. Mayer."

"You're going?" Rose looked from one man to the other. "I'll walk you to the door."

"Thanks. I can find my way out." Percy turned and left.

"Damn Wilson Nye! Damn him! Damn him! Damn him!" Percy pounded the steering wheel with each curse. And he hadn't even invited her to the concert! Well, he wasn't going to do that in front of Wilson. No, sir! Wasn't going to have Wilson splash his private life all over town. And he wasn't going to compete with Wilson Nye, either. Wasn't going to run against him in an election, and wasn't going to ask the same woman out. They'd been through that already. Wilson Nye had already caused Percy enough heartache, and he wasn't going to go asking for more.

Percy had been up at the university, in Burlington, attending the ag school. Lila had asked Percy to please come back for her senior dance, but it fell during the weekend between exams. He'd come back for her graduation, not sooner. Couldn't she find someone else to take her? Percy didn't know Wilson had been pestering her to go out with him the whole time Percy was away. Or how disappointed Lila was that Percy couldn't be there for her. Maybe a little bit angry, too. How else to explain what happened?

In high school, Wilson had been one of the fast ones, the first kid in Orton to own a car, a pathetic Model T that he tinkered with and polished and drove wherever the roads were passable, and sometimes where they weren't. He was always tipping over in gulleys or getting stuck in the mud. That car of his, it was a joke, and everyone laughed at Wilson for his devotion to it.

For the dance, it seems, he'd cleaned it all up. Brushed out the inside. Polished the fenders. Souped up the engine. And tucked a bottle of whiskey in the glove box and a hip flask in his pocket. He must have been sober when he picked Lila up at home. Mr. and Mrs. Winthrop were pretty strict about liquor. Mrs. W. tried heading up the local Temperance chapter, but folks in Orton didn't see the point. If folks didn't want to drink hard liquor, well, then, they didn't have to. No reason to make a law about it. The local movement languished. Even so, the Winthrops never served anything stronger than birch beer. Not a sip of brandy at Christmas or a drop of whiskey for illness, not even when Doc Stoddard prescribed it.

But they'd been drinking. That much was certain. The way Percy figured, Wilson must have spiked Lila's punch. She wouldn't have drunk it otherwise. Maybe she didn't even taste it or, tasting it, didn't know what it was. She wasn't used to it, that's for sure. And maybe she was still mad at Percy, and this was the uncomfortable part for him to admit. Lila must have got tipsy, even a little wild.

There were others involved, too. The Stratton boy had his father's horse and buggy. Lots of the boys had borrowed traps, the kids from the hills anyways. The kids from town just walked.

Well, when the dance ended, everybody headed out. The chaperones hadn't thought this part through, expecting the kids to just go on home, where the girls were expected by midnight. Wilson and Lila and Buddy Stratton and his date—Martha Greenwood that was, now Martha Stratton—and maybe a few others. Percy never found out exactly who all was there, and there must have been half a dozen. But it was Buddy with his buggy and Wilson with his Model T who'd arranged to race down by the flats, just before the covered bridge at the Salmon Hole Crossing. It was car against buggy, Wilson versus Buddy. And their dates. Why they let the girls join in the race, Percy would never know. And why Lila consented to ride in that contraption—to race in it—at night, with Wilson Nye—a drunk Wilson Nye—well, there was no knowing. And no turning back the hands of time. What's done is done.

The way Martha saw it, Lila was game enough and climbed in the front seat all laughter. But when they started picking up speed, she must have got scared. There was a lot of noise—the engine, the horse hooves, the buggy wheels over the gravel and the kids shouting as they took off, so Martha wasn't sure if Lila screamed for Wilson to stop. They were going hell-bent for leather, the horse and buggy starting to pull ahead, when Lila must have stood up. Wilson swerved and Lila fell out.

Martha said it got real quiet real quick, except for the horse panting. Slowly, everyone started to move toward the white lump of Lila at the edge of Brown's field. Then folks started running and shouting, "Lila! Lila!"

Wilson got to her first, but Emmett Hastings yelled, "Don't touch her!" He came running up. "Careful, in case her back's hurt." Emmett knelt down and was about to place his fingers on her neck, but her head was at a funny angle. "Neck's broke," was all he said. He never did check her pulse. Martha said there was no doubt; she was dead all of an instant. Sometimes, when Percy snapped off a light, he thought of Lila's broken neck.

Lila's death was ruled accidental. The first motor vehicle death in the state. Percy was allowed to take his exams two weeks late, after the funeral. He almost didn't, almost quit right there and then. Those whole two weeks, when he wasn't visiting with Lila's parents or staring at the raw dirt over her grave in the cemetery, Percy was out in the field, digging behind his father, considering a return to the farm and the welcome exhaustion of working like a beast of burden, so that he'd be too tired to feel anything but bodily aches and pains.

He was still digging fence-post holes near dusk two days before he was due to take his exams. His pa came out.

"Percy, you got to eat."

Percy kept digging.

His father stood by.

The sun sank.

Percy paused in his digging, and his father gently took the shovel from him.

Percy leaned on his father and sobbed.

When he stopped, his father shouldered the shovel and steered Percy back to the house in the long June twilight. As they neared the house, Arden Mendell said, "Go wash up and have supper. Your mother's got your clothes laundered. I'll drive you up to Burlington tomorrow, so you can finish your term."

That summer—the first one after the accident—Percy fenced new pasture, digging all the fence-post holes in the stony glacial debris that required more pickax than shovel. What did it matter to him how hard he worked? The work is what saved him from grief. After twelve hours of hard labor six days a week, his back ached more than his heart. Only Sundays were tough, with nothing to do. He'd rather have worked, but for his mother. She didn't make him attend church, although when he did, it pleased her.

She did insist he refrain from labor on Sundays, reminding him he was no better than God, and even God took a day off.

When Percy returned to Marlboro, he stood at the back of the auditorium until the very last moment before the Bartok began. She wasn't there.

Even under easy circumstances, a Bartok quartet was difficult to listen to. Today, with all the languor that accompanies a hot afternoon in August, it was that much more difficult.

Percy loosened his necktie. The back of his shirt stuck to the seat, and the stale exhalations of so many equally hot listeners raised the temperature even more. It was a restless crowd, and one of those impossible programs. After the Bartok, they'd be singing to the accompaniment of a clarinet. And if that wasn't bad enough, there was more clarinet in the next piece, a Schumann trio with a German name as long as the alphabet. Maybe he shouldn't have come. On the other hand, there was the Mendelssohn quartet at the end, which might be worth waiting for.

Percy squinted at the stage in an effort to pay attention. The men were sawing away with their bows, bodies swaying, damp patches blooming all over their shirts. The cellist nodded to the violins, and they all attacked a note together. And again. Their strokes were synchronized to one another and to the sound they made. Then they split into four voices, but even from his seat near the back of the hall, Percy could see them looking at each other, sending important signals with their eyes, their eyebrows, their eyelids even, as if there were yet another layer of language beneath the notes.

It was so different from the orchestral music on his records, where a conductor asserted autocratic command. Even the recordings of the concerti, with the virtuosi and orchestras talking back and forth to one another—all that conversation was mediated by the maestro. These four musicians were all tangled in each others' musical lines and eyebeams. It was like swimming naked. That intimate.

Even though he hadn't listened attentively, the Bartok saddened him, and Percy decided to go outside and sit under a nearby maple instead of brave the heat of the hall or the woody complaint of the clarinet. He just wasn't in the mood. Enough of the high notes escaped through the open doors to keep him connected to the concert, and the shade beneath the tree consoled him with its hint of coolness.

Percy had his eyes closed and his back against the tree trunk, when he heard a car climbing the hill and stop. It was Manny Rubin's green Rambler. The back door opened, and Rose stepped out. She leaned into the open window and said something to Mrs. Rubin. She may have even planted a kiss on her daughter-in-law's cheek. Then she stood back and waved as the car performed a U-turn and drove off the way it came.

Rose was just adjusting her dress at the waist when she looked up. He liked the way she squared her shoulders, and walked straight over.

Percy stood and acknowledged her with a nod, and fanned himself with his program while she made her way up the bank.

"Why aren't you inside?" Rose called, across the shrinking space between them.

Percy raised a finger to his lips.

Rose covered her mouth with her hand. Her eyebrows rose high above her widened eyes as she shrugged off her faux pas. "Why aren't you inside?" she asked again, this time in a stage whisper, and standing right beside him.

"Come into the shade," he said, touching her arm and directing her to the relative cool beneath the tree. "It's too hot in there." Percy watched to see how she'd take this. "And I don't care for the German." He thrust a program before her.

She held it at arm's length, moving her head from side to side and making a face. She handed it back, "I understand. Not the greatest program in the world."

"I'm thinking of leaving," he said.

"You are?"

"Oh, I might hang around for the Mendelssohn. That ought to be good."

"I have no choice. The kids are off to go swimming. At some pond."

"You don't like to swim?"

"I love to swim! In the ocean!" She shrugged and made a face. "The water here's so thin. And so—so *brown*."

Applause escaped from the auditorium.

"I'm sorry I missed the Bartok," Rose said. "But the kids weren't ready." She sighed. "I'm not used to living in a family anymore." She smiled up at Percy. "It's a bit of a relief just to get away."

Strains of the Schumann trio drifted on the hot air.

Percy could only imagine the tumult of three generations living under one roof. "The other night—" he hesitated. "Well, I intended to invite you, offer you a lift to the concert." His eyes were focused on something invisible, a long way off. He felt her eyes on him and turned to meet them.

"You don't like Wilson Nye, do you?"

Percy frowned at the amusement in her voice. "No," he said quietly.

Rose was shaking her head. "Well, he doesn't like you much, either."

Percy folded his arms across his chest.

"There must be some story there?" Rose tilted her head, as if she could tease information out of him.

Percy forced a stiff smile. "Are you going to come in for the last piece? I think this one's nearly over."

"I don't have a ticket. I'll just sit outside on the grass."

Percy nodded, and they parted.

Rose didn't like Wilson Nye much either. After Percy stomped out, Rose shrugged as if to say, "What can I do?" She seated herself across from Wilson and said, "So, you went to a national convention!"

"Sure did," Wilson grinned.

"And you voted for Margaret Chase Smith!" Rose sank back into the couch with her eyes closed and her hand over her heart.

"Well," Wilson coughed and crossed his legs. "I was part of the Vermont delegation."

Rose opened her eyes and Wilson cleared his throat again. "But that's just politics." He shifted forward in the chair and leaned toward Rose. "I don't want to talk politics. I want to talk about you." He smiled. "Where did you do all your dancing before you came to Vermont?"

Rose felt the heat rise to her face and looked away. Staring out the window, she told him about the dance halls with Lilly and Esther. "So long ago," she said, "like a far-off dream." She smiled abtractedly at Wilson and waved her hand as if tossing the past away.

Wilson caught her hand. "It's like a dream to sit here with you, Rose. A dream that you came to Orton and walked into my life."

Rose stared at her hand inside his. Age spots. Well, what did she expect? She sighed. It was nice, to hold hands. She looked up and smiled. Wilson squeezed. He was struggling out of the deep upholstery. He was going to lean forward to kiss her! She leaned away. Headlights swung into the drive, and Rose dropped Wilson's hand. "They're home!" She stood up. "It must be late!"

Wilson cleared his throat and heaved himself out of the chair. He towered over Rose. "Well, I guess it's time for me to be going home myself." He patted the top of her head.

Rose stood at the screen door and watched Wilson pass Manny and Jeannie and Wendy and Martin, each nodding to the other as they mumbled "goodnights" on the porch steps.

The next night, when Wilson again dropped by, they dragged the lawn chairs away from the house as if they were teenagers, sneaking out of sight. They sat companionably, listening to the evening noises of insects and birds.

Silence fell with the dusk, and Rose exhaled. "It's nice to have some peace and quiet," Rose sighed.

"Umm," Wilson agreed.

"Sometimes," Rose admitted, "I get tired of always being with the kids." She paused. "And probably," she said, sighing again, "probably, they sometimes get tired of being with me."

"Aw, Rosie. How could anyone get tired of being with you?"

Rosie? What kind of talk was this? She stared hard at Wilson's profile in the dimming light. Was this Avram Schuyler all over again? Was sitting outside the same as accepting a soda at a dance? Had nothing changed in fifty years?

Without turning his head, Wilson asked into the night, "Hey, Rosie, how about coming over to my house on Sunday? You can cook me dinner. It will give you a chance to get away. And I'll take you for a drive. I'll show you around Vermont."

Rose was grateful for the dark. "Actually—" She stopped to soften her tone. "Actually, I'm busy Sunday." She didn't have to say anything else. What business was it of his? But she could smell his disappointment rise like a bad odor. "On Sunday," she explained, "I'm going to a concert. To Marlboro."

It was quick thinking to remember about the Sunday concert, and a good idea. A chance to be alone. By herself.

How could she have been so naive? *Rosie*, that's what tipped her off. Only Sam ever called her that.

She sat on the grass and listened to the Mendelssohn quartet. The sadness of the opening chords pulled Rose right back to Sammy's last days, sitting beside his hospital bed while he lay ashen. She just held his hand, until that, too, became painful. But he never complained, even as the cancer ate his insides. And it all happened so fast. What? A matter of weeks. He comes home from work one day, earlier than Rose, and before Rose is even through the door, she knows something's wrong.

"What's happened?" she demanded.

"Rosie, calm down!" He put his arms on her shoulders, it was that bad. "I just don't feel good. Mr. Bauer told me to come home early. See a doctor, maybe."

"A doctor?" Rose unwound her scarf and removed her hat and coat. "What for? What's the matter?"

"I just don't feel so hot," Sam tried to shrug it off. "Like my guts are twisted or something."

"You plugged up? I should make you stewed prunes?" Rose bustled the groceries from her cart onto the counter. "I bought lamb chops. You think you can eat?" It wasn't really a question. Of course he could eat. Only the dying don't eat. And that's how Rose learned how bad it was, because Sam didn't touch his baked potato that evening, and Manny ate Sam's chop. A fourteen-year-old, what else could you expect? The boy would eat the box the cereal came in if she let him, he was that hungry all the time.

They sent Manny to school as usual the next day. They didn't say anything. Why worry the child? Together they walked to Dr. Jacob's office in Sheepshead Bay. By the time they arrived, Sammy was shivering, unable to get warm even inside the doctor's overheated waiting room.

"You want I should come in?" Rose asked when the nurse called Sam's turn.

Sam shook his head. Rose pulled needlework from her bag and was so engaged in counting stitches that the nurse had to tug on her sleeve. "The doctor would like to speak to you," she said, and led Rose down the hall.

The violin's tremolo matched the vibration of her knees at that moment. The hall elongated into an endless black corridor, and Rose didn't think she'd ever reach the door. The nurse turned into the doctor's study and motioned for Rose to take a chair. "Dr. Jacobs will be right in."

For a brief moment, Rose heard the sighing of strings from the quartet. Their plaintive melody was as dissonant as Dr. Jacobs's voice as he took the seat behind his large desk and said, "Mrs. Rubin, your husband needs to go to the hospital."

"What's wrong?" Rose stuck her chin out, as if that could interrupt the flow of discordant news. "Is he going to be okay?"

Dr. Jacobs steepled his fingers under his chin. "I don't know. That's why we need to admit him. He has a large mass in his abdomen."

"What's a mass?"

"A growth. Possibly a tumor. Probably. He'll need surgery to find out."

"And then?"

"It depends on what we find."

The notes of the violins in the Mendelssohn mimicked the anxiety that made Rose's hands tremble on the way to the hospital; it

99

was the sound of her voice catching as she gave her address to the nurse.

Not until the surgeon came into the room, with Sammy sitting on the side of the bed in his hospital gown, did Rose began to feel the pluck and courage of the third movement. The excitement of doing something! He was a young doctor with dark hair, soft features, and a friendly, comforting manner. The way he explained the surgery, he made it sound like a tune–up—one of those routine services that people with cars were always performing curbside on a Saturday afternoon. The sort of thing that Milty Katzenbacker could do. How hard could it be? And wasn't Milty always bragging about how much better his car ran afterwards? That's what the operation would be like. Rose was sure of it.

But the terror struck just the way the opening of the fourth movement sounded. Sammy under the knife! All the things that could go wrong! And Manny at home, wondering where his parents were! Rose would have to go home and tell him. Maybe bring him back. A visit would do his father good.

But what if something should happen while Rose was gone? The agony of deciding: Go? Stay? And not knowing how long the surgery would take, or how long Sammy would be under. That's what the doctor said, he'd have to put him under. Why do they talk like that? It sounds like they're going to bury him, "Put him under." But that's not what they mean. They're just talking about the anesthesia.

Rose talked inside her head all the way back to the apartment and fetched Manny. When they returned to the hospital, Sam was in the recovery room, but they couldn't see him yet. The nurse said that he was resting comfortably, and that the surgeon would be by to tell Rose how the operation went.

Dr. Heller found them on the stiff lobby seats. Manny was leafing through old *Life* magazines, while Rose sat with both hands clutching the handle of her purse.

The doctor looked different in street clothes, older than when he wore green pajamas. There was more gravity in his face, too. How could Rose have thought he looked boyish? This was not the face of a cherub. This was the face of the Angel of Death. Rose took a quick bite of air and held her breath.

"Mrs. Rubin? And?" He held his hand out to shake Manny's.

"This is Manny, my son." Rose stood to face the doctor. "How's Sammy?"

"Your husband is resting comfortably, Mrs. Rubin."

Rose's heart gladdened. A sweet melody.

"But I'm afraid we don't have good news."

The dark cello sawed across her guts.

"We found a large tumor. It's malignant, and the cancer's spread diffusely throughout the abdomen." Dr. Heller paused to let this information sink in. "I'm afraid there is little we can do for your husband, beyond pain relief."

"Can't you just take it out?" Rose demanded, her voice rising and shrill.

Dr. Heller placed a hand on her arm. "We removed some of it, but the cancer has spread. There's no treatment for the disease when it has progressed this far." He paused. "I'm sorry."

Rose stood stunned. It was Manny, in his gawky adolescence and in a voice that cracked in the asking, "How long does my father have to live?"

Dr. Heller looked at the man-boy. "You look like your father," he said. Then he looked at his shoes and spoke softly. "I don't think he will survive more than a few weeks."

Rose found her voice again. "Can he come home?"

"We'll see. He has a large surgical wound that needs nursing care. We'll keep him here until that's drained. After that, it depends on how well he rallies and how much pain he's in."

"Pain?"

"Yes. Pain from the disease."

And Rose knew Sammy would never come home.

Percy caught a snippet of gossip from the buzz in the audience as the musicians took their places. "The Guarneri's debut!" echoed from seat to seat. It was a mystery to him how so many in the audience knew each other and what was going on behind the scenes. He felt like the kid outside the candy shop, with his face pressed to the glass. His shoulders sagged into the seat as the four men on stage adjusted their music.

The opening chords were as melancholy as Percy, and he felt the notes deep within, as if his internal organs were weeping. This was the sound of his own loneliness, of his life drawing to an end as solitary as the bull pine in his meadow. He imagined the field without the pine defining the landscape, but instead of emptiness, a forest of seedlings sprouted with the violins taking flight from the bass notes of the cello. Wind ruffled through the leaves; the tall meadow grasses rippled. The four voices tumbled over one another. Naked limbs entwined in one another; a man and a woman twisting in the sheets; a perfume of musk and the delight of skin on skin. Percy blushed.

How could such young men know the sadness that followed? The first violinist, with his chin jutting out over his instrument: he was just a boy. The violist had his eyes closed as his arm pulled the melody from his fiddle. It was a melody of middle age, a bittersweet song that surely these boys were too young to fathom. How did that young man playing second know how to run a counter melody of such convincing complication? Only the cellist, whose notes were like ballast to the music plowing through the waves, looked old enough to have maybe touched the troubles this movement lamented.

Plaintive, yes, but hopeful, too, the violin sang above the others' pizzicato. There was hope. There always is. And just look how they pluck in unison with only the briefest nod from one another, then pick up their bows and run away with the music.

If the music were any less, it would be embarrassing to watch these men twist and bend. The four of them heaved as one in a torment of sound, sound Percy knew in the darkest hours in his own home, and blushed to acknowledge in the heat of so public a place. How odd, all these people sitting cheek-by-jowl next to strangers and listening to such naked emotion. How public a place for such intimacy. How voyeuristic to watch the four young musicians perform. And the music. How did Mendelssohn capture such exquisite agony in sound so that it could be re-created here? Why would he want generation after generation to know such private thoughts? For surely, listening to this music was like sitting inside Mendelssohn's brain while the composer, perhaps in the dishabille of his nightshirt, working at a small desk by the attic window of his bedroom, confessed his longing and sadness to paper in a series of dots that translated to these sounds, on this afternoon.

Percy shook his head. It was a brave thing, to write music. And braver still to play it with such vigor. The audience hesitated to break the melancholy spell as the quartet sounded the final chord. After a moment's silence, like a grand pause held under a fermata, the audience burst into applause. Percy didn't clap, but sat with his head bowed, so grateful to have heard the murmurs of his sad heart spoken aloud.

After the concert, Rose stood under the tree where Percy had been and watched the crowd spill out of the auditorium. She recognized him right away. It wasn't so much his close-cropped white hair as his spare frame that stood singular in the crowd. He wasn't taller or thinner than the other men, but he seemed stronger, firmer, more vital. His white hair spoke more of wisdom than age. But his eyes, which had twinkled with annoying amusement that time at the library, his eyes now looked so sad.

He walked over, but for a moment, neither spoke. People were crowding into cars, waving their good-byes, rushing back to their weekday lives.

They spoke at the same moment.

"Such sad music—"

"The music was so sad—"

Both smiled. Percy nodded for Rose to continue.

Rose shook her head and sighed. "It's like looking for *tsuris*, listening to music like that." She saw the question in Percy's face. "Troubles," Rose translated. "*Tsuris* means troubles." She raised her eyebrows. "You don't speak Yiddish?" Rose shrugged. "And why should you? It's a language of *galus*, exile, meaning it thrives in the ghettos of the homeless." Rose looked closely at Percy. "You've lived here all your life, what would you know of exile?" Rose's gaze drifted over the tree-tops and sighed.

"Where are you from?" His voice was so gentle, it hurt.

Focused on the distant view, Rose said, "I was born in a muddy little village called Zolochev. I came to this country when I was nine, and I've lived in a city ever since." She turned to face Percy. "This is the first time I've been in the countryside since I was a small girl."

Manny's green station wagon pulled up beside them.

Percy reached for the door handle. He hesitated. "Well, I hope you like it here."

Rose could tell he meant it.

He opened the car door.

She slid in.

Manny made a wide U-turn, and Percy waved them off, calling, "So long!"

"That's the man from the Fourth of July, isn't it?" Jeannie asked as they drove away.

"Percy Mendell." Rose cleared her throat. "He stopped by the other night. While you were at the movies."

"I thought that was Wilson Nye?" Jeannie squinted, trying to match the face of the trim man who'd just slammed the car door with the portly, mustachioed one who slunk out of the house the moment they drove in.

"Yes, that was Wilson Nye," Rose sighed.

"But *that* wasn't Wilson Nye!" Manny growled.

"Manny!" Jeannie scolded. "Watch your voice!"

"Well, listen to her! Does she or doesn't she know who she's keeping company with?"

"I'm not 'keeping company' with anyone." Rose's voice was hard. "Percy Mendell stopped by last Tuesday while Wilson Nye was visiting. Mr. Mendell didn't stay long. It was Mr. Nye who you saw when you came home."

"It's okay," Jeannie patted Rose's arm and glanced sideways at Manny.

Manny relaxed. "My mother, the Belle of Orton." He shook his head. "You better watch out, Ma, or you'll end up marrying one of these guys."

"Manny!" Jeannie nudged him.

"Let him say whatever he wants," Rose said. "But I've buried two husbands. That's enough." Rose looked out the window so she wouldn't have to talk.

The sadness of the Mendelssohn clung to her, and the memory of Sam dwindling in the hospital bed, until there was nothing left but an empty husk, which they put in a coffin and buried in a city of headstones. Even the apartment was empty. Rose and Manny could both be home, but with Sam gone, the place was hollow. And Manny, he had friends, homework, high school. She was just a widow, alone in the silent apartment.

It was the silence that finally drove Rose out. Three months after the funeral, Rose took the train into Manhattan and walked from the subway to Irving Place, where she joined the line of concert-goers like herself, people willing to stand in line from five until eight to buy a dollar ticket to the Peoples' Symphony Concerts. A dollar! It had only been a quarter when she was a girl.

The afternoon was a warm one, rich with the fragrance of spring. The air had the feel of velvet. And the ritual of standing in line, of climbing the stone steps of Washington Irving High School, the great vault of the entry, the squeak of the wooden seats—nothing had changed in all those years. Rose forgot about Sammy and remembered before she was married, when she would go to every concert she could.

It was at the Peoples' Symphony she first heard the Brahms cello sonatas and recognized the expression of longing. It was there that Rose listened to Mozart's sonatas for piano and violin and fell in love with the order of sound. She was young, and this music taught her to hope for just such conversation with a lover: two voices stating their purpose and echoing their opinions back and forth. It was where she heard Dvorak's "American" Quartet and *kvelled*, rejoiced, she was American.

Rose made a habit of going to concerts again. She brought a book to read while she waited for the box office to open. By some miracle, it never seemed to rain or snow on the Saturday afternoons of concerts, although occasionally it was very cold. Too cold to read.

It was not yet six o'clock on just such a bitter afternoon in 1944, when Rose wondered whether or not to risk stepping into a nearby coffee shop when the well-tailored gentleman behind her echoed her thoughts.

He leaned forward, "We'll still get tickets if we go somewhere warm for an hour, no?"

It wasn't that his language was accented—whose in Rose's world wasn't?—but that it was educated, she could tell right away.

Rose shrugged.

"You'll join me?" He tilted his head to the side and shrugged back.

Rose hesitated.

"My name is Isadore. Isadore Mayer. I teach at Hebrew Union College. I'm a widower and my children are grown, so you are not to worry that I'm just trying to pick up a stepmother for little orphans. I'm cold and I like your face. It's nice to have company in a tavern, and I wouldn't enjoy sitting all warm at the bar if I knew you were freezing out here. So," he crooked his elbow for Rose to hold on to, "Pete's Tavern is just around the corner. Come. A little brandy will chase the winter out of this day."

Rose threaded her arm through his. He smelled good. Sam had never worn cologne.

He took her to Pete's. They sat at the bar. He ordered brandy.

"I've never had brandy before," Rose confessed as she held the snifter to her nose. The fumes burned her eyes.

"Sip it, just so." He demonstrated. "Let it sit a moment in your mouth, then swallow."

He watched her as she followed his instructions. Could he see her cheeks burn? A mellow warmth seeped down her chest. "It tastes like the cello." Rose's voice was husky with the drink.

"Exactly," he nodded. "That's it exactly." He studied her a moment. "So, you're a poet?"

Rose laughed. "A milliner!"

"Did you make that fetching hat you are wearing?"

Rose automatically lifted her hand to her head and patted the cashmere cloche with the velvet ribbon. She nodded.

"A woman of many talents, I see." He sipped and regarded her. "So how is it a lovely woman like you stands in line by herself on a Saturday night?"

"I like music," Rose said.

Isadore shook his head. "Rose, Rose." He stopped and looked directly at her. "Do you mind that I call you Rose? You may call me Dory. That is the name my family uses." He waited for Rose to nod her consent. "You like music, so you come to a concert. My question must appear foolish to you. But what I want to know is why such a lovely woman who likes music comes out on such a bitter cold night to listen to music by herself." He gulped the last of his drink.

"I'm not lonely when I listen to music. When I'm listening to music, I forget I'm by myself." Even with her coat on, Rose felt naked under Dory's gaze. He seemed to be reading her soul.

"And Mr. Rubin doesn't like music?" He looked at her slyly. "I'm trying to find out if you're married. If your husband is going to fling a glove in my face and demand satisfaction!"

Rose chuckled. "You must read novels!"

He bowed in confession.

"My husband died five years ago. My son is overseas."

"Ach." He summoned the bartender and settled the bill. "Now I understand. A woman who has buried a husband and sent a son to be a soldier—it's nothing for such a brave woman to stand a little while in the cold. Come!" Isadore held open the door to the street. "It's time to secure our places. Maybe they'll open the box office early on account of the weather."

"You must be a newcomer to these concerts," Rose said. "Tickets go on sale at seven-thirty and not a minute before." They rounded the corner, where the line had grown. "We'll have to wait, but we'll get in. It doesn't get iffy until the line turns the corner. I think the weather is in our favor."

"The weather is very much in our favor." Wordlessly, Dory positioned himself to protect Rose from the wind. "If it wasn't so cold, we wouldn't have gone for a drink."

Rose nodded.

"So, do you know what music we're going to hear?"

Rose didn't.

"I should tell you?"

Rose nodded.

"Tonight, we're going to be treated to two piano quartets, one by Beethoven and one by Schumann, and neither of them well known. Beethoven's Opus 16 was written as both a quartet and a piano quintet for winds. It premiered in 1797. Beethoven played the piano part for the quintet version, and according to one witness, he began to improvise in the third movement, the rondo, to the evident pleasure of both himself and his audience—and to the visible displeasure of his fellow musicians. Every time they put their instruments up to their mouths, expecting to resume playing the music as written, Beethoven disappointed them with new flights of fancy. Ultimately, he took pity on the wind players and let them finish playing the piece." Isadore looked at Rose. "Can you imagine that kind of showmanship?"

Rose shook her head. "How do you know so much?"

It was Dory's turn to shrug.

Rose's eyes narrowed. "Do you play?"

"A little," he confessed.

"How much is a little?"

"Oh, I join some friends now and then. We play quartets together."

"What instrument?"

"The instrument of your brandy." His eyes twinkled.

"Cello?"

He nodded.

And that's when Rose knew she'd met her new partner in life.

5 | stitch & bitch

The Tuesday after the Marlboro concert, Rose eased herself into Sally Boyce's front seat and sighed, "It's good to get away."

"I know what you mean," Sally said, nodding her head so her brown curls bobbed. "We all feel that way—a little break from routine."

That was it exactly. Rose needed a break from the daily routine of morning projects around the house after breakfast, quiet reading after lunch, an afternoon outing—always swimming if the weather was fine—and dinner followed by board games or books. Except for the swimming in the thin lake water—no salt! no waves! no undertow!—they were all activities Rose enjoyed, but not every day at the same time with the same people. Even the kids—Rose loved her grandchildren!—but they never left each other alone, always pinching and tattling, whining, teasing, tormenting one another, so that Manny threatened to spank them and Jeannie sent them to their rooms. Just Manny and Jeannie's tones of voice—booming and shrill—were fatiguing. Rose shook her head and sighed."I hate to admit it," she sighed again, "but I'm tired of my family."

"Oh," Sally said, taking her eyes off the road and looking Rose full in the face, "You don't have to apologize. Tuesday nights are as much for complaining as quilting." She faced forward again and spoke directly out the windshield. "We call our club 'The Stitch and Bitch.'" She glanced sidelong at Rose.

"*Kvetch und krechtz! Oy!*" Rose laughed and slapped her knee. Her whole body shook.

Sally smiled and raised her eyebrows.

Rose spoke through her laughter, "*Kvetch und krechtz!*" Breathless with laughing, Rose spoke between gasps. "It means—complain—and sigh—like I've been—doing since I got in the car. And now you tell me, we're going to 'Stitch and Bitch.'" Rose wiped her eyes on a Kleenex and caught her breath. "All my years in America, and I never heard such a phrase. Never heard anything in English so close to Yiddish—with the same—the same *oomph*." She sighed once more, relaxing into the car seat as they bounced onto the pavement. "*Oy!* I feel better!"

"What was that phrase you used?" Sally asked.

"*Kvetch und krechtz!* Complain and sigh. To *kvetch* is to whine, never be satisfied. And *krechtz*—" Rose sighed, "is like that. It's still complaining, only with sound effects. Like a person who won't speak up but will moan and sigh, and when you ask them what's wrong they reply, 'Wrong? Wrong? Who said anything was wrong? Is it wrong for a son to forget to call his mother on her birthday? Is it so difficult to pick up the phone and say Happy Birthday Ma, I should like to know?' So, when someone *krechtzes* and you ask them what's wrong, it's like an invitation to *kvetch*. The two go hand in glove."

Sally glanced at Rose. "You're very funny."

Rose shrugged. "In my world, this isn't so funny; it's true."

"Your world?"

Rose looked at her carefully. "Have you ever met a Jew before?"

Sally frowned. "I think Mr. Kramsky's Jewish. Kramsky's Dry Goods, downtown." Her face brightened. "He has the best price on fabrics." They parked beside the Evening Star Grange. "It's where we all buy our yard goods." Sally tilted her head toward the door. "Come in and meet the gals."

Inside, nearly a dozen ladies were seated around a large quilt suspended over a frame. Several glanced up, greeted Sally, and eyed Rose, but no one's hands hesitated for even a moment.

"This is Rose Mayer," Sally announced as she pulled up two chairs to the quilt's edge.

"Oh!" said Irma Bassett, who turned and smiled. "I'm so glad you could join us! Rose, here, knows a thing or two about needlework, if I'm not mistaken."

Rose shrugged.

"Here, let me introduce you." Irma's voice was bumpy as a washerboard. "This is Anna Mae Parsons, mother of the bride who we're making the quilt for." Anna Mae nodded as she rethreaded a needle. "Next is Mary White, of White's Dairy. It's nice to see you here, Mary."

"Thanks. It feels good to sit down." She smiled at Rose and tucked her tawny hair behind her ears. "I've been in the kitchen all day, between fixing dinner and making relish, now that the cucumbers are coming on."

Sally nudged Rose with her elbow, "See? I told you it was 'Stitch and Bitch.'"

Mary blushed. "I didn't mean to complain," she sighed.

Charlotte George snapped a thread as she spoke. "And one of the rules is you can't say anything nice about your husband all evening."

"For some of us, that's no hardship," offered a plump woman

with dimples on either side of her smile. "I'm Florence Darling, and I haven't had a good word to say about Harold for these past twenty years or more no matter what day of the week, but Tuesdays especially. And I'm pleased to meet you, so welcome to the club."

"Don't worry, Rose. It took me a while before I could say anything bad about Lloyd," Irma rumbled.

"But that's because Lloyd's perfect," Florence winked.

"Have you ever quilted before?" Mary asked.

Before Rose could speak, Irma answered, "I'd rather know whether she's ever been married before?"

"Here!" Sally passed Rose a spool of white thread and a book of needles.

Rose opened her purse and removed her eyeglasses and a roll of fabric tied with ribbon. The women around the table eyed her movements. Unrolled, the fabric contained four slots with a pair of scissors in each one, each different. Rose removed the smallest, which trailed a long loop of ribbon tied to one of the handles. This she lowered over her head, so the scissors hung from her neck. She rolled the scissors case back up, took up the thread, cut six pieces something less than a yard long, and started threading six separate needles, which she stuck in the edge of the quilt, for later use.

"And you told me you never quilted before!" Irma clicked her tongue. "Look at you! You're putting the rest of us to shame!" Irma scanned the faces surrounding the quilt. "Why didn't we ever think of that?"

"I've never quilted before," Rose said, adjusting her half-glasses low on her nose, "but I've earned my living with my needle. If there's one thing I know how to do," she paused, "I know how to sew."

The ladies looked at one another.

"So, I'm watching what you're doing, and you're going through all the layers with what? about ten stitches to the inch?"

"Eight is fine," Florence said.

"Ten is better," Anna Mae cut Florence a look.

"And what is this pattern you're doing?" Rose traced the star in a circle that a quiet woman on her left was completing.

"That's the quilting pattern." Irma leaned over to inspect the work. "Martha, maybe you could trace the pattern for Rose. Rose, this is Martha Stratton on your left."

Martha leaned toward Rose and spoke very softly. "You don't really need a pattern, not if you have a good eye." She flattened the quilt in front of Rose. "See how we've stitched this pattern at regular intervals? You can do one right here. It's just a circle, and inside it you make a much smaller circle, and on the small circle you add four long triangles alternating with four short triangles, like rays of a star."

Rose nodded, eyeballed her field of work and started to stitch.

"What do you think of Orton so far?" Anna Mae asked.

"It's different. That's for sure." Rose held one hand beneath her work, to guide the needle back into the fabric, making quick, even stitches.

"You're living with your son?" Mabel Robinson raised her eyebrows. Rose remembered her: Mr. Greenwood's sister-in-law, the one who got Barrett to stock sour cream.

"I thought it was your daughter, Mrs. Rubin," Anna Mae looked over at Rose for only a moment, then continued her stitching.

"Jeannie's my daughter-in-law," Rose spoke as she sewed.

"Why didn't she come?" Charlotte challenged.

"She's a gardener," Irma spoke up. "Doesn't sew."

"Isn't it funny how some women take to gardening and others to needlework?" Florence mused. "I can't stand the dirt, and I can't get anything ever to grow."

"You either have a green thumb or a sharp tongue," Sally quipped as she snipped her thread.

"You mean no one here's a gardener?" Rose asked.

"Mary gardens," Charlotte wrinkled her nose, as if the words smelled bad. "But she's a farm wife; she doesn't have any choice."

Without lifting her eyes, Rose could see the others shoot glances across the quilt, a silent language that was lost on Charlotte.

"Mary puts us all to shame, with her energy," Irma spoke mildly, as if neither Mary nor Charlotte were present.

It was just like in the factory, this kind of banter, but without the whirring power drives turning the belts and making the sewing machines hum. A girl might complain about a neighbor always stinking up the toilet, and it would turn out that the neighbor was the cousin of the girl across from you, and she'd be offended and insult you back and hard feelings would rise until Faith Solomon smoothed things over with her unswerving good nature. She'd just start talking about her married sister's new baby, or the window display at Wanamaker's on Fourteenth Street, or even the newly bloomed flowers in Washington Square and the whole feeling in the room would slowly shift from bad to something lighter, as if there were carefree happiness to look forward to, as if the hours after work were really filled with fun and leisure, and life was comfortable and everyone was happy with their lot.

The quilting ladies fell into a smooth silence of stitching broken by Sally saying, "I haven't heard any complaints this evening, and I told Rose that's what we were famous for. Don't make me into a liar."

"Let's let our guest start," Charlotte said. "What's the worst thing your husband ever did to you?"

A conversation of fleeting glances crossed between the others.

Rose just kept stitching and said, "Died. Two of them. I've been widowed twice."

Charlotte blushed. "I'm sorry," she mumbled.

"There's nothing to be sorry about. What can we do about death?" Rose shrugged and changed her empty needle for a newly threaded one.

"But aren't you lonely?" Martha Stratton's voice was barely above a whisper.

"Are widows the only ones who get lonely? Sometimes I was lonely when I was married."

"Have you come to Orton looking for Husband Number Three?" Charlotte asked.

"Who needs to get married again? At my age, all a man wants is a housekeeper and a nurse. No thank you!"

The ladies laughed.

"Didn't I see Wilson Nye's car parked at your house last week?" Sally asked.

"Wilson Nye!" Mabel shook her head. "Now there's a character!"

"What kind of character?" Rose asked. "I know Percy Mendell doesn't care for him."

The women around the table all started talking at once.

"Percy Mendell! I should say not!"

"So you've met Percy, too?"

"Are there any other bachelors in town? I guess there hasn't been a fresh widow in these parts for some time!"

"Percy Mendell in love. Now that would be a spectacle worth watching!"

"Percy and Wilson rivals! Oh no! Not again!" Mabel moaned.

Sally agreed. "There's enough heartache between those two already. Rose," she said, looking serious. "Be careful!"

"Careful? What do you mean?" Rose asked.

"Wilson Nye killed Percy's fiancée."

"Killed?"

"Well, not murder."

"Might as well have been, from the stories I've heard."

"It was an accident." Martha Stratton spoke softly. "I was there."

A heaviness oppressed the room.

"Lila Winthrop fell out of Wilson's car," Martha said in her barely audible voice.

No one spoke.

Martha continued. "I'm not saying Wilson Nye was blameless. He and Bobby set up the foolish race to begin with. And there was liquor. No denying. But everyone's suffered long enough, Percy Mendell most of all. He was wild about Lila, and he's been grieving her ever since."

Rose snipped her thread, plucked a loaded needle from her arsenal, and continued quilting.

"But it's not all heartache," Mabel said. "Percy's over that. For goodness sake, it's been more than forty years! That's not the trouble between Percy and Wilson."

"Then what is?" Charlotte demanded.

"It had to do with the land adjoining the Interstate," Mabel said.

"That's right," Flo Darling nodded.

Anna Mae shook her head side to side. "I'd heard something about that. It's not true, is it?"

Irma shrugged and Sally spoke. "Percy's been closed-mouthed, but he stopped talking to Wilson after Wilson bought up Holland's

Farm right where the Waterchase exit went in, and he resigned from the selectboard about the same time. Percy won't serve on the local board as long as Wilson's on it."

"What do you think happened?" Rose asked, her hands idle.

"It's just speculation," Martha warned.

"It's more than that." Sally's voice was stern.

"Aye," Irma agreed.

"But you don't know for sure," Charlotte sneered. "Folks are just jealous that Wilson Nye is rich, that's all."

"But just how did he gain his money?" Irma asked, raising her eyebrows.

"He told me he's in real estate," Rose prompted.

"Real estate!" Sally spat the words. "*Land theft* is more like it."

"But you don't *know*!" Charlotte snapped, slapping her hands on the edge of the quilting frame.

"It's not hard to figure out!" Sally glared. She shifted her gaze to Rose. "When the thruway was built," Sally waved off in the direction of the highway, "the state had to buy up all the land for the right-of-way."

"And the deeds are all kept in the town hall," Irma added with urgency.

"And the selectmen acted for the town," Sally explained.

"And they were supposed to do so 'without prejudice' I think the term is." Irma butted in again. "Meaning the state wanted to buy the land at fair market value and tried hard to keep speculators out of it. They were just going to buy the land they needed for their superhighway, and keep mum about the rest."

"It was the location of the exits that was so secret," Sally reminded Irma. "The point is, the location of the exits was supposed to be a secret so that the state wouldn't have to pay more for it."

"And so that no one would buy up that land even after the

state had its right-of-way, you see. Buy it for development, that is." Irma's deep voice added weight to her words.

"That's right," Sally agreed. "The land around the exits would become valuable. The state knew that. It's where people get off to buy gas and use the restroom, maybe spend the night in a motel."

"If there's a motel," Irma added.

"Exactly."

"So?" Rose asked.

"Well, as selectmen, both Percy and Wilson knew where these exits were going to be, they knew whose land was being taken for the exit in Orton and the one in Waterchase."

"Percy, he helped the farmers whose land was taken. He helped them fight for cattle crossings under the road, and urged the road builders not to divide pastures and farms where they could help it."

"But Wilson—" Mabel pressed her lips together, saying no more.

"Well, Wilson bought up Holland's field and the woodlot at the corner of Allard's and all those parcels that would end up right near the exits, see?"

Rose shook her head. She didn't see.

"Wilson went to the owners. He knew which was the valuable land, because he was a selectman. And he knew what the state was offering for it. So he went and offered a little bit more."

Rose's lips parted.

"And then as soon as the thruway is finished, what does he do?" Irma had a glint in her eye and ice in her voice. "He sells an acre of land for what he paid for all fifty. And he does it again and again. Sold the land to the Esso station at one corner, and the Texaco at the other. Sold the land to the Howard Johnson's. He made a fortune!"

"And Percy resigned. Hasn't barely spoken to Wilson ever since.

It's been what? Nearly ten years by now."

Charlotte cut short the silence. "You don't know any of this for a fact!"

"It's all in the land records, if you want to know," Sally said. Her voice had a hard edge.

"That just proves it's all legal!" Charlotte insisted.

"Legal isn't the same as right," Martha said, so quietly everyone was silenced.

Rose asked Charlotte, "Why are you so eager to defend Mr. Nye?"

Charlotte glared at Rose. "Jews aren't the only ones allowed to be rich!"

"Charlotte!" several women gasped.

"Don't 'Charlotte' me!" She stood up and collected her sewing things, grabbed her handbag, and made for the door, where she tossed her parting question like a grenade, "What would a Jew know about our affairs anyway?" The door slammed and she was gone.

Rose sat very still.

Mary White was the first to speak, "I'm so sorry."

Rose didn't move.

"She's young," Anna Mae offered.

"And she's not very happy," Martha added.

The ladies stared at their idle hands in the long silence, waiting for Rose to say something.

Young and unhappy. Same as Hitler's youth. Young and unhappy. What trouble that caused! Rose sighed.

"That's a *krechtz*," Sally whispered just loud enough for Rose to hear.

Rose met Sally's eyes. "So what else can I do?" She shrugged. "There are anti-Semites everywhere." She sighed again.

"So *kvetch* a little."

The other ladies looked puzzled.

Rose chuckled. "*Kvetch, krechtz.* It's the way of the world. What can an old lady do?"

"What are you two talking about?" Irma demanded.

"*Kvetch und krechtz,*" Sally said brightly. "It means 'Stitch and Bitch.'"

"In what language?" Anna Mae asked.

"In Rose's language!" Sally crowed.

"It's Yiddish," Rose picked up her needle and started quilting again. "It's good for complaining." She looked up and smiled. "After all, it's the language of the Jews."

And everyone relaxed.

By the time they were ready to break up, the quilting on Berenice Parsons's wedding quilt was nearly completed. "One more week and we'll have it finished," Anna Mae said with satisfaction.

"You'll come back, won't you?" Martha laid her hand on Rose's.

Rose regarded the faces of the ladies looking at her. Mary White said, "If you come, I will too! No matter what chores are waiting at home."

"I'd like to learn how to can vegetables," Rose told her.

"There's nothing to it," Mary shrugged, "Except back–breaking labor."

Rose escaped after lunch and walked up the hill, in the direction of Boyce's. She longed for the security of a sidewalk; there was nothing but wilderness on either side of the dirt road. Wilderness and stone walls. The road wasn't even flat, but crowned in the center and sloped into ditches where the road met the woods. The only way to walk straight was to claim the high ground in the middle, so Rose did, alert for the sound of approaching cars, and feeling both scared and giddy at her audacity. Walking down the middle of the street!

The pebbles underfoot hurt her feet, so she turned to go back. But that was her question. Should she go back? Back to Florida? Back to Brooklyn? Or to Teaneck and live with the kids?

She'd already changed her plane reservation—twice. When she'd arrived in Vermont, she didn't think she'd last two weeks, and now, here it was coming on two months. But Manny and Jeannie would be going home soon. Summer was almost over, and they wanted her to live with them. Jeannie wanted to return to the classroom. If Rose were there, she could feed the kids lunch, so they didn't have to stay at school all day, and she could be there in the afternoons, when Jeannie had meetings. She'd sleep in the finished attic, with its own bath.

At the beginning of the summer, Rose would have considered it. But a summer with her children—well, it was enough. Manny was so gruff, so easily irritated. If he's this impatient when she's well, what would he be like if Rose became sick, God forbid? No, living in the attic, no matter how nicely finished, was not her cup of tea. Who would she have to talk with? What people her own age? Teaneck was for young families. It was no place for a grandma to live.

But what did that leave her? Finding an apartment in Brighton, where she'd lived with Sammy and raised Manny? Did she still know anybody there? She left Brighton when she married Dory. So, should she take an apartment in Flatbush? How could she pick up that dropped stitch, especially after they'd broken up the household, said good-bye, moved away? She'd been gone seven years, although how it could already be that long didn't make sense. No, that chapter of her life was over, finished.

So? She should go back to Florida? For what? To listen to Sadie September *kvetch* about her arthritis and hear Beulah Morris *kvell* about her son the lawyer or her daughter who's married to the doctor? Or worse yet, endure Aileen Friederman complain about Alan's virility, as if that *putz* had a *shlong* worth opening her legs for. Rose, for one, didn't believe Alan Friederman could get it up anymore. More to the point, if he could, he hardly seemed the type to *shtup* his own wife. For this, she should spend the winter in Florida? She didn't think so. But then what?

Rose moved to the side of the road as Sally's car approached. "Hello!" Sally greeted her, slowing the car. "Do you have time for some lemonade?" Sally asked. "Hop in, I'll drive you up to the house."

Rose followed Sally past a warren of dark rooms and into the kitchen, with two stoves.

"Is that a woodstove?" Rose asked, pointing at the old range next to the new one.

"Yup," Sally patted the cold iron. "It's a great thing in winter. Keeps this end of the house warm. Keeps tea water at a boil all day. Great for slow cooking soups and stews. Oh! Don't get me started!" Sally placed the pitcher and two glasses on a tray and headed toward the front door. "I'm mad about that cook stove, and Eamon, he just makes fun of me. But that's because he cuts most of the firewood."

"My mother used to chop firewood," Rose blurted.

Sally stopped. "Your mother had a wood–burning cook stove? I thought you lived in a city?" She pushed the screen door open with her hip, and held it for Rose to pass. It slapped shut behind her. "Have a seat." Sally nodded at the rockers and placed the tray on a table.

"Ooh," Rose stretched her feet out in front of her. "That feels good," she said, flexing her sore ankles.

Sally plucked the green foliage of plants growing near the porch and held the stems out to Rose. "Mint," she said.

As clean as soap.

"Want some? It's delicious with the lemon."

Rose nodded.

Sally sat herself. "So, did you have a woodstove for cooking?"

Rose sipped her lemonade and nodded, "I think so." She closed her eyes and saw her mother in the dim light of long ago. Her mother, a bundle of skirts and shawls, a kerchief covering her head. It seemed as if she always wore the same black dress, no matter the season. And she was always bustling—chopping, stirring, kneading, scrubbing. Never still. Even when she sat down, she had a needle and thread in her hand. Rose peered through the years into her childhood kitchen, where a stone stove loomed in the gloom. Only a small window allowed light from the outside, and an oil lamp hanging above the table. Her mother bent over to feed wood into the firebox below the oven, like a small cupboard built into the wall. There was also a stove top where she boiled water, rendered chicken fat, fried blintzes.

Rose sighed. "It was so long ago. I was so young. I remember something different from what you've got, something more like a wall of bricks that would stay warm for days. It was the only heat we had in the winter."

"Did you live in the country?"

Rose nodded. "We had a cow. Chickens. It was my job to collect eggs. And sometimes, I carried a hen down to the butcher." Rose sipped.

"A butcher for a hen? Why didn't your mother just do it herself? Especially if she split her own wood? That's what my mother did: axed the birds right on the chopping block." She tipped her glass and drank.

"In our village, we had a *sochet*, a special kind of butcher. So the meat would be kosher."

"What's that?"

"Kosher?" How could she explain the dietary laws? "It's how Jews eat."

"What do you mean?" Sally sat forward. "Jews eat differently from other people?"

"Religious Jews, yes." This was complicated. "Jews eat kosher meat, butchered by a *sochet*. To be kosher, an animal has to be in perfect health, and it has to be butchered with a sharp knife, a single stroke across the neck. Instant. With a blessing."

Sally's eyes were sharply focused.

"And then, Jews don't eat meat and milk at the same meal. And they don't eat pork. Or shellfish. Only animals that chew their cud and have a cloven hoof."

"Why?" Sally leaned back against the rocker and rattled the ice in her glass.

Rose shrugged. "Why? Why not? What difference does it make? God says so, that's why."

"So how does your family manage? Is there a *sochet* in Brattle-boro?"

Rose slid back into her seat. "I don't know. Manny and Jeannie, they don't keep kosher. Neither do I, not strict, anyway."

"You mean, you can choose?"

Rose considered this. Did she choose? Her mother kept kosher. Two sets of dishes, two kinds of soap. In their crowded tenement, with the deep, stone sink, Rose learned to wash dishes according to Jewish law. Blue soap for *milchedig*—most of their meals were dairy. Less frequently, the red soap, for *flayshedig*, meat. How often did they have meat? Maybe for Sabbath, but not always.

Rose set her lemonade on the side table next to her rocker. "My mother kept kosher. But it was easy. She always lived among Jews. In a Jewish community. There was always a kosher butcher even though we couldn't always buy meat. And eggs from hens kept separate from a rooster."

"But hens lay better when there's a rooster around!" Sally said.

Rose shrugged. "Jews don't eat blood. If the egg has a blood spot, you can't eat it." Rose smiled at Sally. "Who wants to risk the money on eggs that maybe you can't use? So you buy them from a kosher dealer, that's all."

"What about you? Do you keep kosher?"

"For my second husband I did. Two sets of cutlery, two sets of plates. Separation of meat and dairy. It made a difference to him. He was observant that way."

"And you weren't?"

"It's how I was raised, but Sam and me, what did we care? We were Americans! Who needed the headache of such Old World things?" The two women sat silently before Rose added, "Of course, we never ate anything *trayf.*"

"*Trayf?*"

"Not kosher."

"And there are certain foods which are not kosher, even if they're butchered by a *sochet?*"

Rose nodded her approval. "Listen to you! You'll be speaking Yiddish before I finish my lemonade!"

"But this is interesting." Sally leaned forward in her seat. "Without you, I'd never learn any of this!"

"What's so interesting? That Jews eat funny?"

"Rose, I've never been out of Vermont in my whole life. All I know is Orton, Waterchase, Norwalk." She waved her arm in the direction of the dirt road out front. "I've been to the state fair, but

I've never been to the state capital! Having you here is like—it's like going on a trip. Think of all the places you've been: Europe! New York! Florida! And you haven't just been there, you've *lived* in all of those places." Sally shook her head. "Me? I was born in Waterchase. I married Eamon right after high school. Bought this place about two years later, and we've been here ever since."

"You've lived in one place your whole life?" Rose looked down at her dusty shoes. "You're lucky." Rose sighed. "Here I am, sixty-four years old, and I don't know where to call home." Rose looked away, across the pasture, hoping Sally wouldn't see her eyes welling up. "I don't want to go back to Florida. I never liked it there. It's full of old people." Old people with nothing to do. Okay, so a few of the ladies walked on the beach.

She leaned back into the rocker and pushed it into motion with her foot. The runners thunked against the porch boards as Rose rocked back and forth. She patted her chest with her fist. "My whole life, I keep leaving. Always making a new home. Never staying in one place. Never putting down roots." Rose stopped the rocker. "I'm tired of it, tired of always packing up and moving on."

A breeze lifted the warm air, gently stirring the day lilies bordering the porch. Rose lifted her arms and let them slap down on the arms of her chair as she sighed, shaking her head. It was hopeless. She was homeless. Again.

The breeze died down. Sally followed Rose's gaze out to the road. In a calm, uninflected voice, Sally asked, "Why don't you stay here?"

A week later, at breakfast, Rose announced her decision.

"But Ma, you can't stay!" Manny set his cup down so hard coffee splashed onto his hand. "Ow!"

"Here, I'll get it." Jeannie handed him a dish towel and blotted the table with a sponge.

Rose rebuttered her unbitten toast. When she thought she could control her voice, she asked, "And why not?"

"Nobody will be here! The place isn't winterized! How will you manage? You don't even drive!"

"I'll manage."

"How? How will you get groceries, for God's sakes?"

Rose shrugged. "I'll call a cab."

"Mom! This is Vermont! There are no cabs! There's no public transportation! There's no trash pick-up! There's no delivery of the *New York Times*!"

"So I'll walk."

"Walk?" Manny boomed.

"Yes, Manny. Walk. It's what you do with your legs, what people did before God gave us cars."

"It's two miles just to Greenwood's Store!"

"So, I'll walk two miles."

"And it's two miles back!"

"So I'll walk four miles. I'm not such an old woman. I'm healthy, *kayn aynhoreh*. Praise God."

"You'll walk two miles downhill, and then carry your groceries two miles up? What about when it snows?"

"I'll wear boots. Now stop!" Rose pushed her plate away and smoothed the placemat before her. "All I'm asking is that you let me stay here, and I don't see that's such a big deal, since you were planning to shut the house up. So I'll use the oil and electric. I'll pay for it. I'm not a pauper. You want, I'll contribute to the property taxes. Charge me rent."

"Forget the rent. You're my mother!" Manny bellowed. "What about your apartment? You're going to pay rent in Florida all winter?"

"Shh. Manny, calm down!" Jeannie pressed down on Manny's shoulders, as if she were forcibly keeping him in his chair.

"*Mach nisht a tararam!*" Rose muttered.

"*Don't make such an uproar?*" Manny translated. "Calm down?" He glared.

Rose shrugged. "It's only money. Maybe I'll sublet. Beulah Morris might take the apartment for her children. People down there, they always need a place for visitors."

"This is insane!" Manny appealed to Jeannie. "An old woman living alone in this house all winter!" He gestured toward Rose. "She'll freeze!"

"Now just a minute! Who said I was old? I'm sixty-four. So? It's not how many years you have, it's how you feel. And I feel fine, *kayn aynhoreh.*" She stared at the two of them, Jeannie still standing behind Manny at the opposite end of the table. "Instead of yelling and shouting, can we just talk calmly?" Rose waited a moment. "Sally Boyce said the people who you bought the house from lived here all year." She let this sink in. "So, what did they do?" Manny took a deep breath like he was about to say something, but Rose held her hand up. "Stop yelling at me and telling me where I can't live and what I can't do and start telling me what has to be done to make this place livable for winter."

"Do you know how cold it gets?"

"Not yet!" Rose set her chin in the air.

"How are you going to shovel the snow?"

"I'll buy a shovel. Where's a paper and pencil? I'll start a list."

Jeannie fumbled by the phone for a pad and pencil.

"Thank you," Rose said, taking them from Jeannie. She wrote *snow shovel* at the top of the page.

"You'll need heating oil. Lots of it," Manny said. "And you'll still be cold."

"I'll manage."

"This is just a summer house. I want you to be comfortable. And I don't want you to be lonely. What about all your friends in Florida?"

"My friends in Florida?" Rose rolled her eyes. "A bunch of old ladies, that's what. And a couple of old men trying to court me on account of their wives is dead and they need someone to look after them." Rose stopped for a deep breath. "Look, Manny, I nursed Dory into the grave, may he rest in peace. And before that, it was your father, God bless. I got no desire to bury another old man. It's my turn to live a little."

"So live! No one's saying you shouldn't. But what about moving back to Brooklyn? We'll find you an apartment, in your old neighborhood. Or come stay with us! The attic is finished. You'll have your own bath."

"You're so worried about me walking up a hill, what makes you think I can be climbing up and down stairs all day? Besides, it's not fair to Jeannie."

"I wouldn't mind, Rose," Jeannie said, squeezing Manny's shoulders. "It could work out well."

"No woman wants to live with her mother-in-law," Rose frowned.

"But I really wouldn't mind. If you lived with us, I could go back full-time, because you'd be there for the kids."

"No thank you."

"What?" Manny roared. "They're your grandchildren!"

"Of course they're my grandchildren!" Rose paused to lower her voice and Manny interrupted.

"Don't you love them?"

"Yes, I love them, and I love you, and I love Jeannie." She nodded to each as she named them. "But I want to stay here!"

"The house isn't winterized," Manny glared.

"This is an old house, *nu?*" Rose clasped her hands in her lap, out of sight. "What did the—whatstheirnames—the Pickles—"

"Pickerels," Jeannie prompted.

"What did the Pickerels do? They lived here year 'round."

"They were Vermonters," Manny drawled.

"So?" Rose shrugged. "What difference does that make?"

"Mom, there's no heat! The pipes will freeze! Then, what will you do?"

"What do you mean, there's no heat? Every chilly morning you turn on the furnace. We all stand over the register until we warm up." Rose eyed Manny with her clear, blue eyes.

"But that's just for a few minutes, to take the chill off. It's not the same as trying to heat the whole house."

"Don't treat me like a fool, Manny."

Manny just glared back.

Jeannie broke the uncomfortable silence. "I'm surprised you want to stay, Rose. Back in June, you didn't want to come."

"I know." Rose shrugged. "So I changed my mind then, and I changed my mind now. I want to spend the winter here. At least try. If I don't like it, I can always go back to Florida."

"I can't believe this!" Manny blurted. "You were so against us buying this place. You didn't even like it when we moved to Teaneck. You're a New Yorker! Anything outside the five boroughs might as well be the moon!"

"Then why did I move to Florida?"

"I thought you liked Miami?" Manny reined in his voice.

"What's to like? It's full of old people."

"It's warm there! Half of the old neighborhood lives there now. You even said it was convenient," Manny trumped.

"It was convenient." Rose paused and looked Manny in the eye. "When Dory was alive. It was for Dory I moved to Miami. For retirement. Now there's a *meshuggeneh* idea."

"What's so crazy about retirement? I can't wait to retire!"

"For a man, maybe. But for a woman, what changes? I still cook, clean, cook, clean. What's retirement? And Florida? What's there? The Miami Symphony Orchestra? Maybe they're not so bad, but the old men in the audience, so deaf they don't know they're humming and tapping their feet? Or the Miami Ballet, it's even worse. Sadie September, who buys a subscription with me. Every time a ballerina crosses the stage, Sadie, she whispers in a voice loud enough to waken the dead, '*Oy*' she says. '*She's so thin!*' Like Sadie should make the girl a plate of dumplings and sour cream."

Jeannie hugged her sides as she shook with swallowed laughter.

"You're spoiled, that's all," Manny explained. "You've lived in New York all your life."

"I lived in New York all my life until I moved to Miami. Now I don't live in New York any more."

"So move back!"

"'Move back!' he says, like a person can go backwards in time. It isn't so easy, Manny. It wouldn't be the same. Half the old neighborhood is gone. They've all moved away—or died."

"Well," Manny sighed. "If you think Miami is the end of the earth, what makes you think Vermont in the winter will be any better?" Manny stood up.

Rose looked up at him. "You're just a boy, Manny." She shook her head. "You're a good boy, but you're too young to understand."

"I'm pushing forty, Mom. Try me." He moved next to Jeannie and held her hand.

"Miami," Rose said, shaking her head. "There's always sirens.

Ambulances up and down the avenue like it's an air raid or something. Sirens screaming 'another stroke!' 'another heart attack.' Enough already. I want quiet."

"You'll get quiet all right." Jeannie tugged Manny's hand, and he swallowed whatever else he was going to say.

Rose looked at the two of them. "I wasn't a city girl all my life, you know."

Manny and Jeannie stood very still.

"I was born in the country." Rose gestured out the window.

Manny said, "That was the Old Country, Ma."

"That's right. The Old Country." Rose folded her hands on the table before her and spoke to them. "And all these years, I only remembered the fear and the cold." She looked up at her son and his wife. "But after being here all summer, Manny, I remember being a girl." She nodded. "It's like a room of memories has been unlocked. Going barefoot. Wading in the stream. Picking berries. All these things bring back my childhood." She looked up at her children again. "I had a mother who loved me. A brother and sister. Others who died. They were different people then, your grandmother and Aunt Lena. We were poorer. And frightened. But there's something else about that time I need to remember. I don't know what it is yet. All I know is I need to remember it here."

"Okay, Ma," Manny said, shaking his head. "If that's the way you want it."

"Yes, Manny. That's the way I want it." Rose paused. "Enough said."

6 | in the wilderness

After she'd waved them off, Rose reentered the house, and the silence wrapped its arms about her like a warm night, even though it was not yet noon. Just as country silence hummed with the noise of insects and weeds, so this new silence echoed with Manny's voice, telling her she was making a mistake, and the kids pleading, "Oh, Grandma! Come live with us!" Only Jeannie said nothing, for which Rose was thankful.

Well, maybe she would end up living with them, like a live-in maid, in the attic, under the eaves.

Rose wandered through the house, touching lamps, dragging her fingers along the top of the bureau in the hallway, pushing the curtains aside and looking out the window. Here she was, finally alone, and she couldn't sit still. She could finally read without interruption for the rest of the day and—what?—she was too restless to sit down.

Out the window, the leaves fluttered on a gentle breeze, the movement adding new shades of green to the rainbow of greens that colored the hills and fields. Who could imagine so many different greens? Like corduroy and velvet and linen, each cloth a different green, each shade another celebration of living. *L'chayim*. So different from the muddy countryside of her youth.

Standing at the window, Rose fell back into the Old World. The autumn sun slanted into the kitchen where her twin's four-year-old body lay side by side with the challah, as if they'd be blessing him along with the Sabbath. Her mother was scrubbing Israel's face, red as a beet with the fever just that morning, and now as pale as the flour dusting the kneading board. Mama was cross. "Look at your dress!" she scolded. "And your hands! You're covered in mud!"

Papa moaned into the corner, his shawl-draped shoulders rocking in prayer. Dova, her older sister, handed Mama a pressed sheet, snapped it open, and while it hung like a curtain between the kitchen and Rose, Rose slid under the table, wiggling between the forest of chair legs.

Hiding there reminded Rose of the time Mama pulled her into the hayloft when a troop of soldiers pounded into the square, and the village held its collective breath until the hoof beats subsided down the road without stopping. It was like that, sitting among the commotion of legs while Mama and Dova wound Israel in his shroud, Mama checking the fading daylight, urging Dova to stitch faster, the knock at the door that could have been Rose's heart pounding out of its cage, but it was Yonkel, the undertaker, and his boy, Lemuel. Goodness! Rose could still remember their names. So many years.

Yonkel lifted the bundle. It was almost sundown. No time even for grief, just hurry, hurry, hurry, before the Days of Awe, before the blowing of the shofar. Mama, Papa, Dova, Yonkel, Lemuel, they all crowded out of the house, forgetting Rose, Israel's other half. They'd been birth mates, playmates, a pair. And now, he was leaving for a separate grave.

The mourners formed a small huddle of dark figures retreating into the dusk toward the cemetery at the edge of the town. Rose stayed under the table, imprisoned by the furniture and Mama's dry-eyed command to bury him before sundown, to cover the mirror, to sit *shiva* on the Day of Atonement, which fell on the Sabbath that year. Double holiness. Rose sat under the table—hands and face unwashed, her ordinary dress not redeemed for a clean one. She sat, alone. Even though Rose did not follow them to the cemetery, to this day—even now, standing alone at the window of her son's country house on the other side of the world—Rose could still hear the pebbles and damp, worm-eaten earth thump into the hole with Israel bundled at the bottom of it.

Did he whimper as the clods weighed him down? Rose didn't believe Israel was really dead, just sleeping. She'd wished Mama hadn't been in such a hurry to bury him. Maybe he would have gotten better. A miracle, maybe. Isn't that what God was good for? And how was it her mother didn't cry?

Mama stood at the threshold, washing her hands from a pitcher at the doorway, Dova right behind her. Papa *davened* at *shul*, prayed with men at the synagogue. Her mother lit the Sabbath candles under the tent of her kerchief, Dova in her shadow. It wasn't until Rose bumped against a chair that Mama remembered her. She grasped Rose's wrist so tight, Rose still felt the burn to this day, still hurt from the fierce hug that followed, still choked in the suffocating folds of Mama's clean apron that smelled of cold air, damp ground, risen bread, and the onions flavoring the stew. Rose wanted to die there and then, with her face in the folds of her mother's fabric. She didn't want to let go. She didn't want to be alone or separate. She didn't want to live if Israel had died. And he must have died, because they'd buried him. They'd buried him, and she was left alone.

She was four, almost five, and she could still remember, like it was yesterday.

And Dova? When was the last time Rose thought about her?

Dova married Elihu Sametz and stayed in Zolochev. Everyone told the young couple to emigrate with Rose's family, but they refused. Elihu had old parents. Even though he was a young man, he had an old heart. He was a good student, a star pupil of Rev Mordechai. His heir, maybe. And Dova, she was old-fashioned, too. She wanted to make a life just like her parents', except that it would be her own. Her own kitchen, her own candlesticks, her own Sabbath, everything her own.

The following spring, at that last seder before Rose and her family left, Mama tried to talk Elihu and Dova into changing their minds. "Come later," she urged. "We'll get established. We'll save. We'll send for you. You can raise your baby in America," for Dova was already round with expectation. But Elihu stood behind Dova, with his hand on her shoulder, and Dova shook her head no.

At the time, Rose thought Dova was so romantic, to stay with her young husband and have her own baby. At the time, that's just what Rose wanted to do when she was older. Marry. Keep house. Have children. But in America, it wasn't so easy, keeping house. And they'd only been in their railroad tenement—with three boarders who got fed before she did—a few months maybe, maybe longer, when the letter came saying that Dova died giving birth, along with her baby.

This time, her mamma wept. A flood of tears sent her to bed, leaving ten-year old Rose to cook for the boarders, to care for Lena, to negotiate the crowded streets. Was it any wonder she loved school? It was so much easier than home life.

Eventually, her mother stopped crying. She resumed her place in the kitchen. And she let Papa make Rose leave school. During those years of taut silence between Rose and her father, Rose's mother spoke for each, as if she were a member of the diplomatic corps translating for two hostile countries. And like any good functionary, she did so without emotion; she appeared to take no sides, so that both Rose and her father thought Hannah was on theirs.

Only later, when Rose announced she and Sam planned to marry, did she discover how wrong she was. "He's not religious!" Mama objected.

"Neither am I!" Rose shot back. At which, her mother dissolved. "Do what you want. Who am I to stop you?" Her mother whined in the small voice of defeat. "I've done what I could."

"You brought us here," Rose said, meaning America. "Now it's up to us to make the best of it."

"I wish we'd never left," her mother squeaked between sobs.

"Well, we're here." Rose was emphatic. "It wouldn't have been any easier if we'd stayed. We have a better chance here."

"Chance of what?" Her father loomed in the doorway, having overheard the whole conversation. "Chance to defile the Sabbath with work? Disobey your parents? Covet your neighbor's possessions? Forget your God?" Spittle formed on his lips as he fumed. "That's all America is—a place where there are no commandments!" His eyes held Rose's in hate. "Go! Go! Go marry your *shaygets*! Go and be damned!"

"He's not a *goy*. He's a Jew. From Zolochev, just like you!"

Her father blinked, then his shoulders sagged. "Another *schlemiel* in this *goldeneh medina*," he muttered. Another simpleton in this fool's paradise. It wasn't until later that Rose realized her father had broken his silence.

A month later, when she left to marry Sam with witnesses supplied by the rabbi, her mother pressed a few dollars into her hand, and the silver candlesticks. "Here," her mother said. "I wish for you to be happy. May your children bring you joy and not *tsuris*, heartache." At the time, Rose thought her mother had given her a curse instead of a blessing. Later, Rose realized her mother was just explaining the way of the world.

Kinder. Children. *Tsuris*. Troubles. They might as well be the same word. What were children if not worries and suffering? And hadn't Rose learned that lesson well enough, on her own? Her first baby, a perfect girl with the lips of an angel and the tiniest hands and feet, the child who broke her open—Rose thought she'd split in two before the baby came out—and who cracked her heart when, instead of thriving, the baby turned blue, then gray, and died.

The doctor assured her that it wasn't her fault; the child had an incomplete heart, and there was nothing anyone could do but recover and try again. To this day, Rose isn't sure her own heart ever healed, although her womb did. Two years later, Manny was born.

He came out easier, but all red and wrinkled and angry from the start. He latched on to her breast and sucked until her nipples were sore, and still screamed for more. He howled through the night and nursed through the day. Rose thought she'd birthed a leech, not a boy; he was always attached to her, always guzzling, always demanding more. She started him on cereal and banana even before the pediatrician advised it, but it was the only way she could sate him, and it seemed to work. By the time he was six months old, he'd switched his energies from feeding to exploring the world, forcing Rose into constant vigilance. Instead of pinning her to a chair while he nursed, he now kept her in constant motion; she followed him around the apartment, clearing dangers out of his way. Within a week of starting to crawl, Manny had showed Rose every hazard at knee level, which Rose moved to higher ground, so that the apartment looked like a depot for misplaced objects, with books and bric-a-brac stacked on top of the end tables, and all the dishes and soap powders on the kitchen counter.

Rose gave Manny pot lids and wooden spoons to play with; she tried singing to him; she tried to play peek-a-boo and tell him stories, but he wasn't interested in anything that didn't include constant motion and serious noise.

Rose couldn't wait for Sam to come home and take the boy out or, if it was raining, to go outside herself. Anything to get away, to hear quiet, to be alone.

Well, here she was. Alone again.

Rose sighed and let the curtain fall, turning to view the domestic landscape of her new home. The sofa cushions still held dents from when Jeannie and Wendy had sat reading fairy tales the night before. Rose sighed and plumped the cushions. The echo of Manny's complaining voice irritated her as she stacked the old newspapers in a crate beside the fireplace. He must be unhappy, he's so grouchy all the time. Or was it only her he was impatient with? He didn't pick on Jeannie, thank God. At least he knew he had a good wife. So, a man might get impatient with his old mother. What's new?

Rose plopped down on the seat cushion she'd just plumped and sank into the deep chair. Manny's irritation with her was new. He wasn't like this before Isadore died. What did he care where she lived? Did he ever say she shouldn't move to Florida? Was Florida so far away when Isadore was alive? No! But now, he feels responsible, like Rose was another burden across his back. Like she was an unwanted child.

Rose had wanted another child, but—but what? What if she had another Manny? She couldn't take another baby so demanding. Besides, it was tempting fate to ask for another. So many things could go wrong—a club foot, a cleft palate, a mental condition, God forbid. Besides, how could she not dilute her attention to the one if she had another? He'd act out, have tantrums, go bad, like those hooligans from downstairs, running wild while Millie Shoshkiss tried to stop the howling of the newest one rooting for her breast. It's too much, what God wants from a woman, to bear children and raise them and cook and clean and earn a little besides. But maybe it was wrong to pray against having more? Maybe all the babies were God's punishment for her misuse of prayer?

Three times she'd found herself in that swollen second month. Please God, not again, she leaned heavily against the door, made herself hurry up the stairs to the apartment, even though she was too tired to rush.

Breast soreness, that was always the first sign. She'd try to ignore it, get down on her hands and knees and scrub the kitchen floor with extra vigor, or carry a heavy load of wash up to the roof, to hang. But she never let more than a week go by, or it would be too late. Complications, or more than Dr. Benson could handle.

So, down in the basement, where she fetched coal, or in the vestibule opening the gold flap for the mail, or maybe just outside on the landing leaning against a mop, she'd confide in Mrs. Furgang, or Carola Palovski, or Hannah Rosensweig, or even dark little Sylvia Bogosian. Word would spread down the street from pursed lips to coiled ear, detouring the heavy-lobed Italians, who birthed babies yearly, and cried more often. Before another week went by, the gaunt man in the dark coat would be striding up the street, his flag of white hair bent into the wind or under the sun or against the rain.

Every time, he told her Sam could get snipped or use the condoms he left for her. Rose felt bad for the doctor, that he didn't understand about a man's pride. All the housewives agreed, their husbands would die before stuffing themselves inside a balloon, or worse, having any part of it cut off. And Dr. Benson wasn't just a doctor, but a man. They all thought he should have known better than to suggest.

Each time, Rose promised, "I'll give them to him," as she tucked the condoms in her apron pocket. She didn't like to look into his eyes, though. Not just because she was lying, but because his eyes were so sad, as if it pained him to do this messy work. But if he didn't? The women would do it themselves. When Rose promised she wouldn't—she promised she'd get hold of him, and about this she wasn't lying—she looked him in the eyes. She'd heard what happened to Bertha Hausmann, who tried to take care of it herself, leaving six orphans. But how many children could a poor woman raise? feed? clothe? educate? What chance had these brats if they were all part of a happenstance litter?

Rose fished the quarters from the broken teacup and laid them in the doctor's washed hands. Bless God she had one healthy son.

"Avoid relations in the middle of your cycle," Dr. Benson urged even as he folded his long fingers over the quarters and pocketed them. "Rest today and tomorrow."

"Thank you, Doctor." Rose sat in Sam's upholstered chair with her feet up and her hands wrapped around a glass of tea held to the crampy well of her belly, emptying itself onto damp rags.

Was it so wrong to pray against life? What was prayer, anyway, but a way to express troublous thoughts?

If one person prayed for a child and another prayed to stay barren, whose prayer would God grant? But maybe the problem isn't with praying but with the man they prayed to. What's it to God, one child more or less? Even Sammy, he wouldn't have minded another child, never mind they couldn't really afford it. What did it really matter, money? Sure, like the Italians across the street afforded it, sleeping three to a bed and the babies in the bureau drawers. No, Rose only had a wanted child. And she gave him everything she could.

Rose sighed, shaking her head. She'd knitted Manny a sweater, and what did he do? He lost it at school. So Rose marches down to Lincoln High, to check in the Lost and Found, and he yells at her in the school corridor.

"Mom! What are you doing here?"

"I'm looking for the sweater you lost!"

He glanced around, to see who might be watching.

She stuck her chin up. She'd brushed her hair, put on lipstick. She wore nice clothes. "So what? You're embarrassed by your own mother?"

"Ma!" Manny took her by the elbow and steered her down the hall.

She shook him off. "Don't you 'Ma' me. I knitted you a sweater and what? You lose it! You think yarn is free? You think I can go and make another, just like that?" She snapped her fingers and stopped in the middle of the hall, right in front of the office, whose wall was glass from the waist up. Mr. Kaplan was talking to the school secretary. He saw Rose, nodded to the secretary, and opened the door.

"Hello." Mr. Kaplan straightened his tie and buttoned his jacket as he strode toward them. "Manny, is this your mother?"

Manny glared at Rose and said, "Yes, Sir."

"Hello, Mrs. Rubin," Abe Kaplan said, extending his hand. "Manny's a fine scholar. You should be proud of him. I hope he's thinking about going on to college. He'll make a good teacher."

"A teacher?" Rose blurted. "A professor, maybe. Or an engineer." She didn't see the look that passed between the principal and her son.

"I'm sure he'll do well, whatever he goes into," Mr. Kaplan said, walking them toward the great double doors at the end of the hall.

That night, Manny stormed into the apartment. "Ma! Don't come to school!"

Rose stopped stirring the cake batter. "What? I shouldn't come to school to find the sweater my boy lost? It's a free country. I'm allowed."

"Here's your damn sweater!" He tossed the green v-neck onto a kitchen chair.

"You found it!" Rose put the mixing bowl down. "Good." She picked it up and folded it neatly and handed it back to Manny. She was just reaching up to pat his cheek when he shrugged her off and backed away.

"I didn't lose it." He folded his arms across his chest. "It was in my locker."

"You didn't lose it?"

Manny just glared.

"So, you don't like it, is that it?"

His arms slipped down to his sides and his face turned red. "I hate it! It's too big! And I'm going to be a teacher. An ordinary teacher. Not a professor and not an engineer. Got that?"

Before Rose could say anything, he'd stormed out of the apartment in nothing but his shirtsleeves. "You'll catch your death of cold!" she yelled after him, but the apartment door had already slammed shut.

So what could she do? He didn't like the sweater. Well, why didn't he say so? He'd watched her knitting it for weeks, holding it up, measuring it against him. It wasn't so easy. The boy grew daily, how could she knit something that would fit? So she made it a little big. She walked down the hall to the bedroom and tucked the sweater into her bureau drawer. Maybe later, he'd change his mind. Maybe he'd change his mind about being a teacher, too. Being a teacher wasn't so bad. It was a good job. But. But it wasn't the same as being a professor. A professor was like being a rabbi. A New World rabbi. Rose slid the cake into the oven and started shredding cabbage. She had potatoes ready to boil, pot roast. It was a good dinner. He'd be back to eat. He wouldn't stay mad. She wouldn't nudge about being a professor. Poor boy. He was becoming a man, and with no father to guide him. What would Sammy have said? "Leave him, *Rosela*. Leave him be. He's got to figure it out for himself." Rose sighed as she grated carrots. She couldn't argue. Sammy was right. He had to find his own way.

Rose tried to get her bearings, but she didn't recognize the room right away. The noisy silence of Vermont. She pushed herself out of the chair. Had she been too pushy? He'd done what he wanted, anyway. He joined the army. He picked his bride. He became a teacher. He'd done fine. So why was he so angry? Still? She didn't even make him wear the sweater.

Rose could knit herself a sweater. She'd have to. She had no winter clothes. She looked around the now familiar parlor and smiled. As if she'd placed the last piece in a jigsaw, Rose now knew what she had to do: sew a wardrobe for a Vermont winter.

7 | the guilford fair

By the end of her first week, Rose had settled into a daily routine, walking down to Greenwood's to fetch her milk, her newspaper, and whatever small grocery items she needed. It was a long walk, and not some easy stroll along a beach with a bunch of gossiping hens. Returning home, uphill, was work, and she felt it; her body ached. Maybe that's why she fell asleep so early. A confirmed night owl all her life, Rose now found herself dozing in her chair after supper and going to bed before ten.

In no time, Rose started waving at the cars who passed her on the road, and she said hello to fellow shoppers at Greenwood's. Barrett Greenwood himself always greeted her like they were best friends, which at first made Rose suspicious, but she soon looked forward to it. When she entered the store on the first Sunday of her sojourn, it was Rose who said, "Hello, Mr. Greenwood. How are you?"

"Just fine, thank you. Nice to see you, this morning." He nodded. "And I have a special item here today you might just enjoy."

Rose tilted her head like a bird waiting for crumbs.

Barrett pointed to stacks of thick newspapers laying along the floor. When Rose didn't move, Barrett came out from behind the counter and led her closer to them. "It's the Sunday papers!" he said, triumphantly. "Lots of folks who don't take the daily take the weekend edition. And some who only read the *Phoenix* during the week ask for the *Rutland Herald* or the *Boston Globe* on Sunday." He turned to make sure she was still following him. "And there's some—especially in the summer, like your son—who order the Sunday *New York Times*." He stopped at the last paper lying at the end of the row. "I hope you don't mind," Barrett said, stooping to lift her paper. "But I took the liberty of reserving a copy for you." He held it so she could read the front page, with "Mayer" in black marker written across the top. "Here it is!"

"Oh," Rose broke into a great smile. "Thank you so much!" She held her arms out to receive it. "I forgot I had to order in advance." Her name stared back at her. Rose saw that the other papers on the floor had her neighbors' names written on them. She looked back at Barrett, who was beaming down at her. "Thank you, Mr. Greenwood."

"It's my pleasure, Rose."

Rose blushed and followed Barrett back to the counter. "Would you like me to put it in a bag, make it easier to carry? That's a mighty hefty paper to carry up that hill."

Before Rose could answer, the sleigh bells attached to the door jangled and Percy Mendell walked in.

"Good morning, Percy!" Barrett boomed. "Maybe this kind gentleman will give you a ride? There must be seven pounds of newsprint here."

Rose and Percy mumbled greetings to one another. "This young lady here has this heavy paper to get home."

Bending ever so slightly at the waist, Percy replied, "It would be my pleasure."

He picked up his Sunday *Herald* and escorted her out to the car.

"You don't have to go out of your way." Rose slid into the front seat.

"No trouble at all." Percy closed her door and walked around to the driver's side.

"I walk up the hill every day." Rose settled the paper on her lap.

"So I've heard. But that's an awkward burden to carry." He nodded at the thick newspaper and started the engine.

"I love the Sunday *Times*!"

"Doesn't have much local news in it, does it?"

"It's got a metropolitan section!" Rose flipped to it and saw the headline: "Jews To Celebrate Rosh Hashanah at Sundown." A new year already.

"I take the *Herald*," Percy said, glancing at his paper lying between them on the seat, "so as to keep abreast of what's happening around the state."

"But what about what's going on in the nation? And around the world?"

"Oh, there's always some of that. Can't hardly escape world news nowadays, not with the radio and television and all." He stole a quick look at her before steering the car around a curve. "Besides," Percy continued. "It's local politics that matters."

"How can you say that?" Rose glared at Percy's profile.

Percy shook his head. "What we do at Town Meeting has more effect on us here in Orton even than what the legislature does up in Montpelier, and the laws they make up there make more of a difference to a Vermonter than anything that happens in Washington. Or it ought to. Washington ought not be meddling with folks' lives."

"Well!" Rose faced front and folded her hands on top of her paper. "I see we don't agree about that!"

After some silence, Percy said, "It must take all day to read a newspaper that big."

Rose tried to match his friendliness. "You develop a system. There's certain sections you just skim. I don't even bother with the sports."

"You don't follow baseball?" His eyebrows arched up.

Rose sighed. "Not since the Dodgers left Brooklyn." There was real resignation in her voice.

"If you're going to live in New England," Percy advised, "you have to become a Red Sox fan."

"Next, you'll tell me I've got to vote Republican!"

Percy's eyes darted sideways, then back to the road again. "I wouldn't ever tell anyone how to vote." In a low voice, Percy added, "And I certainly couldn't recommend anybody vote for Senator Goldwater."

"Glad to hear it."

"He's too extreme." Percy's mouth was set in a thin, grim line. He parked in front of Rose's house.

"So, will you vote for LBJ?" Rose asked.

Percy frowned, and Rose regretted the question.

"You don't have to answer." Rose tried to smooth over her gaffe. This wasn't Brooklyn. People here didn't just hurl opinions at one another and shrug them off. "I'm sorry," Rose said, touching Percy on the arm.

Percy flinched as if her hand burned him. Then he blushed.

"Oh, I didn't mean to startle you," Rose apologized again.

"No, no. That's all right." Percy placed his hands on the wheel and stared out the windshield even though the engine was off. "I've never really thought about the national scene independently from state politics, you see. We just elect our town representative and our county senators. Then we pick the best man among them to go to Washington." Percy hesitated. "Used to be, all the election-eering went into the primaries—picking the right candidate from the start." He shook his head. "It was just a matter of which fellow was the best choice, and the whole system worked like a ladder right to the top. It was easy to cast a vote." He paused. "But it ain't so simple anymore." He shrugged and looked at Rose. "Tuesday is primaries. Local elections. Statewide offices."

"Is Mr. Nye running against Mrs. Aitcheson in the primary?" Rose asked.

"He should do."

"But he's not?"

"He's on the ballot as an Independent. More than likely, he'll split the vote and the seat will go to Barney Johnson, the only Democrat in all of Orton—just about. How you call that fair representation, well I certainly don't know."

After a moment, Rose sighed. "Well, thanks for the ride."

"Oh!" Percy hurried around the car to open her door.

It was a short path from the car to the house, and Rose was nearly there when Percy spoke up. "Guilford Fair tomorrow. A real country fair, with livestock and farm goods and the like."

Rose hesitated.

"Live politicians, too. Trying to win votes."

Rose perched on the porch step.

"Would you like to go? I'd be glad to take you."

"Thanks." Rose hugged the paper in her arms. "But I've already got plans." She regretted the words as soon as they were out of her mouth. "Tomorrow is Rosh Hashanah," she explained. His face was blank. "The New Year." Still, nothing registered. "It's a Jewish holiday," she explained. "I think I'll stay home."

"Oh." He looked disappointed and relieved all at once.

Rose raised a hand to wave. "Well, thanks again for the ride."

Percy nodded. "So long."

Rose slammed the paper on the table. Why did she turn him down? What was it about that man, anyway? No matter what either of them said, they kept bumping into each other's sore spots, like those cars down at Coney Island, where kids drive into each other on purpose. Were all Yankees so thin-skinned? Or were they just too polite to raise their voices?

She filled the kettle and slammed it onto the stove, striking a match with force and waiting, arms crossed and foot tapping, for the tea water to boil.

The local paper was a joke. She couldn't believe it the first time she read, "Miss Williams returned from visiting Mr. and Mrs. John Baker at their camp in Lake George." This was news? And the patient list from the hospital! Can you imagine? You get sick, you go to the hospital and you get your name in the paper? Unbelievable!

The *Phoenix* had come out with an endorsement for Johnson; she had to hand them that. And for Hoff, the Democratic governor who was running for a second term. And they came right out and said Goldwater was no good. No argument there.

The *Phoenix* had also endorsed the Republican senator and representative seeking reelection. Well, she had no opinion, but maybe she'd have to form one. Where was she going to vote, come November?

The water boiled. Rose fixed herself tea and opened up the Week in Review, spreading it across the table, the way she liked. By the time she'd read through the Book Review, the magazine section, Arts & Leisure, and Business, it was mid-afternoon. Rose tidied the paper in a neat pile and reread the headline announcing Rosh Hashanah. Imagine, she had to read it in the paper to find out! Out here in the wilderness, who knew from Rosh Hashanah? It's not like she missed *shul*. But all her life, there'd been feasting and song—happiness for another year. Another year. Now that was something to be thankful for. A new year. Here she was, starting a new life in a new year. It called for celebration!

Without even thinking, Rose opened the pantry and started pulling flour, baking powder, salt, soda, cinnamon, oil, honey, almonds off the shelf. Rose baked by rule of thumb: for every cup of flour, so much leavening; for every egg, so much sugar. For this cake, she increased the flour on account of the honey. She found nutmeg, cloves, and ginger, and added a pinch of each. Jeannie, she knew, baked by the book. Delicious cakes, if you liked sweet. Frosting that stuck to the roof of your mouth. So much sugar, it made you pucker. But they were gorgeous. Too pretty, maybe, to eat.

Rose, she liked a down-to-earth cake. At home, she even used brown flour. She slid the cakes in to bake and made herself a hard-boiled egg sandwich. On account of the new year, she stirred honey into her tea. As long as you had honey, one way or another, you were sure to have a sweet year, and that's what mattered. She always let Manny have a teaspoon of honey on the first day of school. So what, it wasn't strictly Rosh Hashanah, but it was a new year of studies, and learning should be sweet, *nu?*

The next morning, Rose assumed Greenwood's would be closed, on account of the holiday. Labor Day, not Rosh Hashanah. So she'd walk over to Sally's; she had the cake to deliver. She was wrapping it in waxed paper when Sally knocked at the screen.

"Yoo-hoo! Hi there, Rose!" She pulled on the door. "The door's stuck!"

"Just a minute! I've got the latch on." Rose bustled over and slid the hook.

"You don't have to lock the doors around here."

Rose shrugged. "I feel safer. Come," she said, waving to Sally to follow. "I was just wrapping up a present for you and Eamon.

153

Honey cake, for the New Year."

"New Year?" Sally asked.

"The Jewish New Year. Fifty-seven-twenty-five."

"Fifty-seven-twenty-five what?" Sally still didn't comprehend.

"Years. Since Moses led the Jews out of Egypt. Or from the day he received the Commandments on Mount Sinai." Rose stopped and turned. "You know? I don't know! All I know is that it's fifty-seven hundred and twenty-five years since the day the Jews started counting."

"And you celebrate with honey cake?"

"That's only the beginning. We have from now until Yom Kippur—that's ten days—to consider our sins, then we ask God to inscribe us into the Book of Life for another year. But why we do it in September and not January?" Rose shrugged. "You got me."

"It makes sense to me!" Sally said. "Better to celebrate the harvest—celebrate having enough to get you through another year, is more like it."

"You know," Rose nodded, "you could be Jewish. Sit down." She pulled out a chair. "I'll make us both a cup of tea."

"No, no! Rose, you are so thought-provoking I completely forgot! Eamon's waiting outside. We're headed down to the Guilford Fair and we stopped by to pick you up."

Rose's hand flew to her head, then fluttered down her dress. "But I'm not dressed!"

"Rose, you're better dressed than any woman in Vermont. If you dress any better, you'll make enemies instead of friends."

"This Guilford Fair? Is this what Percy Mendell told me about yesterday? Some kind of cow contest, I think he said?"

"Percy asked you to the fair?" Sally's eyes popped open.

Rose shrugged.

"And you turned him down?" There was awe in her voice.

"How was I supposed to know from a fair?"

"Hang the fair! Percy Mendell has been the most eligible bachelor in Windham County for over forty years, as near as I can make out. And there's any number of single women who've set their caps at him over the years. Women have dreamed of Percy Mendell asking them to the fair. Heck! I know gals who'd shovel a barn if he made it sound like a date!"

Rose fiddled with the waxed paper folded around the loaf of honey cake.

"And you turned him down?" Sally repeated.

Rose sighed. "How was I supposed to know? Besides," she raised her eyes to meet Sally's, "I'm not looking for a date! I'm too old for that nonsense!" She picked up the cake and held it out. "Here, I made this for you."

"Thanks." Sally held it to her nose. "Mmm. Smells good."

"A honey cake, to wish you a sweet new year."

"That is sweet. Thank you, Rose." A horn sounded. "That's Eamon, wondering where we are."

"What if we run into Mr. Mendell?" Rose asked, suddenly awkward.

"We run in to him, we run in to him. It's a free country."

Rose stared hard at Sally, then they both doubled over in laughter.

The horn tooted.

"Okay, already, as if he could hear me," Rose said. "You go tell him I need five minutes to get ready."

"But you look fine!"

"Sally, I'm not going to any farm party in my house-dress. You got to let me put on some clothes, powder my nose. Go!" Rose shooed her with the back of her hands. "Go tell that man of yours he'll just have to wait."

At the fair, Sally steered Rose into the Farm Hall. "This is what I want you to see." They walked down an aisle between long rows of tables set up end to end, draped in clean muslin and laden with baskets spilling over with summer squash, bouquets of peppers, heaps of tomatoes, glossy eggplants, purple beets, nosegays of radishes, and heavy braids of onions whose pungent aroma was both sharp and sweet.

"It's like a museum," Rose whispered.

Sally chuckled.

"This looks too good to eat," Rose said, stopping in front of a mound of artfully arranged tomatoes. "Look," Rose said. "These look like modern sculpture, like they're made out of polished stone. And what's this?" Rose fondled a smooth fruit. "A yellow tomato? I've never heard of such a thing!"

"There are yellow and orange ones," Sally said, guiding Rose toward the canned goods. "And then there are all sorts of things people do with green tomatoes."

"You mean unripe tomatoes?" Rose moved forward at Sally's prodding, "Or a variety that's supposed to be green?"

"Unripe." Sally nodded toward the jars arrayed like bowling pins at the end of a lane. "Here we've got green tomato pickles, green tomato relish, green tomato mincemeat, and stuffed green tomatoes."

Rose followed Sally down the aisle, past an army of canned food. Sally stopped and lifted a half-pint jar. "Just look at this!" She scowled, tilting the jar from side to side so its purple contents slid away from the glass. "It's too loose. And this one," she said, holding a darker jar and rotating it on its side without budging its contents, "is too stiff."

Rose looked from one jar to another. "What is it?"

"Grape jelly!" Sally set the jars down with force. "One of canning's basics, yet neither of these got it right, and they're the only two entries this year. If only I'd known, I could have put some up and won first prize!"

"You know how to do this?"

Sally nodded. "It's easy."

"Tomatoes, too?"

"Of course. Tomatoes are a cinch!"

"I told Jeannie I'd preserve what I could of her garden."

"I'll show you. You'll pick it up in no time."

Sally led Rose past the midway toward the cow shed. "Eamon's probably watching the oxen. He's always threatening to raise up a team of his own."

"What would he do with a team of oxen?" Rose wondered.

"Oh, go to fairs, mostly. But look!" They'd approached the livestock pen where a shaggy man in dirty overalls was maneuvering a pair of huge beasts yoked with a heavy, hand-hewn beam. "That man actually farms with his team, if you call it farming," Sally said. They stopped at the rail. The animals came to a halt on command, their eyes glazed. "That's Harlan Knight," Sally whispered in Rose's ear. "Used to have a reasonable operation till the highway came in. Lost half his land. As if that weren't bad enough, he fell in love with his own daughter. Near ruined him. He's dislocated in time. Farms old-fashioned. No electricity. Just grows food for his own use. Self-sufficient." Sally shook her head. "Sad man."

"What happened to his daughter?"

"Not so loud!" Sally turned Rose away from the fence. "She was sent away."

"Sent away?"

"Instead of jail. She tried to throw the baby away."

"You mean she bore her father's child?" Rose's whisper was

hard and harsh.

Sally nodded.

"And this man," Rose turned back to the thin man in the ragged clothing whose salted hair and beard were so long they could have come out of the Old Testament, "This man got away scot-free?"

"Well," Sally said. "He wasn't punished by the law, if that's what you mean. But look at him." She nodded in his direction. "He hasn't exactly gotten off easy."

The two watched Harlan Knight maneuver his team into a first prize. Sally said, "Eamon's not here. Let's go check the horses. Who knows where he's got to? And I'm getting hungry. How about you?"

"I'm always hungry in Vermont."

The two strolled across the fairgrounds.

"There's Wilson Nye," Rose said, pointing him out in the center of a knot of fair-goers.

"Politics," Sally said tersely.

As soon as he saw them, he hastened over.

"Hello, Rose!" Wilson held her hand longer than a handshake. "Hello, Mrs. Boyce."

Sally just offered a cold nod.

To Rose he gushed, "I never I thought I'd see you here." He gestured at the fair unfolding around them. "I thought you'd be too sophisticated for something as hick as this."

"Is that what you think of your constituents, Mr. Nye?" Sally's question was all ice.

"No, no." Wilson feigned easy-going dismissal. "I just thought Rose, here, a New York sophisticate and all—" He let his sentence fade.

"And what are your plans for after the election?" Sally inquired.

"Well, we'll just have to see what comes up on the docket, won't we?"

"I mean, when you lose. You don't stand a chance against Mildred Aitcheson, and you know that. Or you're a fool," Sally said.

"Mrs. Boyce, I'd be a fool not to try. And while it's very likely that Mrs. Aitcheson may best me, a little opposition is always a good way to keep a politician honest, don't you think?"

Sally acknowledged this speech with raised brows.

"But," Nye continued, "if I'm not elected, I'm thinking of going down to Florida." He turned toward Rose, "Which I believe is your home turf?"

"I lived there," Rose admitted.

"Indeed. It's unusual to see summer people at the fair. You all usually fly home by Labor Day. What keeps you here?"

Sally cut in before Rose could. "Mrs. Mayer is staying in Vermont."

Rose laid a hand on Sally's arm to calm her, "That's right. So if you're looking for a place to rent in Florida, my apartment's available."

"How very generous."

"I'd charge you rent!"

"Of course, of course!" Wilson smiled. "Now, if you'll excuse me." He nodded and turned.

"Whew!" Sally breathed a sigh of relief as soon as he stepped away. "What a creep!"

Rose remained silent.

Sally looked shrewdly at Rose. "You haven't been encouraging Wilson Nye, have you?"

"Not encouraging him. No." Rose replied truthfully.

"But he's been sniffing your skirts," Sally stated flatly.

"Sally!" Rose stopped in her tracks.

"Well?" she asked.

"Well what?" Rose demanded.

"Wilson Nye?" Sally's voice was impatient.

"He's stopped by the house," Rose admitted.

"Paid calls, you mean?"

"I suppose you could say so, though it seemed pretty innocent at the time."

"There's nothing innocent about that man, Rose. Watch out!"

"You don't have to worry about me!"

"And don't rent him your apartment!"

"Why not? I could make a little money, maybe. And it would keep him at a distance, *nu?*"

Sally threw up her hands and let them slap at her sides. "Chances are, he won't pay you. And he'll pawn whatever furniture he doesn't ruin. He'll chase every one of your friends and flirt with every dame who's still breathing. Only Wilson, he'll find the one with a husband, who'll kill him in broad daylight."

"And this, I should prevent?"

Sally laughed.

"Besides," Rose added. "Maybe it won't come to pass. He could always win the election."

Sally raised her hand to her forehead, "God forbid!"

They both laughed.

Percy saw Rose, who'd told him she was staying home on account of some holiday, so why is she over there, chatting it up with Wilson Nye?

Should he go and say hello?

Percy slid into the horse barn, unnoticed. At least the aroma of horse and hay gave him comfort. He greeted a stabled Percheron like an old friend, stroking its nose. As if the horse understood Percy's tumult, the beast whinnied and pawed the ground, then dipped his head and let Percy scratch him behind the ears.

Percy couldn't stop working his doubts, as if they were a piece of corn stuck between his teeth. Did she lie? And what about that Jewish holiday? Was she just making that up? Or was she already keeping company with Wilson Nye and just didn't want Percy to know? She didn't say she already had plans to come. She didn't even know what the fair was! So why did she turn him down but show up anyway? And who was she with, the Boyces or Nye?

"Well, I'll go find out," he told the horse, who blinked and nodded, as if this was a good idea.

Percy hesitated in the shadow of the barn. She was still talking with Wilson. Sally tugged on Rose's sleeve. The gals were moving on, but where were they headed? Percy started down the path, then detoured. He didn't want to run into Wilson.

Sally and Rose were disappearing into the dinner tent. Well, he might as well get dinner, too. But was chasing her the right thing? She'd already turned him down. Maybe he should take the hint. And if somehow—he didn't know how, but maybe—it was an honest mistake. If there were a reasonable explanation for her saying she has one sort of plans one day and ends up having another sort of plans the next, well, in that case, he didn't want to make her feel uncomfortable, as if she'd done something wrong. Even if maybe she had.

No, no. Percy turned and headed away from the tent. He wasn't going to accidentally on purpose run into her. This wasn't high school. He shook his head and chuckled to himself, and walked directly into Wilson Nye.

"Well, if it isn't the Extension Agent himself, surveying the work of his disciples!" Wilson held out his large palm for Percy to shake. Percy nodded but kept his arms swinging as he walked past.

"Rose Mayer's gone over to the chicken barbecue!" Wilson called after him.

Percy swiveled and stepped back, placing his hands on his hips. "And why would I want to know that?"

"Just passing on some friendly information, pal." Wilson draped his arm across Percy's shoulder and said, "Now smile for the camera."

Percy tried to shrug Wilson's arm off him, but looked up just as Greg Warner's flash popped. "Great!" the tall man said. "Now, one more. Come on, gentlemen. A little closer. Percy, how about cracking a smile. It's a fair!" Another flash. "That's better."

"Hey, Greg," Wilson let go of Percy. "What are the chances of you running that photo on the front page?"

"Don't you dare!" Percy glared. "It will look like I'm endorsing him, and I'm not doing any such thing!"

"You supported those other Independents at the convention," Wilson reminded him. "You didn't have any problem with them nominating Smith for President. Don't you think I could do as good a job as a woman?"

"You running for the State House or the White House?" Percy came close to sneering as he hurried after the photographer.

Greg was one of those tall men whose every step covers more than a yard, and Percy, of just average height, didn't get a break until Greg stopped to set up his camera and flash.

"Hey, Greg!" Percy stopped next to the photographer.

"Hello, Percy." Greg continued to fiddle.

"I'm serious about not printing that photo," Percy said.

"I know you are." Greg turned the crank that wound the next frame of film into place.

"So, promise me you'll not print it." Percy held his hand out for a friendly shake.

"Wish I could," Greg said, straightening to his full six-foot-three, and keeping both hands on his apparatus, "but that's an editorial decision. You'll have to talk to Mr. Rice about that. It's his paper."

Percy put his hand on his hip again. "Couldn't you just spoil that picture? Expose it in the sun, or something? Maybe ruin it in the darkroom?"

"Aw, come on, Percy. Don't get your shorts all twisted over a little photo. Besides," Greg was scanning the scene through his viewfinder, trying to locate a new photo to frame, "there's lots of folks don't know the story of bad blood between you two. Most folks won't even blink. To them, it's just two prominent men at the fair." Greg winked, "So long!" and loped off, leaving Percy speechless.

His eyes followed Greg's rangy form as the photographer knelt on the ground to snap a shot of a little girl eating cotton candy. Now why couldn't he just satisfy himself with those kind of pictures instead of stirring up trouble? What had Percy ever done to turn Greg Warner against him? Or was Greg just one of Wilson Nye's admirers, out to help his buddy? Politics sure made strange bedfellows. Percy rubbed his chin and shrugged, then continued on his way, only he wasn't sure anymore where he was going.

Even though he was hungry, he didn't want to risk the big tent. Besides, according to his watch, he was due over at the sawing contest. They were probably waiting for him to begin.

It felt good to walk purposefully again, and he strode past the prize pigs and fancy poultry. Percy nodded and waved to friends as he made his way down to an open glade.

The sun rained into the clearing, where a stout log lay cradled in a buck horse. The strong, shirtless men stopped milling about and stood aside in loose pairs as Percy approached. Percy greeted them, picked up the clipboard and stopwatch, briefly reminded the men of the rules and called the first pair to the saw.

Two brawny youths took their places, one on each end of the long blade straddling the log, and at the signal, started to work. Sawdust flew, sticking to the damp skin of the sawyers, whose muscles glistened with sweat.

A few of the spectators heckled the men, but mostly, it was the sound of the saw biting through the hardwood that filled everyone's ears. The buzzing was as hot as the sun beating down without relief until someone yelled, "Hey!" and the log thudded to the ground in two pieces. Momentary silence. Then some cheering and general chatter while the roustabouts positioned a new log into place on the horse.

"Next up!" someone yelled as soon as the log was installed. A father–son combination took their places across from one another. The whistle. The noise of the blade. This time, the crowd hushed, but not for long. The log thumped in two. Men cheered; the roustabouts hoisted a new log into position; another pair came to the fore.

Percy keyed into the rhythm, blowing the whistle and starting the clock; watching keenly for the single log to become two; stopping the clock; recording the time. Unaware of the heat, the time, the dent in his heart, he just kept the contest going until all the young men and all the small boys had a chance to beat the woodsmen: men in middle age who cut timber for a living, and who, despite some fat padding their bellies, could still best the young bucks. It wasn't until the sawing was finished, the winners announced and the general visiting over, that Percy remembered that Rose had been at the fair.

Was she still there? He didn't know. Did he want to find out? He didn't know that, either. He turned down an invitation to drink beer with some of the men and headed off in search of lemonade and a flower. His Rose.

Well, listen to him! It just wasn't true! And he gulped his long drink without tasting it, then ordered another and sipped it, his back to a tentpole, checking the landscape for a white-haired woman in a brightly striped dress. But he didn't see her anywhere. By his watch, it was unlikely she'd still be there. Wilson Nye was gone, too. Maybe it was time for Percy to call it a day.

But he wasn't ready to leave, so he made his way through the farm hall. The sight of the polished vegetables and the festive jars filled with pickles soothed the wrinkles from his forehead and cooled him some. Made him feel glad. These were the end product of all that labor; the gems given up by the land. A gladness, like the space that was church, filled his chest as he wondered, yet again, at the miracle of wind, rain, and soil yielding up such colors. Such tastes.

He let his fingers trail over the taut skin of a tomato, the smooth surface of an eggplant, the spines of a cuke. The yellows and purples, greens and reds. He shook his head. Up to this moment, he'd been having a black and white day.

He palmed a jar of pickled beets. Here was not just the miracle of earth, but of labor as well. The work that comes after the harvest. The farmwives who put the food by. As pretty as rubies. More precious, maybe. So far, Percy hadn't done more than can beans. He had beets in the garden. And onions whose tops had withered. He needed to pull them up and let them cure. But before he could go and start pickling beets, he had tomatoes to process. Rows and rows of tomatoes waiting to be canned.

8 | canning tomatoes

Monday, after work, Percy started. Tomato sauce, he figured, was easier than whole tomatoes. He wouldn't have to bother with scalding the skins off; he could simply run them through the food mill and reduce the sauce on the stove.

Even so, it took a while just to wash the forty-five pounds of tomatoes required for seven quarts. It was more tomatoes than fit in the sink, even using both sides. Damn Addie's harebrained idea! He was going to put that old sink back on the wall, and soon. Then he'd have enough room to process a garden like his. As it was, he had to work in shifts, rinsing fruit, filling the dish rack, then stopping to quarter the tomatoes into a pot in order to make room for more. Nor could he find find Addie's giant saucepan either, so he had three different pots simmering on the stove, and the oversized canning kettle heating up, too. He could already see that he was in for more than one night's work. Well, he could at least get the sauce made, maybe even reduce it some. He'd have to put it up on the morrow, unless he didn't plan on sleeping, that is.

It was past eleven before Percy wiped the last splatter of tomato puree from the counter, and he still had pots to wash. The sauce, at least, was ready to can. He'd reheat it as soon as he returned home from work the next day.

He shook his head, remembering how John Ready teased him back in June. It seemed reasonable back then to plant two dozen tomatoes. Now he wondered what he was thinking. How many quarts of tomato sauce did an old bachelor need? Maybe, in fact, he should be putting up pints, a more likely size for someone living alone. But that would take twice as long in the canning! Well? What else did he have to do?

He was too weary to think. He'd been standing in the kitchen since after supper and his legs ached with the effort. Placing his hands on his low back, he arched backwards, as he'd seen Addie do any number of times, and no wonder. Maybe he should have been a bit more sympathetic? Had he been too hard on her, like she complained of all those years?

Percy wandered into Addie's side of the house and sank into her sofa. Addie would never have abided his legs stretched out so. She was always so prim. It was a drain, really, minding your manners in your own house. Percy closed his eyes and imagined Addie seated in her sewing chair, peering over her half-glasses with unmistakable disapproval in her eyes, but saying nothing. Just taking up another stitch in her embroidery—or crocheting, or knitting or mending or whatever it was she was doing at that moment—and setting her mouth in a stern line of criticism.

Oh, Addie! She were a rare one! Didn't even have to speak to let you know her mind. Though of course, she'd just as soon beat you with words as not. Never spared you one if two or three would do. But when you got her back up, there was no listening for her. She didn't care what you had to say in your own defense, or defense of anyone who she thought had transgressed.

"No, no. Percy." She shook her head the way a hen ruffles its feathers. "I don't want to hear about it. I know the facts about those Wagner twins, and if they aren't the ones stole Lester's car and took it on a joy ride till it landed in Smith Brook, well, then, I suppose it's the bogey man who did. So, don't go telling me about evidence and what the sheriff has or has not been able to prove. There is such a thing as upbringing and character and I'm afraid what those boys got wasn't much of either. And them always mad for motorcars and machines, like the time one of them—Orren or Emmet, I can't never keep them straight—had that motorcycle and tried driving over Drake's chicken shed, like he was in the circus or something. It's a miracle those boys are still alive. Though, if you ask me, identical twins with cowlicks like that—mark of the Devil, and don't you try to tell me otherwise."

Percy didn't. Speeches like that just took his breath away. Besides, what could you possibly say in reply to a woman whose brain worked like a cattle prod, setting off unconnected jolts? Percy thought the way current traveled down a fence line, keeping his thought charged until it arrived at the gate where an idea could pass through to the next pasture.

On the way home from work the next day, Percy stopped by Greenwood's for some pint-sized canning jars.

"Good thing you don't want quarts," Barrett said.

"And why's that?" Percy wanted to know.

"Why, Mrs. Mayer wasn't in here but two hours ago and bought me out. Said she's canning the tomatoes her daughter-in-law left in the garden."

"Is that so?" Percy looked at Barrett to see what else he might know. "And did she carry them up the hill?"

"Oh no!" Barrett stroked the sides of his belly through his apron. "It was Sally Boyce who drove her down and showed her all the merits of one kind of jar over another, and ascorbic acid versus lemon juice. A whole course in tomatoes, if you ask me." Barrett rocked back on his heels. "Seems like Sally found the star pupil she's been longing for all this while." Barrett slapped his sides and stood straight. "That Rose Mayer, she is a bundle of energy if ever I saw."

"Canning tomatoes?" Percy asked, his hands resting on his cardboard box of Mason jars. "With Sally Boyce?"

"She and Sally seem thick as thieves. Sally even dragged Rose off to the Guilford Fair. Can you imagine Rose, from New York City, going off to a country fair?" Barrett's belly jumped up and down as he laughed.

"Sally took Rose to the Fair?" Percy asked. "You're sure about that?"

"Sally and Eamon! Honked for her. She was completely unprepared. Not even dressed yet, or so she said. If you ask me, it's hard to imagine Mrs. Mayer except all done up. Why, even when she walks in here, after tramping down that great hill to pick up her paper and whatnot, she always looks done up. Not like the ladies around here." Barrett shook his head. "Don't know what it is, but she sure is different."

"She told you this?" Percy's voice squeaked up the scale. "You're sure you're not just making this up?"

Barrett leaned over his counter, all confidential, and wiggled his finger for Percy to lean over and meet him halfway. "Ain't half the reason to run a store to keep track of folk? What do you think I've been doing all these years, Percy, just stocking shelves?" Five-o'clock whiskers dotted the shopkeeper's face. Percy shook his head no. "Anyone can sell canned soup." Barrett stood up, pulled the feather duster out of his hind pocket and waved it toward the shelves. "It's the knowledge you store up here," he tapped his temple with his finger, "that counts."

Percy stood up. "Well, I appreciate what you do for the community, Barrett. I sure do."

Barrett leaned back on his heels again and tapped the side of his nose. "It's also knowing what your customers want to know, and whether the knowledge is good for them." Barrett nodded his head toward Percy.

"Thanks for the jars, Barrett." Percy shifted the box onto his hip, opened the screen door with a jingle, and let the screen slap shut behind him.

Percy slammed his palms against the steering wheel as he drove home. If it's so obvious to Barrett, how many others know? Did Wilson? Why else would Wilson have told him she was in the dining tent? But how could they know what Percy was just finding out? And how was it he liked her so much? The few times they'd seen each other, all they did was argue! Aside from running into each other at Marlboro, they hadn't ever even been on a date.

A date.

Where would he take her?

When was the last time he'd taken anyone anywhere?

Addie. To the hunters' breakfast, because she'd never been and she knew she'd never get another chance. It took a mortal illness to get Addie to try something new, because in health she'd never gone to the hunters' breakfast either to eat or help out. It was just one of those community events she refused to put on her calendar, and there was no knowing why. Just as there was no understanding why, as her life was drawing to its conclusion, there she was, thin as a rail, bundled in countless sweaters and shawls and still cold, sitting at the end of a table with seven beefy hunters packing away eggs, pancakes, sausage, potatoes, and toast like this was the last meal they'd ever eat. Meanwhile, Addie, more bird than woman, pecked at a bit of pancake, but mostly she ran her fork through the syrup and sucked off the tines. The sweetness was the only thing that cut through the metal taste in her mouth, she said. That was her main complaint, that her mouth tasted like metal no matter what she put in it.

The metal taste arrived in September, when she pretty much stopped eating. By the time of the breakfast, in early November, she'd nearly dried up from lack of nourishment. And there was nothing Doc Stoddard could do, not that Addie would let him do much. Wouldn't even go see him until October, on account of feeling so poorly. But when he told her she needed an operation to find out what was wrong, she just said, "No, thank you. I think I'd rather die in the comfort of my own skin."

Doc Stoddard said, "I understand." And he did. At the end—it came fast, a few days after the breakfast she slipped into a cloud of pain—Doc stopped by with morphine injections. The way Addie blinked her eyes after he'd plunged the syringe into her arm made it clear it was the right thing to do. She was gone by Thanksgiving.

At home, Percy left the canning jars on the kitchen table and went in to Addie's parlor, where he sat at the piano. He sat for a long time without lifting the cover, but listening. Lila's music rose in his ears. That Chopin prelude she used to play, all dark and sad now, not like back then, when the music sounded as tender as touch.

Percy lay his head down on the cover of the keyboard, as if listening for the piano's heartbeat. The chords of that nocturne she used to play saddened him further. The melody in the treble breaking away from the chords only emphasized the undertow of death sucking air. That's what Chopin's piano music had come to sound like after Lila died. And why he only listened to symphonies and concertos since then. In the big music, the struggle for life triumphed.

So why was the Chopin rising from the keyboard as if Addie's old upright had turned into a player piano of remarkable sophistication, able to reproduce passion exactly as Lila could pull it so joyously from the hammers and strings? Why is it Lila took such pleasure in commanding such sad music? Did she anticipate her own end? Or was there joy in the accomplishment? Maybe those short bits of happy dance outweigh the funeral march? Even Percy broke out into goose bumps at the memory of those waterfalls of notes, and the thrill of watching Lila pluck them from the keyboard, like magic. Yet even when Chopin danced, the music carried a sadness of inevitability about it. Percy lifted the cover, placed his hands over the keys, and started playing scales.

His fingers moved stiffly. It wouldn't do, stopping for weeks at a time, not if he wanted to improve. Not if he wanted to play decently in his lifetime. He couldn't expect to garden and use his hands roughly, then come back to the piano at the end of the season and have his hands remember how to move. He couldn't lock up his desire to play in the drama of growing food. Just like he couldn't pretend he didn't like Rose.

Starting with C major, Percy played one octave in stately quarter notes; then two octaves in moderate eighths; three in faster triplets; and four in persistent sixteenths. It was all a matter of remembering which note the fourth finger played in each hand; it stayed the same going up and down.

As he played the twelve major scales, a voice inside him chided he should practice the minor scales as well.

All in good time.

For the minor scales he'd have to pull out his *Hannon*, the thick book of exercises, and at the moment, he just wanted to play scales. It was a straightforward way to play without having to think too hard, but hard enough so that he couldn't think about anything else.

On Wednesday, Percy was impatient to leave work for home to practice, to can the sauce that had been sitting in the fridge since Monday, and yes, to harvest more tomatoes. He figured he could practice the piano while reducing the sauce and heating the canning kettle. Maybe the ripe tomatoes could hang on the vine one more day. Figuring out how to use his time was like working a combination lock until the tumblers all fell into place, and he liked how he was opening up the possibility of having more to do outside the office than in it. Maybe retirement wouldn't be so bad.

But the piano didn't go well. With the sauce bubbling on the stove, Percy couldn't focus on his fingering. He'd arrive at the end of a scale a finger short and have to reposition his hands in order to negotiate the path down, and even then, he didn't always get it right. While he practiced, the sauce burned.

At work the next day, he couldn't concentrate. Should he pay a call on Rose? He didn't know how this idea popped into his head, or why he was working it over like a worry stone, but there it was when he got out of bed in the morning. Call on Rose.

Could be he couldn't face another round of tomatoes on his own. Addie was right: It was harder than he imagined. It probably wouldn't be so hard if there were two working at it, the way Rose and Sally Boyce were pitching in to help one another. Could he ask Rose to come and help him? Or John Ready? John would be over in a flash if Percy needed help taking down a tree or moving a boulder or fixing some machine or another. But kitchen work? Not likely.

Percy supposed any number of the grange ladies would gladly give him a hand. Would probably nudge him right out of the kitchen, if he let them. There wasn't a single local lady Percy could name who wouldn't come over and take over, like he couldn't even boil water, regardless of how he'd managed these past forty years. Well, there was one, but she wasn't local. Percy was sure that if he asked Rose to help him with the tomatoes, that's what she'd do. She wouldn't start rearranging the cupboards. But he didn't know if he could just come out and ask her to help.

He still didn't know that evening, when instead of practicing the piano or picking tomatoes after supper, he drove over to Rubin's to call on Mrs. Mayer. But no one was there, so he drove up the hill, to Boyce's.

Steam enveloped him as he stepped in the kitchen door. Immediately, his shirt stuck to his skin and his brow beaded up with sweat.

"Hello, Percy." Sally spied him first through the steam billowing from each stove.

"Why it's hotter than the hinges of Hell in here!" Percy replied.

"Canning time."

"You don't have your woodstove fired up, do you?"

"Sure do," Sally said, pulling a wire basket of tomatoes out of a boiling kettle. She carried the basket to the sink and emptied the tomatoes into a basin of cold water. "All yours," she said to Rose. "Eamon's on the front porch, listening to the ball game," Sally said to Percy. She was already dunking another basketful of tomatoes in the boiling water.

"That's all right." Percy cleared his throat.

The two women exchanged looks, and Percy thought his skin was about as red as the tomatoes Rose was peeling.

"The fact is," Percy ran his finger under his collar, loosened his tie, unbuttoned the top of his shirt, "it sure is hot in here."

"You know the old saying," Sally carried another basket of

scalded tomatoes over to the sink. "If you can't take the heat, get out of the kitchen."

"Well," Percy cleared his throat again. "I'm here because I'm having some kitchen trouble."

Rose's eyebrows lifted, but she continued to slip the skins off the fruit and cut out the cores. When she filled a shallow saucepan with a single layer of naked tomatoes, she carried it to the wood-stove, then returned to the sink, where more tomatoes were cooling and ready to be skinned.

"Kitchen trouble?" Sally asked. "How's that?" Sally gathered another basketful of tomatoes from the half-empty bushel by the table. Next to it stood another bushel, full of ripe fruit.

Percy nodded at the surplus of tomatoes. "I have about as many tomatoes as you have there, but only one novice trying to process it all. It's taken me since Monday to put up five quarts of sauce."

"I thought you were putting up pints?" Sally peered into the pot, checking to see if the skin on the tomatoes had cracked yet. "Barrett said you'd been in to buy pints."

"No secrets in a small town," Percy commented.

"How come you've got so many tomatoes?" Sally wanted to know.

Percy shrugged. "Planted a big garden for a change. Bigger than Addie ever allowed me. And now I've got the piper to pay."

"You could give the tomatoes away," Sally said, carrying more scalded tomatoes to the sink.

"Just a minute." Rose said. "The water's warm. Let me fill another basin." She disappeared into a dark pantry off the kitchen and returned with a large block of ice.

"Here, let me." Percy grabbed the heavy block and hugged the cold to his chest. "Where do you want it?"

Rose bustled to the sink and cleared a place for the ice. "Here."

Percy's hands hurt from the cold.

"Thank you." Rose smiled as he held his cold hands against his hot cheeks. "Hot work, *nu?*"

"Hot work," he agreed.

"Well, Percy," Sally said, checking him with her hip so that she could get closer to the sink. "If you're not here to visit Eamon, we'll have to put you to work."

"I'd be glad to help." He unstrapped and pocketed his wristwatch. "What would you like me to do?"

"You can help Rose there, slipping the skins off the tomatoes. We're almost ready to put up the next canner." Just then the pleasant click-click-click of the kitchen timer ended in a long ring.

"Excuse me." Rose grabbed a pot holder to lift a pot lid as large as a cymbal off the canning kettle. With a pair of wooden lifters, she pulled a jar from the big pot and carried it to the table, where fourteen other quarts stood cooling on dish cloths.

"Wow. You ladies have done a fair bit of work this evening."

"We've been at it since five." Sally placed empty jars into the newly vacant canner, to get them sterilizing. She took sterilized jars from a second kettle for Rose to fill. Sally handed Percy a small pharmacy vial. "Put a half teaspoon of citric acid in each jar. Then Rose will fill them, and you can take the wooden spatula to release the air bubbles and wipe the rims. She can put the lids on. If we work together, we can all go to bed a little bit sooner."

So, Percy measured citric acid with the precision of a chemist, leveling the half teaspoon with a flat-edged knife. The ladies teased him, "It doesn't have to be so exact!"

"Only a novice in the kitchen," Rose observed, "is so precise. After a while," she said, "it's a *pitsel* here, *eppes* there, a morsel this, a little that. I don't think I've used a measuring spoon my whole life."

"Then why follow a recipe?" Percy wiped a jar.

"A recipe is a guide," Rose explained. "Like the directions people around here give: 'Follow the road to Waterchase four, five miles and turn left at the dead elm.' It's different from seeing the route laid out on a map."

Sally nodded to Percy, "She's sharp."

Percy said, "When you put it that way, I understand what you mean."

They finished two more canner-loads before calling it a night. But they were far from finished. Percy was invited to come back with his tomatoes. Together, the three of them put up the fruit from all three gardens. They worked late Friday evening, all day Saturday, and finished up Sunday afternoon. Mostly, they canned whole tomatoes, but they also put up twenty quarts of sauce and fourteen pints of ketchup.

They'd worked hard, hardly talking. It was a little like haying, when you walk behind the trailer, heaving bales. At the start, you think there's no way you'll be able to lift every one of those square bales dotting the field. Too many, for one, and too hot, for another. But you develop a rhythm and you get used to the heat and the scratch and itch, and the guy who's driving knows just how fast to go, and the guys walking behind know just when to signal the trailer's full and hop on for the bumpy ride back to the barn, where you have to haul out each of the bales you just loaded and put them on the conveyor up to the hayloft where the heroes of the day stacked them. When the load was empty, there was a moment of deep peace as you surveyed the pasture and saw fewer bales waiting to be picked up, guessed how far the next load would take you, drank a long draught of spring water, and climbed back on the trailer for another load. Men loading hay didn't talk much. And evidently, neither did women canning tomatoes—and the work was just as hot.

But haying just tuckered you out, whereas the canning revital-ized Percy. As if his brain had been vacuum sealed along with all those bushels of tomatoes, he could concentrate again. He brought home three cartons of tomatoes and left them at the top of the stairs, intending to carry them down to their winter destina-tion any number of times—even walking past them on some other cellar errand—but he walked around them instead. The jars stood at the head of the stairs where he could view them over the rim of his morning coffee and his afternoon tea. Like a problem he couldn't solve, he stared at the cartons and wondered what to do about Rose.

Despite the steam that filled the kitchen, Percy remembered every minute of those three days spent with her with the clarity of bright sunshine. Her straight back as she stood at the sink; the swift competence with which she slid the skins off with one hand, catching the naked fruit in the other; her confidence with the par-ing knife, as she cut out the green core. And she claimed she'd never canned tomatoes before. "Ah, but I know my way around a kitchen," she'd said.

Aye. That she did. And he told her so. Maybe he didn't have that comfort of complete competence among the kettles and cans, but he was at ease with her as he'd never been with a woman, bumping shoulders and hips as they jostled each other at the sink.

Under normal circumstances, fall is a busy time of year in the farm calendar, but this year was busier than ever, on account of Percy's impending retirement. Every farm visit turned into a fare-well, and every meeting a roast, often accompanied by a presenta-tion of a plaque or a gift, or both. It got to be so that it was a relief to return home. Return home and play the piano.

Percy finally did pull out the *Hannon* and played the exercises daily for a month, because to do so was like working out the mathematics of planting a corn field, and he needed the clean, even spacing of seeds in hills after a day of good-byes. Even on the weekends, when Percy worked in his garden, either harvesting the late, cold-weather crops, or putting the hot-weather beds to sleep under a blanket of winter rye, even after that labor, Percy would come in and play scales.

By early October, only Brussels sprouts, kale, carrots, beets, and leeks remained in the garden, so Percy turned to other chores. He cleaned and installed the storm windows. He changed to winter oil in his car. He raked leaves up against the foundation. And he moved from scales to music, sight-reading all the way through *Easy Classics to Moderns.*

It was the early music he liked: Purcell, Telemann, Handel, and most of all, Bach. He ordered a copy of Bach's Two-Part Inventions, but when the music arrived, it stumped him. He could play all the notes in the right hand, and all the notes in the left, but he couldn't get his hands to cooperate with the music when he attempted both lines together. And even when he played the treble phrase, he could tell something was missing. He suspected it had to do with the hieroglyphic notation above the B in the first measure, but he had no more idea what the squiggle meant than he understood Chinese. It was as if suddenly a new letter had been introduced to the alphabet, and he no longer knew how to read. Nevertheless, he thumped his way to the end, occasionally hitting a sequence of notes in a such a way that it touched his heart. But mostly, he just made sounds like shadows of his own longing.

He hadn't seen Rose since they finished canning. It would be awkward to see her again, after those three days in Sally Boyce's kitchen. He imagined Rose in his own. He had a clear picture of her sitting at the table, with her New York paper spread out before her. He'd never seen her in this pose, but he was sure she rested a cheek on her propped arm, shaking her head and talking back to the newsprint. Only playing the piano put an end to this reverie. Only making music soothed his heart.

But his playing was rarely musical, so after St. Louis beat the Yankees in the World Series—no small comfort to a Red Sox fan— Percy made an appointment with a piano teacher, and on a cool but bright Wednesday after lunch, he walked from his office on Main Street to Mrs. Salerno's home on High.

She lived in a converted carriage house behind a Victorian manse. As Percy approached the garden, where the tattered leaves of a grape arbor hung over a bluestone patio, the traffic noise disappeared. He wasn't sure if he should knock at the glass door or if there was another entrance, when a diminutive woman of unquestionable elegance appeared.

"You must be Mr. Mendell?" Mrs. Salerno held her hand out. Paper thin skin covered her small bones. "Please come in." She gestured with one hand and pushed her gray hair behind her ear. A pearl ring matched her earrings. She smiled.

"Thank you," Percy managed to say as he stood in a high-beamed room filled with books, paintings, and *objets*, and dominated by a huge concert grand whose shiny black surface reflected the earth tones of the velvet upholstery. The kitchen, he could see, was behind a screen of open shelves, and through an alcove whose shutters were pushed aside, he saw an imposing four-poster.

Mrs. Salerno glided toward the piano. Percy followed in the cloud of her darkly spiced perfume. She indicated the piano bench, and he sat, but not comfortably. Her tailored skirt, starched blouse, and boiled wool jacket—all of a quality to last a lifetime and withstand any change in style—affected in him a stiff formality.

"May I remove my jacket?" he asked.

"Please," her voice quavered. "And roll up your shirtsleeves. I want to see your wrists." She remained sitting while Percy stood between the piano and bench, looking for a place to stow his tweed. She took it and draped it over the straight back of her chair. "Now, shall we begin." It wasn't a question but a command. "A C-major scale would be fine."

Did he even remember how? Her eyes, faded with age as they were, penetrated his fears. Percy's face was hot, but his hands were stiff and cold, and the eight notes of the scale sounded like the bungled effort of a child.

"Relax," she smiled. "Warm up as you would at home."

Percy played the exercise he always started with: quarter notes, eighths, triplets, and sixteenths.

"Now," she said, leaning over the top octaves and placing her hands on the keys. "You must learn where the accents fall." She played the scale.

"How do you do that?" he blurted before she even finished.

"What?"

"Your scale sounds—like music," Percy shrugged. "Mine sounds like—like sound."

"Watch," she struck a note. "I let my wrist sink before I lift my finger. That gives each note a rounder shape. Try it."

Percy tried it, striking the note too hard.

"Again." She placed her dry hand on his and guided him. "There. Try it yourself."

He did, and it sounded better.

"But, you can only do that for the quarter note scale. For the eighths and sixteenths, you must accent the beat." She played triplets, "ONE-two-three, ONE-two-three. And so on. Sixteenths are ONE-two-three-four, ONE-two-three-four." She demonstrated. "Now you try it."

Percy laid his hands on the keys again. He had to stop thinking about his incompetence, concentrate only on the notes. Nothing else.

"That was better. That's how I want you to practice scales at home."

Percy nodded.

"Do you have a metronome?"

Percy frowned, "I don't think so."

The piano teacher pinched her arched eyebrows together. "This is a metronome." She picked a wooden box in the shape of a pyramid off a stack of music books and wound a key in its side. When she set it down and released the metal arm from a bracket, the arm swung back and forth like a pendulum, making a click-ing sound at each side of the swing. "You set the speed here." She moved a small metal weight down the arm. He could see numbers and notched lines. "Here, try sixty." It was hard, actually, to play the first scale that slowly, but it was comfortable for the eighths. Even the triplets worked, if he pushed himself to keep up. But the sixteenths—they ran away and his fingers tangled.

"Get yourself a metronome, and work on this scale until you can play it at ninety-six."

"I can barely play it at sixty!"

Mrs. Salerno nodded slowly. "Patience."

"I thought it was 'Practice'!"

She held his gaze steady. "Practice is important, but patience is more so. Patience. Humility. Faith. That's what you need to play the piano."

Percy sat still as the blood drained from his face. He'd always thought of himself as a patient man. Maybe he was wrong about that? Maybe he was even a little arrogant about being patient?

Maybe this piano playing was a test of his faith. Faith in what? In himself, maybe.

"Now, what else are you working on?" The teacher stood beside him and placed his copy of the *Inventions* on the music stand. "Which ones are you playing?"

"I can't get past the first one," Percy lamented. She caught his tone of self-pity.

"You must break it down into its parts."

Percy explained how he could play each line by itself, and how he didn't know what all the musical symbols meant. When he finished speaking, he felt as if he'd undressed before a stranger, admitting so much ignorance.

Mrs. Salerno decoded the music for him, writing out the mordent that had confounded him, and explained how to synchronize the beats in the right and left hands.

Breaking each beat into four equal parts clarified the music so that when Percy left the piano teacher's house, he saw the golden oak leaves still hanging on to the trees. The glory days of fall color were past; nevertheless, Percy delighted in autumn's browns and golds. Storing the harvest's bounty was like hoarding gold. Like stacked wood. Canned tomatoes. Like the promise of music.

But as soon as he arrived home and sat at the piano, the wisdom of the afternoon's lesson deserted him, and he played worse than ever. He tried to forgive himself, but charity was not among Mrs. Salerno's directives. He was to be patient, yes. And humble. Okay. And have faith. Well.

9 | yom kippur

Rose placed her jars of tomatoes in the pantry so she could send them home with the kids in October. Usually, they'd just close the house Columbus Day weekend. But not this year, no matter how much fuss they made. *Oy*, the hints they dropped on the phone. *You're not frightened up there all alone at night? Aren't you cold?* These kids, what do they know about change? About being uprooted? Here, maybe for the first time in her life, Rose could put down roots— little threads growing out of her toes and into the earth, this green earth of Vermont.

Rose held a quart jar out to admire. She'd give Jeannie back her own tomatoes. *Pri hagofen*, like in the prayer, fruit of the vine. Only they weren't grapes turned into wine, but jewels floating inside the glass. Rose placed the jar on the kitchen table, like a bouquet. Who cares? If she thought it was a centerpiece, that's all that mattered. Not that there was anyone to argue with. But she could hear Manny making fun of her, just the same.

After all the bustle of canning over at Sally's, Rose's own kitchen seemed pale and small. No steam to raise sweat on her scalp. Swear to God, her hair was soaked to her head by the end of the evening, like she'd been swimming without her bathing cap. Sally and Percy, too. Water dripping over their brows; Percy's shirt sticking to his skin.

She had to admit, he did okay in the kitchen. At first—when he measured the ascorbic acid so precise—Rose was sure he'd be one of those fellows who takes an hour and a half to boil a three-minute egg. But Percy surprised her. They bumped into each other while they worked side by side, like they were friends. Friends who agreed with each other, like when a jar was filled, or if a rim needed to be wiped again. It got so they communicated without talking. Their gestures spoke. It was nice.

Nice, but now what? The future was a dark room, and she was just feeling her way along the wall. Maybe she'd find a doorknob to turn, a threshold to pass through. Just what the room on the other side would look like, Rose had no idea. Surely, there would be light at the end of the passage. There always was. All she could do was wait. Meanwhile, she had her life to get on with.

Every morning, she walked down to Greenwood's, where she picked up her daily *New York Times*. It was funny how in Florida she just read the paper on Sunday and that was enough. But here, the paper kept her company, as if it were an old friend. How else would she know that Tuesday night was *Erev Yom Kippur*, the eve of the Day of Atonement? The trees, they should tell her? "Atone for your sins!" like it was written in the wind? Or maybe the birds would all flock to *shul* to repent? The other day, she saw a buck with antlers like a coat rack grazing by the apple tree in the field. The shofar was a ram's horn, not a deer's. And there was no one else in this empty landscape who even knew the meaning of Yom Kippur. Just Rose, Rose and the *New York Times*.

In Florida, they'd all fasted until their mouths felt hollow and they could taste their own bad breath. After sundown, the gang gathered at Aileen's, where they feasted on blintzes and sour cream, gefilte fish, noodle kugel—soft, comforting foods that rounded out a day-long fast.

So was Rose going to fast this year? Or was she just going to walk to the store, as if it were any ordinary day? Not when her friend the *Times* reminded her that tomorrow was the holiest day of the year. Jews the world over would be petitioning God to be inscribed in the Book of Life for another year. And Rose would, too. After all, here she was starting not just a new year, but a new life. Surely, that merited God's attention. And how did you get that attention? By dressing up and going to *shul* and mumbling your way through the service? Or by overeating at the end of the day? Well, maybe those things worked when you were part of a group big enough for God to notice. But Rose figured she was the only Jew in Windham County—maybe the only Jew in all of Vermont! She didn't figure God knew where Vermont was, not when so many in New York, Philadelphia, Miami, Tel Aviv, even, were all clamoring for His attention. She could hardly expect Him to glance in her direction, especially when she hadn't exactly made her voice a regular part of the chorus.

Well, she'd gotten along pretty well without Him so far, why was she worrying herself now? Maybe it was just that here she was, alone in the world, at the end of one year—the garden finished, the trees starting to turn, the air cool despite the sun's shine—and at the beginning of another: seasons ahead that were to her unknown. What did she know from foliage? Or winter, with drifts of snow and brittle nights? Family could worry her, and friends could tell her how to prepare, but until she'd seen the trees burst into autumn flame, or the world erased in the white of a winter storm, these seasons were just as vague as the ocean when she used to stand on the beach and look out to sea.

Rose braided and baked a challah. The ceremonial bread came out of the oven just as the sun set. She lit two candles with traditional prayers blessing the Light of the Universe and God, for bringing her to another holiday season. She recited a prayer for the fruit of the vine and sipped wine. With her hand over the warm bread, she praised the fruit of the earth, then tore a piece and placed it in her mouth. It tasted like life itself.

Outside her kitchen window, dusk gathered into night, and Rose sat sipping wine and nibbling bread. The candlelight bounced off the bare window and stared back at her like the eyes of a wild animal. Rose met its gaze, challenging whatever beast was outside to come in. But nothing entered, not even the ghosts of her husbands, who visited her the last time she kept vigil. This time, instead of her neighbor's apartments pressing in on her from all sides, trees circled her house from across the lawn, and the wind knocked at her door. But no one walked in. Not Sam. Not Dory. Not her parents, may they all rest in peace. Not even Manny's voice, with its permanent edge of annoyance. At first, Rose heard nothing but silence, a silence so profound, she could perceive the shadow of her own breath. She was replete with light, and as calm as the blue flame that burned steady at the wick.

Rose sat, watching the candles burn until she heard music play. It was the rondo of a Mozart sonata for piano and violin—something she'd heard long ago, back at the Settlement House, maybe—and it filled her heart. But she couldn't figure out where it was coming from. She pressed her face against the window and saw only the immense, star–speckled sky. She stepped out the back door, where the music was no louder, but filled her ears as her eyes soaked in the sparkling points of light spattered across the night sky. She drew a deep breath and exhaled. Only then, in that brief moment when her lungs were empty and before she inhaled again, did the music pause. And that's when Rose learned she was listening to the music of her life, and it came from within.

The next day, instead of walking down the hill to the store, Rose stayed home to atone. It was her job to ask forgiveness of people she'd offended over the year; God didn't intercede on behalf of man's transgressions toward man. And surely Rose had offended, but who? and how? Did she have to go back to Florida to beg pardon from Sadie for saying unkind things behind her back? For keeping the wrong change from the grocer? For cursing the Republicans for nominating Goldwater? Well, the election would take care of that.

Just as surely as Rose had offended her fellow man, she was sure she could make amends. Okay, so she liked to argue. She even liked to criticize. *Nu?* So, who didn't? Besides, the time for all that was passed. The *Yamin Noraim*, the Ten Days of Penitence, were over. Now it was the Day of Atonement. A day to repent.

"For the sin we have committed before Thee, O God of forgiveness, forgive us, pardon us, grant us remission." The words streamed into Rose's mouth the way saliva flows after tasting a lemon. Her father uttered these words fifty-six times, for fifty-six categories of sin, beating his breast with every utterance. Her mother, too, rocked in the corner of the kitchen, wringing a handkerchief as she mumbled in Hebrew, sometimes fiercely clutching Rose and Lena to her side, to include them, Rose supposed. Who else was "we"? The whole tribe of Jews? Could a Jew pray alone? Was she still part of a tribe if she lived alone among *goyim*? Would she be included in the collective prayers of all the other Jews *davening*, rocking back and forth in prayer, in synagogues throughout Brooklyn? Which was her tribe, anyway? She'd never belonged to one congregation, not to any. Dory invited her to go to synagogue with him, but she

preferred to stay home. It wasn't her place, she told him, and he kissed her on the forehead as he left, wrapped in the cloak of his own need to belong to the "we" and "us"—those who hope for a clearing of the communal conscience. Rose had trouble enough just with her own.

She could have performed *shlogn kapores*, even by herself. She could have asked Sally for a live chicken, and swung it over her own head, the way—back in the Old Country—her mother had waved a hen over them. Dova, Israel, and Rose would stand absolutely still, Rose feeling sorry for the chicken and frightened of her mother, whose eyes fell far away while her voice rose as if from a well of fire as she repeated three times, "This be my substitute, my offering, my atonement. This hen shall meet death, but these children, please God, shall find a long and pleasant life of peace." In New York, her mother substituted coins knotted in a kerchief for the chicken, chicken being too expensive to sacrifice, while the coins could go for *tzedaka*, charity. Rose could simply make a donation. But to who? The Orton Public Library? The volunteer fire brigade? Or maybe she should send some money to Israel, to plant a tree?

So many questions, and Rose had only herself for the answers. But what if she was the riddle? Could she solve the puzzlement of herself? And why had these questions never occurred to her before? She didn't know. All she knew was she was grateful when the sun came level with the treetops, the moment for the *Ne'ilah* to begin, time to make the final request for forgiveness for the year. Rose stood on her front porch while the sun dropped below the horizon. The modest heat of the day vanished with the light, and the first stars came into view as Rose stepped into the New Year.

She was just washing her supper dishes when Sally's car pulled in and honked. Tuesday night! Rose grabbed her sweater and scissors.

"What's the project for tonight?" Rose asked as she slid into the front seat. "Do we start on someone else's quilt, now that we've finished with Berenice's?"

"We'll start something new tonight," Sally grinned.

"How do you decide who gets to do a project?" Rose asked.

"You'll see."

"Well, I certainly enjoyed the quilting. Maybe I'll start a quilt of my own. A log cabin, maybe. With all my scraps. Or a crazy quilt." Rose watched the dark night rush past as they hurtled down the hill.

"I thought you were going to sew some winter clothes?" Sally asked, her brows suddenly furrowed.

"Umm." Rose peered out the car window, amazed at how the woods were even darker than the night. "It's so dark," she said. "And it was so bright, such a beautiful day."

"Perfect fall weather," Sally agreed.

The lights from the Grange Hall beamed into the night.

"Here we are!" Sally chirped. "And it looks as if the gang's all here."

"How can you tell?" Rose asked.

"The cars."

Rose sighed. "I'm such a pedestrian, I don't notice these things."

"You will, in time," Sally assured her. "In a small town, when you wave to your neighbor, you don't only know who it is, but where they're going."

Rose sighed. "I'm still not used to it." But how different was it, really, from the building where she and Sam lived, where Manny grew up? Wasn't that just like a small town? So, nobody had cars, they all knew each others' business just the same. How could you help it? What, with one phone in the lobby, you heard whatever anybody had to say. And everyone's laundry up on the roof, you knew how often your neighbors did their wash, and the condition of their underwear and sheets. In the summer, with the windows wide open, you could hear things you'd rather not. Sometimes it was yelling and cursing and maybe a slap or two followed by some tears and a door slammed. Or maybe it was panting and a grunt, or the squeak of a mattress that you'd rather not hear; it was embarrassing, and made you wonder if your neighbors heard you, no matter how hard you tried not to make noise.

Rose and Sally walked up the steps in silence. Sally opened the door. All the ladies stood in a huddle facing them and shouted, "Surprise!"

Rose checked over her shoulder to see what they were all looking at. Then she felt her face on fire. "What's going on?"

"It's Rose Mayer Night!" Irma Bassett announced, pulling Rose by the hand into the room.

Rose looked from one face to another, each one crinkled in a smile. She shook her head. "Sally, what's going on? You're in on this, aren't you?"

"We all are," Sally grinned. "We're going to help you make some winter clothes. That's our project for tonight."

Rose stood speechless.

Mary White came forward, holding a hank of soft flannel. "This is for a winter nightgown. Unless you prefer pajamas."

"Pajamas are warmer," Flo Darling piped up.

"Pajamas are too confining," Irma countered.

"Why don't you ask Rose what she prefers?" Mabel Robinson raised her voice over several heads in front of her to be heard.

"Well, how cold is it going to get?" Rose asked. "I've got to stay warm this winter without the benefit of a man."

"Flannel sheets!" Florence suggested. "That's what you want. With flannel sheets and a hot water bottle you'll be as warm as if your husband were snoring beside you, only not so bothered."

"Not everybody thinks it's a bother," Irma corrected.

"If you had Harold for a husband, you might think different," Florence smiled. "The man doesn't miss a night!"

"Are you bragging or complaining?" Irma demanded.

"Ladies, ladies!" Anna Mae tried to restore order.

Rose asked, "Flannel sheets? I've never heard of them."

"Oh, they're so cozy!"

"You can buy these things?"

"Mann's carries them, but they don't come cheap."

"If you don't mind sleeping on a seam, you can make them for the cost of yardage."

"With a felled seam, maybe?" Rose wondered. "Horizontal, across the mattress?" She shrugged. "I'll look into it."

"Wait a minute. What size bed are we talking about? If it's just a twin, I have extras," Flo Darling offered. "Why don't I lend you a pair, and you can try them out for yourself."

"Ladies, ladies!" Irma Bassett called out. "Let's get to work!"

Rose returned home that night with the pattern pieces cut for two flannel nightgowns and all the parts for a pair of silk-lined woolen slacks. The next day, Irma stopped by with a sewing machine for Rose to borrow. Rose offered her a cup of tea and a chat, but was relieved when Irma said, "Another time. I have to run."

She set the machine up in the corner of the parlor where the windows faced south and west. The nightgowns took no time at all, even with the faced yoke. Rose embellished the sleeves and bottom with ruffles, so she didn't have to hem. Only the buttons and buttonholes had to be finished by hand. She laid the night clothes aside and considered the pants.

These would take more time. First of all, there was the lining, to which Rose added an on-seam pocket, so she'd have a place to put her tissues. Then the waistband had to be faced and inter-faced, and the side zipper installed. The light faded before she was finished, so she carefully laid the pinned garment over the ironing board and closed shop for the evening.

After dinner, Rose returned to the parlor to read, but every time she looked up and saw the sewing machine in the corner, she shook her head at the wonder of such friends. Sure, back in the apartment house, the women always helped each other out, but out of duty, not—*love*. Well, what other word could she use? These Orton ladies didn't have to buy her fabric. They didn't have to include her in their club, even. She'd never belonged to a club before, not counting the union. Back in the old building, you didn't have a choice—you just did for one another in order to survive. When Sylvia Bogosian came home with a new child, you brought her a dish of something, and went in one morning to clean. The ladies in the building, they talked in the hallway and divvied up the days so a new mother could rest. You did it because it was the right thing to do.

What did Rose know of these ladies of Orton? They were kind. They'd embraced her. They'd helped her get started on some warm clothes so she could stay the winter. They asked her to join the book club at the library. They drove her into Waterchase and Norwalk when she needed a ride. And they left her alone.

Rose woke in the morning to the silent sun streaming in her window, and fixed herself coffee as the refrigerator hummed and the water pump kicked on. She watched the meadow from the kitchen window. By now, she was familiar with the way the shadow of night receded from the landscape, the same way waves washed backwards into the sea after they'd exhausted their crashing momentum. And even though Rose awoke at the same early hour, night lingered a little longer each morning, so that for the first time in her life, Rose became aware of the earth's rotation around the sun.

"It's the autumn of my life," she told the landscape.

The weather remained warm at midday, so that Rose took her book or her needlework out to the porch to sit in the sun. When she looked up, she saw the brilliant maples at the far end of the meadow. The sharp color the leaves cast against the pure blue sky took her breath away. She'd never seen anything like it, and something about the flaming hillsides and the crisp air touched her deeply. Rose didn't like to talk about it—she didn't even have the right words—but looking at the autumn landscape filled her with a sense—a sense of home.

And the air! It was so clear, yet spiced with a scent of decay that was oddly satisfying. It frightened Rose a little, to like the aroma of dying so much. But she did. As much, maybe even more, as she liked the sound of the leaves crunching beneath her feet when she ventured off the road and crossed the meadow that spread below the house. Leaves drifted against the stone wall, and Rose waded through them, as if she were walking in the shallow water along the shore. The trees surprised her with their kaleidoscope of color. She interrupted her walk a hundred times to pick up a leaf that called to her from the ground. The big dictionary was now stuffed with leaves pressed between its pages.

Even though Rose spent a good deal of her time alone, she never felt lonely. Sally usually dropped by for a cup of tea, or to take Rose somewhere. She'd even had visits from some of the other ladies, who stopped by to drop off a gift of freshly laid eggs, a jar of home-raised honey, a warm apple pie. As for not having a car, it certainly didn't stop Rose from getting around. Every Tuesday at the Stitch and Bitch, the ladies told her when each of them was going to town. Days when she didn't shop with one of the ladies, Rose walked down to Greenwood's Store. She didn't lack for company, and she was too busy to feel lonely. In fact, as Columbus Day approached, Rose started to worry about Manny's visit with Jeannie and the kids.

10 | columbus day

"So, Ma, we've come to rescue you. Are you ready to come back with us?" Manny asked as soon as he walked into the house.

"Manny!" Jeannie scolded. "Say 'Hello!' Hi, Rose." She kissed her mother-in-law. The kids tumbled into Rose for hugs.

"Come in! Come in!" Rose herded them into the kitchen. "I've got a nice fire going. The kettle's hot. We can all sit down and have tea and *mandelbrodt*, fresh made."

"Mmmm. Smells good," Jeannie said.

Manny was in the parlor, inspecting the woodstove. "It looks like you've got this going okay."

"And why shouldn't I have it going okay? Don't sound so surprised. Eamon showed me how, and I have nice warm house."

"It's hot!" Manny countered.

"So take your sweater off and sit down. Come, have some tea." Rose bustled about, handing out cups and saucers. "Kids, here. A friend gave me this honey, from her own beehives. Put some in your tea. Or dip your cookie in it."

"Sit down, Rose," Jeannie pleaded. "We have everything we need."

Rose sat. Teaspoons clinked. Wood shifted in the fire. Rose sipped her tea and waited.

"Oh!" Jeannie set her cup down hard, splashing her tea. "I have groceries to bring in!"

"Groceries?" Rose asked.

"I always bring up meals when we come for the weekend."

"I already cooked." Rose shrugged and placed her cup in the saucer. "There's a nice roast chicken for tonight, and brisket for tomorrow. It can just stay in a low oven while we go down to the village, the Heritage Festival."

"We've never been." Jeannie looked over to Manny.

"We have to close up the house—" Manny interrupted himself. "Usually, that's what we do."

"That's why we've never been down to the festival," Jeannie explained. "But I guess this year, all we have to do is put the garden to bed."

"Which reminds me," Rose said. "I canned your tomatoes. They're in the pantry. Don't forget to take them home."

"You canned the tomatoes?" Jeannie asked.

"Are you sure they're safe to eat?" Manny said. "We're not going to get botulism or anything?"

"I did it over at Sally's. So far, she hasn't poisoned her family," Rose said, a little stiffly.

"Well, there's always a first time," Manny quipped.

"If you don't want them, leave them here. I'll use them."

"You're really going through with this?" Manny said, shaking his head as he stood up to stretch. "Well, I better get the storm windows in place. Did you buy fuel oil?"

"And firewood," Rose said. She cleared the tea things onto a tray. "There's a job for you kids. You can stack wood. It's out in a big pile beside the shed. In a minute, I'll come out and show you."

"First, let's bring in everything from the car."

Rose kept tripping over the boxes and bumping into people, the house was so crowded. "Go," she said to Jeannie. "You go dig in your garden and I'll finish dinner."

"You're sure you don't want any help?" Jeannie asked, one foot out the door.

"I'm sure." Rose nearly shooed her out of the house. "Go!"

Rose roasted her chicken and potatoes and cooked spinach and set the table in peace. But every time she opened the fridge, she had to search through all of Jeannie's packages and half gallons of milk so that she felt like a visitor in her own home. By the time they'd finished the dishes after dinner, Rose was exhausted and went to bed.

She woke hours before the others, started the fire, put up a large pot of coffee and waited. By the time the kids straggled down in their pajamas, she could have walked to Greenwood's and back. Tomorrow, she would.

"We brought you bagels and lox," Jeannie said, handing deli packages to Rose.

"Now this is a treat," Rose said as she helped Jeannie set out the pink fish. "And bagels! You can't find them in Vermont. You can't even get good rye. I've started baking my own bread. Whole wheat."

"Next time, I'll bring you some you can put in the freezer."

"She could live with us and have decent bread every day of the week," Manny said.

"Just slice the bagels!" Jeannie glared as she handed them to him.

It was late morning by the time they all piled in the car and headed down to the village. Rose should have walked. She could have met them there. At least they were out of the house.

"It's just like the Fourth of July!" Wendy said, as they parked the car behind a line of others.

"No it isn't." Marty sneered. "There's no parade!"

"But look at all the booths!" Wendy eyed the tables of candied apples and pies.

"I want to look at the rummage sale," Jeannie said, peering at the piles of housewares under a striped tent.

"There are used books, too," Manny said.

"Come first to the Grange." Rose shepherded them toward the hall. "There's something there I want to show you."

Irma Bassett greeted them. "Hi, Rose! We were getting worried you weren't here! We thought maybe someone was supposed to pick you up and forgot."

"Just off to a slow start," Rose replied.

"I see your family is up."

Rose nodded.

"This must be your son," Irma said, turning toward him.

"Manny Rubin," Rose said, making the introduction. "Irma Bassett."

"Your mother is quite a seamstress," Irma said. "We don't know how we've managed all these years without her. Nice to meet you." She nodded and continued downstreet.

They started to walk on when Shirley Greenwood stopped them. "Hello, Rose. Hello, Mr. Rubin. Mrs. Rubin. Nice to see you. It's a good time of year to visit."

"We always come up Columbus weekend," Manny said.

"Do you?" Shirley smiled. "Well, enjoy yourselves."

"How do you know all these people?" Jeannie asked.

"It's just like you said," Rose shrugged. "You just meet them."

"But you've only been here, what—about six, seven weeks since we left."

"Is that all?" Rose shook her head. "It seems as if I've lived here forever."

The Grange Hall was crowded with people milling about each of the needlework displays the ladies had set up the day before. Rose hadn't seen it; she'd stayed home to get ready for her kids. And there, prominently displayed was a mannequin wearing the three-quarter coat Rose made for the winter.

"Rose!" Mary White rushed up to her. "There's a lady from New York who wants to meet you. Over there!"

Rose followed Mary's gaze and saw the woman in question. Who else but a New Yorker would wear a suit and heels to a day-time event at the Grange? Even Jeannie knew better. Like the Orton women, she wore a woolen skirt, cardigan, and Oxfords. This stranger, she had her hair piled on top of her head, and eyelashes with such heavy mascara Rose wondered at the strength it took to keep her lids up.

"Here she is!" rippled through the room. The crowd parted to allow Rose to pass. The elegant woman turned and regarded her.

"Hello," she said, in a voice as deep as a man's. "I've been admiring your work."

"Thank you." Rose's chin was in the air.

"You're quite good, you know."

Rose didn't reply.

"You're good enough to work in New York."

Someone behind her guffawed.

Rose said nothing.

"Are you interested in a job?" The woman arched her penciled brows.

"It depends," Rose said. "I only do custom."

"I see." The woman fingered the cloth. "I couldn't interest you in production?"

Rose couldn't help smiling. "You couldn't interest me in moving back to New York, if that's what you mean. But if you ever want a custom-made outfit, just give me a call. Rose Mayer, Orton, Vermont."

The woman nodded, "I will."

Rose turned and left.

"What was that all about?" Manny wanted to know.

"A lady offered me needle work in New York!" Rose laughed.

"Did you take it?" he asked. "You could commute in by bus."

Rose walked out of the Grange and into Wilson Nye.

"Rose! How wonderful to see you!" He took her hand as if he were going to kiss it and shook it up and down. "And this must be Mr. Mayer," Wilson pumped Manny's hand. "How do you do?"

"Rubin," Manny corrected him.

"Hello, Ruben. My name's Wilson. Wilson Nye."

Manny pulled his hand away. "Manny Rubin. Rose Mayer is my mother."

"Wonderful woman, Rose. We're so glad she's here. Only wish I could get her to go out with me." He winked at Rose. "If I can't get you to come on a date with me," Wilson leaned toward Rose, "I sure hope I'll get your vote—or I'll see you in Florida!"

Rose just shook her head. To Manny she said, "Let's go look at the books."

"What does he mean, he'll see you in Florida?" Manny demanded. "And where are you going to vote?"

Rose said nothing.

"You're not going to vote here, are you?"

"I'm registered."

"You're kidding!"

"No, I am not kidding!"

"But you don't know anything about local politics!"

"I don't? Wasn't that just a local politician, Ruben?" Rose chuckled. "Not that I'd ever vote for Wilson. I'd date him first."

"You're going out with that guy?" Manny's face was red.

"Calm down. I'm your mother. I'm a grown woman. I can look out for myself." Rose paused. "And yes, I'm going to vote in Vermont."

It took a week to clean the house after the kids left, in part, because they had rain, and Rose couldn't finish washing the sheets until new high pressure blew in, making it safe to hang laundry again. When the weather cleared, it was a different season. All but the brown oak leaves had fallen to the ground. Summer was over. Night arrived early and left late.

At Greenwood's, the conversation turned toward the elections. Rose asked Barrett, "Does Wilson Nye stand a chance?"

Clipboard and pencil in hand, Barrett paused from his inventory and considered. "Rose," he said, frowning. "Please don't take offense at my asking—"

Rose tilted her head. "Go on."

"Well, it's a small town, you know."

"People talk," Rose prompted.

"Yes. That's right. People talk." Barrett regarded his order sheet a moment.

"People talk about me. Is that what you're getting at?" Rose asked.

Barrett placed his clipboard on the counter and leaned over. "That's just what I'm getting at. That's exactly right."

"*Nu?*" Rose raised her eyebrows. "So what do people say? About me?"

Barrett leaned back on his heels and folded his hands across his chest. "It's not about you. Not really. But you asked about Wilson Nye, and I'd like to tell you, but—" Barrett looked at the floor, then the counter. He took the pencil from behind his ear and tapped the eraser against the cash register.

"But what?"

"Well," Barrett's eyes swept over Rose's face then settled on the toes of his shoes. "I don't want to hurt your feelings, is all. Not if you're serious about him."

"About who?"

"Wilson Nye."

"Wilson Nye!" Rose's chest rose with her voice. "You've got to be kidding!"

Barrett stared Rose in the face. "You're not?"

Rose leaned over the counter. "Who told you this lie? Who's spreading rumors about me?" Rose straightened and squared her shoulders.

"Now, now," Barrett's voice went mellow. "Don't get all worked up!"

"Don't get all worked up? When someone's slandering me before I have a chance to make a name for myself! How am I supposed to live in a place if people make up stories!"

"Hey. You're taking this too much to heart. And I was just checking my information, which I guess isn't true." Barrett shook his head. "But I should have known that. And I'm sorry, Rose. Really I am." Barrett was now leaning across the counter on his elbows, wiggling a finger for Rose to step close.

Rose bent toward him.

"It was Wilson, you see, who was bragging about going with you to Florida. Said maybe instead of selling you a house in Orton, you would be moving in to his."

"*Oy!*" Rose clapped her hands on her mouth.

"He has an apartment back of his house, but the way he said it—" Barrett shrugged. "Well, it was like maybe you were already sweethearts and keeping company. You know?"

Rose frowned.

"So, I just wanted to check, make sure I wasn't hurting any feelings when you asked about Mr. Nye—as a politician, I mean. But I guess I hurt your feelings anyways. I'm sorry."

Rose shook her head and attempted a smile. "So, Wilson Nye thinks I'm going to spend the winter with him?"

"He's insinuated you two were an item."

"An item?"

"Yeah. You know. A couple."

Rose shook her head.

Barrett leaned further over the counter. "Rose," he whispered.

Her eyebrows lifted.

"I'm glad it's not true."

Rose sighed.

"And Rose." He was still leaning over the counter. "I'd say Wilson Nye has about the same chance of winning the election as he does winning your affection."

Rose gave him a hard look. "But if someone like you could be mistaken, could believe what he said about me, then voters might mistake him, too?"

Barrett nodded slowly. "That's exactly right."

"So people might actually vote for him."

Barrett nodded again.

"Especially if they didn't want to vote for Mrs. Aitcheson, but didn't want to vote for a Democrat, either."

Barrett stuck his pencil behind his ear. "That's what folks are worried about."

"So, there's a chance he could win?"

"There's a chance."

"Or he could split the vote, and Barney Johnson could win."

"That's a possibility."

"So who do you think is the best candidate?"

Barrett shook his head. "Oh, no, Rose. I don't go telling folks how to vote. But I'll tell you what. Shirley and me, we'll pick you up Thursday evening and take you down to Waterchase, where you can meet the candidates and listen to what they all have to say."

"Thursday?"

"Seven o'clock."

"I'd like that, Barrett. I'd like that very much."

"Fine then. We'll call for you at half-past six."

Rose didn't recognize so many people at the candidate's forum, on account of it being held in Waterchase. Nearly all the seats in the town hall were filled, and a good many men were leaning around the doorway, as if undecided about actually attending. A long table with a podium in the center spanned the front of the room, and the candidates were just taking their seats behind it.

"What's Percy doing up there?" Rose leaned over to ask Barrett. "He's not running for office, is he?"

"Percy? No. Why, he's the moderator."

Just then, Percy banged the gavel and brought the room to order.

Rose thought maybe he'd gone up in smoke, evaporated with the steam from the canner, it had been that long since she'd seen him. He looked well, maybe a little tired.

Rose didn't catch what he said, but the audience laughed. His face relaxed when he smiled. Rose sat up to listen.

Percy was explaining the rules, how each candidate had two

minutes to make a statement, and then the audience could ask questions. They'd start with the hopefuls for state senate, followed by ten minutes of questions, then they'd move on to the candidates for representative from Waterchase, Norwalk, and Orton, in that order. "Any questions?"

The audience remained silent.

"Then, we'll begin."

By now, Rose was used to the Republican rant against Governor Hoff, and as far as she could tell, it was mostly on account of him saying that everything wasn't perfect in Vermont and then having the audacity to try to fix it. The Republican candidates for the state senate complained that Hoff had "run down the state"; they accused Hoff of enlarging state government at the expense of local control; and they complained that he took too much credit for saving the Fairbanks–Morse plant up in St. Johnsbury.

The Democrats reminded the audience that it wasn't Hoff who said Vermont's educational system needed to be overhauled, but a commission appointed by Keyser, the Republican governor Hoff unseated. Same thing for Vermont's government. The present bureaucracy had grown higgledy–piggledy. Yes, Hoff was asking for reorganization of state government, but to streamline it, not make it bigger. And finally, the Democratic candidates pointed out, the governor supported the amendment to the Vermont Industrial Building Authority that allowed the state to give money to existing industries, like the Fairbanks plant, and not just to new ones. The only thing wrong with Hoff's administration, the Dems argued, was a Republican–dominated legislature that stonewalled his initiatives at every turn.

Well, Rose would help these fellows out. At least she could do something at the state level. God forbid Goldwater was elected; he'd get rid of everything but the Pentagon, and it would be left to the states to take care of health, education, and welfare. Rose was still hopeful that LBJ would win, but it couldn't hurt to have people closer to home willing to take care of folks. Wasn't that what government was for?

"No," Mildred Aitcheson spoke. "Government is not our Big Brother, and we don't want government taking our money and telling us how to live. We want to educate our children in our own communities. We want to help our neighbors out just as we always have. The town poor farm works just fine and puts folks to work who need it. Why change what doesn't need fixing?"

Wilson agreed with Mildred. "If you just give poor people money, why would they ever want to work?"

Barney Johnson tried to explain how the working conditions of the mill worker were different from those of the farm laborer. "Industrial workers are at the mercy of the economy, and if they get laid off, they need something to tide them over. Vermont isn't only a farming state," he tried to explain. "Not anymore. We might not have much industry in our corner of the state, but there might come a day when we'd welcome it and the folks who work in manufacturing. And even if we don't, we have to think as a state, not just as a little town." Rose would vote for him, but even she could tell he didn't have a chance with this crowd.

"Well, Rose," Barrett spoke after the final gavel fell. "I hope that helps you make up your mind."

"Oh, it certainly does!" Rose stood, but Wilson Nye was blocking her exit.

"Certainly does what?" Wilson smiled broadly.

"Good evening, Wilson," Barrett tried to budge Wilson out of Rose's way, but Wilson held his ground. Rose hoped Percy wasn't watching.

"Well, Rose, did we convince you how to vote?" Wilson persisted.

"We?" Rose backed into the chairs.

"The candidates."

Rose was going to have to sit down if he leaned any closer. "Excuse me," she ducked around him. "Hello, Percy," she said.

"Well run show, Percy," Wilson swiveled to join them.

Rose tried to smile. Before she could say anything, a large man in a flannel shirt buttonholed Percy, who seemed eager to turn away. Well, she wanted to get away from Wilson, too!

"This is mere local politics," Wilson spoke confidentially. "We just mirror what's happening on the national scene."

Rose watched Percy become the center of a knot of animated speakers. She turned toward Wilson and sighed, "And how's that?"

"Well, if I had a little woman, I'd send her around like Peggy Goldwater is doing."

"Her silent campaign?" Rose couldn't keep her voice from climbing.

"It's brilliant!" Wilson grinned at Rose. "It helps a man to have a pretty woman by his side, don't you think?"

"I admire Lady Bird's style, the way she's riding that campaign train of hers through the South, talking about common human values, things that bind people together. Not like most politicians, trying to divide people up all the time." Rose placed her hand on her heart. "That would be something, to see the Lady Bird Express! To hear her speak!" Rose finally saw the way Wilson was beaming at her. "Peggy Goldwater!" she said as coldly as she could. "Do you really think women should be seen and not heard?" Rose asked. "Excuse me. I have to find Shirley. She's my ride home." Rose pretended she didn't hear Wilson offer her a ride as she turned and walked away.

It wasn't until she was picking up her Sunday paper that she finally ran into Percy. He walked into the store just as she was settling her monthly account. Barrett was regarding her check at arm's length. "Don't you think you ought to open up an account here?"

"I suppose I should," Rose agreed. She turned toward Percy. "Hello," she smiled.

"Hello," he nodded at her and at Barrett.

An awkward silence.

"So," Barrett cleared his throat.

"How's that, Barrett?" Percy asked.

"Well, how've you been? Don't think I've seen you since the debate." Barrett pulled a couple of newspapers from Percy's pigeon hole. "Here's your papers. Not like you to leave 'em here."

Percy glanced at the Friday and Saturday front pages. "Been busy, that's all." He glanced at Rose's Sunday *Times*. "Excuse me." He walked behind Rose to fetch his thick *Herald* and thumped it on top of his others.

Rose raised her eyebrows at Barrett, who shrugged and frowned.

Percy sighed.

"Rose, here," Barrett nodded toward her. "Shirley and me brought her down to Waterchase on Thursday. To hear the candidates."

"Mmm." Percy flipped through the Sunday paper, glancing at the headlines of each section. "And what did you think?" Percy didn't even look up.

"Who you asking, Percy, me or Rose here?" Barrett couldn't keep the annoyance out of his voice.

Percy straightened and nodded, "Mrs. Mayer. What did you think of the candidates' debate?"

"It was very informative! I learned a lot!" Rose tilted her chin in the air.

Percy nodded but didn't pursue.

"I just hope the factory workers around here have strong unions, that's all."

"And why's that?" Percy folded his arms across his chest and faced her.

"Well, clearly nobody in government is going to look out for them! What happens when they retire? What if a worker gets sick? Who takes care of her? Pays her medical bills?"

"If a worker is smart, he saves up! That's what's prudent."

"Prudent, yes, but possible?" Rose shook her head. "Not always. Not if someone's working for low wages and trying to raise a family."

"If you have to, if worst comes to worst, you sell your lumber, or split off some acres."

"Workers don't have acres!" Rose stamped her foot. "Not everyone's a farmer! Factory workers don't even have a garden to fall back on for groceries! They don't own their own houses! Rent's due on the first of the month, and if they don't have it, they're out on the street by the end of it."

Barrett's head swiveled from Rose to Percy, as if he were watching a tug-of-war.

"Well, why does the government have to step in? Why—as you say—why doesn't the union take care of its workers?"

Rose's eyes popped wide open. "You don't know much about labor, do you?"

"About as much as you know about agriculture, I expect."

They glared at one another.

"Greed," Rose broke the silence. "It all comes down to greed."

"How's that?" Percy asked.

"Unions. Factory owners. Doesn't make a difference. They all want all they can get and give back as little as they can. Government's the same. Takes the taxes, but what do we get in return?"

"Well, we agree about that!"

"Do we?" Rose asked.

"Government taking the taxes!"

"Isn't that what governments are supposed to do?"

"Is it?" Percy asked.

"How else can it take care of its citizens?"

"But why should government take care of us? Folks should take care of themselves!"

"If a country doesn't take care of its people, what good is it? It's people who make a country great."

"People and natural resources," Percy countered.

"But you can't mine the natural resources, or farm them, if you don't have workers fit to do the work." Rose sneered a little when she said "farm." "A fit worker has food in his belly, a roof over his head, a school for his children, police to keep the streets safe—" Rose ran out of breath.

"Why does the federal government have to get involved? Or even the state government? Why can't we take care of ourselves on the county level, say, or town by town?"

Both Rose and Barrett stared at Percy, mouths agape. Barrett just cleared his throat, but Rose said, "There aren't enough people in a town, for one. Especially not a little place like this." She dismissed Orton with a wave of her hand. "You need enough people to put money into the kitty to have enough to share."

"That's socialism!"

"So?"

"This is America! We're not Socialists! We're individuals! Each person should reap the benefits of his own labor! No one will work if they have to give away their wages, or if they know they're going to get them anyways, even if they don't work for it!"

Rose had never heard Percy raise his voice before, or seen his face turn red. "Calm down!" she said.

Percy stepped back. "All I'm saying," he said, "is that workers have to pull their weight, just like farmers do. There aren't any guarantees when a farmer plants seed that he's going to end up with crops, or if he does, that he can sell 'em at a profit. Why should workers be guaranteed wages any more than farmers?"

"Farmers own their business," Rose kept her arms crossed in front of her. "Workers don't. They're not their own boss."

"But farmers take all the risk! Those that own the business have more at stake!"

"Excuse me." Now Rose's voice had an edge. "But what does an industrialist have at stake? His stockholders' money? I have a hard time feeling sorry for him, when he smokes his cigar in comfort while those who work for him labor six days a week on the factory floor!"

"But workers get paid! Payday at the end of every week!"

"What are you talking about? What about speed ups and slow downs and layoffs? Even without them, all a factory worker has at the end of the week is her pay—and believe me, it's not much."

"Farmers work seven days a week and everything they own is at risk. Compared to farmers, wage earners have it easy!"

"You don't know what you're talking about!" Rose stamped her foot. "I worked in a factory! I know what it's like! What do you know about punching a clock or keeping up with a machine?" Her chin jutted out. "Do you know what it's like to be nothing but a kike in a sweatshop? Or to have nothing but your weekly pay to live on?" Her voice wavered. "I spent my lifetime earning a wage and—" Rose looked around the store, "and I don't even have a place to call home!" Rose frowned, determined not to cry.

Percy looked to Barrett, then to Rose and back to Barrett again.

Rose rubbed the toe of her shoe against the worn wooden floor.

The tick of the pendulum clock filled the store.

The motor for the cooler switched on, causing the lights to flicker.

Barrett cleared his throat. "What about the shopkeepers of the world?" Barrett forced a chuckle. "Who's going to look after us?"

Rose shook her head at the floor. "Maybe it's the politicians who can get us out of this mess," she sighed.

"Politicians?" Derision filled Percy's voice. "You mean like Wilson Nye?"

Rose folded her arms across her chest. "At least Wilson is one of your famous Vermont Independents!"

"Wilson?" Percy's eyebrows arched to the top of his head.

Barrett stifled a cough.

"And just where did you get that idea?" Percy wanted to know.

"He's running as an Independent, isn't he?" Rose raised her chin. "And what about at the convention?" Rose asked. "Didn't the Vermont delegation nominate Margaret Chase Smith?"

"The Independents in the delegation did, yes."

"Well, isn't that what we're talking about? Isn't Wilson an Independent?"

Percy let out a long breath. "I don't know what he's got you believing, but Wilson Nye cast his convention vote for Goldwater. He was not one of the Vermonters who voted for Senator Smith."

"He wasn't?" Rose's hands were cool on her cheeks.

Percy frowned. "He was not."

"But—" Rose shook her head, as if the motion would set her straight. "But, he seemed to indicate—"

"*Seemed to indicate.* Well, if that ain't Wilson Nye in a nutshell!" Percy glared at Rose.

Rose looked to Barrett for help.

Barrett shrugged.

"Wilson Nye," Percy sneered, shaking his head.

Before Rose could gather her thoughts, Percy picked up his papers. "I guess I have some reading to catch up on. So long." The bells on the door rattled as Percy swung it open.

"Bye, Percy," Barrett called after him.

The door slammed.

Rose frowned and turned to Barrett. "How was I supposed to know?"

"He's a slippery one, Wilson is."

Rose studied the floor.

"But he's a good man."

"Wilson?" Rose looked up.

Barrett nodded toward the door. "Percy."

Rose shrugged, "But what must he think of me?"

Barrett regarded her for a moment. "I think you've unsettled him."

"I didn't mean to hurt his feeling, but he doesn't have any idea—"

Barrett stopped her. "It's okay, Rose. It's done him good."

"But I was wrong about Wilson Nye?" Rose appealed to Barrett.

"Really. It's okay."

"If you say so," Rose sighed, shaking her head.

"May I give you a ride home?" Barrett asked. "It's no trouble. I'll just call up to Shirley to cover the store."

"Thanks," she smiled weakly, "But I better walk. I need the fresh air."

11 | landslide

By the end of October, when it rained, it rained cold. Some days, Rose just had to stay home. Days she didn't make it to the store, Eamon or Sally would deliver her paper. Once, Barrett himself drove it up after closing. Rose worried at the cost of such kindness until she hit on the idea of baked goods by way of thanks. She made all her favorites—apple cake, *bobke*, sponge cake, pound cake, *mandelbrodt*—and handed them out like calling cards. Recipients *kvelled*—raved—over the treats, so that those who didn't receive them started to stop in and visit, or offer rides, or ask Rose to join them for an outing or a party. Before long, Rose had too many friends. Well, a good number of friends and many acquaintances. But no one, really, to join her relief when LBJ won by a landslide.

Rose walked down the hill early on the Wednesday following the election, to find out the results. More cars than usual were parked outside Greenwood's, and the door was propped open to accommodate the crowd just starting to tire of the electoral post-mortem. Rose stopped on the steps, where she couldn't see who was speaking, but she could hear a man's voice.

"The whole state has gone to the Democrats this time. Not just the governor, but the lieutenant governor, the treasurer, the secretary of state, the auditor, and the attorney general."

"Prouty and Stafford were reelected," another voice countered.

"At least our Washington delegation's stayed Republican," a different voice spoke.

"And the Vermont Senate is still Republican."

"Barely."

"You can't tell me that everyone in this room voted Republican. Some of you folks right here must have voted across the aisle, so stop your bellyaching." It sounded like Wilson Nye.

"Do you know that this is the first time Vermont has ever supported a Democratic presidential nominee?"

"Well, what did you expect, with Goldwater?"

Rose was pretty sure that was Percy's voice, but she couldn't see through the press of woolen-clad bodies.

"Mildred was reelected," someone spoke up, "and she's G.O.P."

"Too bad for Wilson here, eh?"

"I didn't never expect to win Mildred's seat, but I gave it the good college try."

"Hey, Wilson, you ever been to college?"

Laughter.

"What are you going to do now?" someone asked.

"What I've always done, I expect. Sell real estate. Though I'm thinking about going south for the winter. Florida, maybe."

"What you going to do there?"

"I might just marry me a rich widow."

"Anyone we know?"

"Rose Mayer."

"How do you know she's rich?" It sounded like Barrett asking.

"She's a Jew, ain't she?"

"Excuse me!" Rose pushed her way up the steps, through the

crowd. "Excuse me!" The men all took a step back, leaving a space for Rose to face Wilson. "Did I hear correctly?" Rose glared at him.

"What's that, Rose? LBJ's landslide? Or that Democrats took the entire state?"

"No. I heard that part clearly enough."

"Well, it must have made you happy, being a New York liberal and all." Wilson leaned a hand against the counter and crossed his legs, as if he had lots of time to banter. Barrett was behind the counter, inspecting something on the floor.

"Well which am I, a New York liberal or a rich Jew?" Rose crossed her arms in front of her and waited. The room was suddenly still, and very warm.

Wilson straightened up. "What are you talking about, woman?"

"I heard you just now! And let me tell you something, Wilson Nye: I'd sooner marry a Republican than a bigot!" She turned to Barrett. "May I please have my paper?" Barrett handed her the *Times*, and the crowd parted, allowing Rose a magnificent exit.

The nerve! Rose chugged up the hill, hugging the folded paper with her left arm and pumping her right. Announcing that he was going to marry her! Assuming she was rich! Because she was Jewish! If that didn't beat all! Where did that man live? On the moon? And what did all the other men there think?

"Did they all think like him?" Rose asked Barrett the following day.

"No, Rose," Barrett shook his head. "I think I can safely say that Wilson speaks only for himself, which is maybe why he wasn't elected. Didn't even come close."

"How could he say that?"

"Which part offends you most, announcing his intentions or broadcasting your wealth?"

"Wealth?" Rose asked.

"Supposed wealth—according to Wilson."

Rose narrowed her eyes at Barrett. "Don't tell me you think I'm rich just because I'm Jewish."

"It never crossed my mind." He held up three fingers. "Scout's honor."

Rose huffed.

"But Rose, you got to understand. Folks around here—they're not many of them have met Jews, just like we don't see many colored up here. You can't blame folk for what they don't know."

"Ignorance is no excuse!"

"Excuse me, but I think it is."

Rose frowned.

"Not everybody wants to go around learning new things. It's just human nature."

"Human nature to be closed-minded?" Rose shook her head.

"Yup."

Rose thought a moment. Her father not wanting her to work on the Sabbath; her mother, not wanting her to marry Sam, he wasn't religious. She? What chance did she have to be closed-minded?

"Let me prove it," Barrett said, leaning his elbows on the counter. "What do you think about hunting?" Barrett asked.

Rose furrowed her brow. "Hunting?"

"Deer hunting," he nodded.

"So you go out and shoot a deer?" Rose asked. Barrett was her authority on local custom.

"Men, mostly," he replied.

"And what do the women do?" Rose asked.

"Complain."

Rose shot him a hard look.

"No, really, Rose. I'm not kidding." Barrett said. "It's not just that the men go out all day long." He shook his head as if he could loosen the right words. "It's not easy to explain," he went on. "But something, something maybe old and primitive, from before we were civilized and lived in houses, from back when we were cave dwellers, maybe. Well, this something just, just blossoms this time of year. It's like a fever. Hunting fever. The men don't just go out looking for deer to shoot. They get quiet. They stop talking. They don't change their clothes or shave. They become hunters again."

Rose made a face. "Whatever you say, Barrett."

He shrugged his shoulders.

"And how long does this *mishegoss*—this lunacy—last?" Rose wanted to know.

"From the fourteenth to the twenty-eighth of November. That's rifle season. You'd better get yourself a red hat or something," Barrett warned. "We don't want you mistook for a deer." He chuckled. "Bow hunting isn't so dangerous."

"Bows and arrows? Like Indians?"

Barrett frowned at the counter. "Yes," was his quiet reply.

"Well, then, maybe that's when I'll go visit my kids."

The papers that predicted a Johnson victory were right. It was a landslide. Well, it was to be expected when the alternative was Goldwater. Percy knew firsthand; for the first time in his life, he didn't vote straight Republican. Thanks to the Independent Party putting LBJ on their slate, he didn't have to vote Democratic, either. But it still rankled. What was wrong with the party that they insisted on nominating someone nobody could vote for? What's the point in that? What the party needed was more men like Aiken and Prouty in the Senate. At least Prouty and Stafford were reelected. At the national level, anyways, Vermont was safe.

At the state level, he wasn't so sure. He didn't know about this young man, Hoff. Percy would have preferred to see the Republicans take the statehouse back, but he wasn't sure Ralph Foote was the man to do it. Well he wasn't, since he lost.

Percy guessed Rose would be happy with the election results, but when he walked into Barrett's the day after the election, she wasn't there. It was just the usual informal gathering of highly opinionated folks who wanted to take credit for the way things turned out, as if predicting an election after the fact was some kind of rare talent. Percy listened to the banter, only chiming in to gripe about Goldwater.

At least Wilson wasn't elected. Didn't even split the vote, as feared. But that didn't seem to stop the man from running at the mouth. Here he was talking about his plans, like he was still a candidate and anybody cared. Percy wasn't really paying attention to what Wilson was saying, until he heard him say, "Rose Mayer."

And there she was, on cue, bustling through the crowd and glaring at Wilson. "I'd sooner marry a Republican than a bigot!"

Then she was gone.

After what happened down at the store, Percy didn't feel so bad about the election. He pretty much stopped thinking about politics altogether. At home, after work, he sat down at the piano and didn't just practice but made music, maybe for the first time. Again and again, he brought to mind the blank astonishment on Wilson's face as Rose turned on her heel and asked for her papers. Finally, someone who could shut him up!

He played with joy and even performed well for Mrs. Salerno the following week. When he returned home afterwards, he noticed the canned tomatoes still sitting at the top of the cellar stairs. Percy carried the boxes down. As he unpacked each jar, he remembered the comfortable companionship of canning. When they were all shelved, he climbed the stairs buoyantly. Why didn't he just take a drive over and pay a call?

In the early dark of mid-November, Percy turned onto Wheeler Hill Road. What would he say? His high beams swung through the trees as he turned the corner. A startled deer disappeared into the woods. They could talk politics; with the election over, it was probably as safe a subject as any. Percy shook his head and shrugged. He liked their arguments. He rolled down the window for fresh air, rounding the last curve and trying to ignore the heat in his armpits. For goodness sake, he was like a teenage boy.

The stone wall.

The twin maples.

At last, her house came into view.

It was dark.

She wasn't there.

As soon as she entered the house, she knew she'd made a mistake.

"Mom! You're here!" Jeannie approached with her arms spread wide. "How was the bus?" She gave Rose a kiss.

Rose pulled off her gloves and patted Jeannie's warm cheek. "Already, you forgot."

Jeannie stood blankly.

"'Rose,'" she patted her daughter-in-law's cheek once more. "I want to be called 'Rose.'"

"Oh," Jeannie's hand flew to her mouth. "I'm so sorry! It just came out." She pressed her lips together.

"I know. I know." Rose bustled past her. "So where are my

grandchildren?"

Manny walked in from the garage and answered, "I told you already, Hebrew School. Here, give me your coat."

"Five days of school isn't enough in one week?" Rose shrugged out of her coat.

Manny fumbled, and it fell to the floor. He brushed it off with his sleeve. "It's religious school." Manny sighed. "I thought you'd approve."

"Religious school," Rose repeated.

"Yes. They learn about Judaism. They learn Hebrew. Martin, he's preparing to be a *bar mitzvah*."

"Already, a *bar mitzvah*? He's what? Maybe ten years old and he's studying for his *bar mitzvah*?"

"It's a good tradition, to read Torah," Manny insisted.

Jeannie led Rose out of the passage. In the kitchen she asked, "Would you like a cup of tea? Something to eat after your journey?"

Rose turned to Manny. "Of course it's a good tradition, to read Torah. But it's also a good tradition to let children play while they're young, not to rush the cares of the world upon them." To Jeannie she said, "Coffee. I'd like a coffee, please. I need something stronger than tea to take the taste of diesel out of my mouth. That bus is the slowest, smelliest, saddest excuse for transportation I've ever been on. Worse than The Boat, even." Rose stood in the middle of the linoleum and fluorescent palace that was Jeannie's kitchen, blinking at all the shining white enamel. "I always thought a greyhound was supposed to be some kind of fast, sleek, animal, like a cheetah or something."

"It's a dog," Manny corrected her.

"You're telling me it's a dog? The whole bus line's a dog! I'm almost tempted to learn how to drive just so I don't ever have to sit in one of those nasty things again."

"Mom, you're exaggerating. It couldn't be so bad."

"You don't think it's so bad? Have you ever had a man across the aisle take out his *shlong* and show it to you?"

"What?"

Rose shrugged, "A regular *schmuck*, with a pathetic *putz* for a *shlong*. But a man should keep his business in his pants and not go showing it off on a bus, that's all I've got to say."

"You should have reported him!"

"To who? What should I say? An uncircumcised *shaygetz* is on the bus, stroking his *putz*? Tell a police officer? You think I can't take care of myself?" Rose looked significantly at Jeannie. "I just slipped my shoe off and held it up like I meant business, and I hissed, 'Put it away or I'll whack it!'"

"I don't believe this!" Manny put his head in his hands.

"What don't you believe? That I can take care of myself? Or that the guy got all flustered and apologetic? Or that a young girl in the seat in front of me turned around with tears in her eyes and thanked me. The bum had been looking at her—attracting her notice to get himself—well, you know what I mean, I don't have to spell it out. Anyways, it makes me almost think I should learn to drive, at my advanced age. Except that maybe they need old ladies like me to protect young ones. She couldn't have been more than twenty, poor thing. What's a young girl know about a strange man like that?"

"Well, I'm sorry you had such unpleasantness on the bus, but you did the right thing. I'm sure that passenger was grateful." Jeannie tried to steer Rose toward the table, but Rose wasn't finished.

"Grateful! That hardly describes it! She invited me to sit next to her at the next stop, and she talked my ear off from Hartford to New York. *Oy!* Everyone thinks they've got the most interesting problems in the world. *Tsuris* is *tsuris*. They don't change. So, she's in love with a boy in the army. What? She thinks she's the first woman in the world to pine for a soldier? This is an old story. In the Bible, maybe. If it's not, it should be." Rose sighed. "So, is that coffee ready yet? I'll just sit down at the table." She slid on the bench of the breakfast nook. "Listen to me. I talk and talk and talk. It's because I live alone, so that when I get out, I make up for the silence."

"Okay, Ma. You're with us now. You can talk all you want. I got to go get the kids. I'll be right back." Manny kissed his mother on the cheek and went out through the back hall. Jeannie set the coffee service on a tray and said, "Let's go sit in the living room."

"Why bother? Don't make such a fuss. I like the kitchen." Rose patted the table. "Just put it right here and take a load off your feet. You look tired." Rose nodded to the bench opposite. "Do like Sam always used to say, 'Sit down before you fall down.' Some way to talk to a wife, eh?"

"Here," Jeannie passed her a steaming cup and saucer. "There's milk and sugar."

"Black's fine." Rose inhaled the dark aroma and sipped. "Ahh. That's a good cup of coffee." She nodded appreciatively.

Jeannie stirred milk and sugar into hers. She held the cup in front of her mouth and said, "So, it sounds like you got lonely?"

"Of course I got lonely," Rose confessed with a shrug. "Who wouldn't?" She looked across the table at her daughter-in-law and narrowed her eyes. Jeannie avoided Rose's glance by sipping her coffee. Rose set her cup in the saucer with a clang. "I was lonely when I lived in Florida, too. And I bet, by tomorrow afternoon, I'll be lonely here." She leaned across the table, forcing Jeannie to look at her. "It's part of the human condition, loneliness. Aren't you ever lonely?"

"But I have Manny and the kids." Jeannie gestured with her coffee cup.

"And you're never lonely?" Rose raised her eyebrows.

"I'm too busy. I've been substituting quite a lot." Jeannie lowered her eyes again. "In fact, I've been offered a long-term assignment, for a teacher going on maternity leave the first of the year."

Rose said nothing. She knew what was coming. Jeannie wanted her to stay and help out, so she could go to work.

"It's in a second-grade classroom, in Ridgewood, so it's not far away."

"That's nice."

Silence hung between them.

"Well, I think I'll go unpack."

Jeannie lurched to her feet. "I'll carry your bag up."

"You take care of things down here. I can manage."

"But it's two flights!"

"Yes, but it's only one bag." Rose left the kitchen. She didn't want to see her daughter-in-law cry. But she didn't want to be trapped, either.

The two flights of stairs to her attic suite were nothing compared to Wheeler Hill, though the way Manny and Jeannie carried on, you'd think she was an invalid and they should install an elevator. Or maybe they should move up to the attic and let Rose have their room, with the two closets and bay window over the street. Rose didn't think so. Not for a three-week visit, she told them, to their evident dismay. She'd have to be sure to go up and down a few times a day, just to make up the kind of exercise she was used to. Already, after that long bus-ride, she felt stiff.

Rose had arrived on Saturday, and by the time Monday arrived, she was glad to wave them all off to school and have the house to herself. So, for a few weeks she could play Grandma. She walked to the A&P daily, where she always checked out at cashier number two.

"Cold weather's coming," Rose smiled at the cashier as she unloaded her cart. The woman just punched the prices into the register and moved the groceries along. "I wonder if we'll get snow for Thanksgiving," Rose tried again as she placed the last items on the counter. Still no response.

Barrett would have had an opinion on the weather, at least. Why couldn't this girl even say hello? Was it so hard? Here she was, a steady customer already. She'd been in four days in a row, and she didn't rate so much as a smile or a howdy-do?

The other shoppers were just the same, minding their own business like it was against the law to be friendly. Only the fruit and vegetable man was different. He wasn't a young man. There were flecks of gray in his hair. And he peered through reading glasses perched on the end of his nose when he squinted at the scale. He sported a paunch, and a pasty complexion from maybe not enough exercise or fresh air. For all the fruits and vegetables in the world, it was fresh air that mattered, getting outside. Percy probably had ten years on him. Maybe she and Percy didn't agree about farmers and workers, but about not liking the confines of the suburbs—about that, she was sure, they'd agree.

Rose pulled her grocery cart home behind her, stopping at each intersection to negotiate the curb. You'd think the people who put in the sidewalks would think about curbs and shopping carts and baby carriages and maybe make those little dips at the corners, like they did for driveways, where you turned your car in. But it's men who built sidewalks, and they didn't push babies, so why would they ever think of the convenience? Maybe we needed women to build sidewalks? Rose shook her head.

Such thoughts! But what else had she to think about? Every

day, she walked the four blocks from the house to the grocery and back, and the streets were deserted. Not a soul out walking the dog, pushing a carriage, raking a lawn. Just house after house with drapes pulled aside to let in the daylight. But no signs of life.

No kids in the street, she understood. They were at school. But the women? They must hang their laundry out the back door. Or they probably just used the dryer, like Jeannie, never stopping to consider sunshine, or the smell of fresh air on your sheets. Too busy, they'd say. Too busy doing what? Okay, so Jeannie was teaching. It was good to have teachers. But what about children? Couldn't she wait a few more years? It wouldn't be long before Wendy was in Junior High, she wouldn't come home for lunch anymore. She'd be busy after school. Then, Jeannie could go back. But nowadays, it's rush, rush, rush. What's the big rush? People are in such a hurry to get old. Getting old is so wonderful?

Rose walked past house after house, each one isolated on its patch of lawn, so different from the tenement, teeming with life. Or even the apartment in Florida, where at least you said hello to whoever was in the elevator. Even if it was someone you didn't socialize with, you still asked them about their health, or told them something about the weather. Like whenever Rose stepped in to Greenwood's, Barrett always greeted her. And if there was someone else in the store, she said hello. She'd met lots of people that way, knew most everybody in Orton by now. And if she didn't know someone, Barrett would tell her.

"Know who that is?" he'd ask as Rose passed a customer on his way out as she was on her way in.

She'd shake her head no.

"That's Abel Towne." Barrett paused.

Rose would raise her eyebrows, waiting for more.

"Served in the Senate for nigh on thirty years." Barrett nodded solemnly. "Born and raised right here in Orton, too."

"Democrat or Republican?" Rose wanted to know.

"Rose. Rose." Barrett frowned. "What does it matter? He's an old man now. Served his time well, and they weren't easy times. First, the Depression. Then the War. Now the boom."

Rose nodded at the litany of disasters.

"Only I'm not so sure about the boom," Barrett said, pulling out his feather duster and waving it over the tops of tinned goods closest to the register. "If you ask me, the boom passed Vermont over. Excepting for the Interstate, what sign of a boom have we had here? Mostly, our young folk go away for better jobs."

Rose shook her head. Who was she to know Vermont's problems? She used to think it was a problem there were no sidewalks along the dirt roads. Now her feet ached from walking on the pavement. And the woods, the chaos of them still frightened her a little. But here all the trees were lined up along the curb like hydrants for dogs to piss on. There was one, a triple-trunked maple on Queen Anne Road, whose roots had pushed up the sidewalk, so it was hard to steer the cart around it. But she didn't mind. It was as if the tree had *chutzpah*, the nerve to protest being confined to the narrow verge of lawn between the sidewalk and the street. There was a maple on Wheeler Hill like that; it had pushed over the stone wall as if the giant rocks were mere pebbles. A tree—if there was one thing Rose had learned to admire, it was the power of a tree.

Suddenly, Rose tired of the neat suburban landscape, where every house was a mock Tudor, with an azalea in the front garden and a slate path bisecting the lawn to the front door. Her limbs went limp with fatigue, and it took all her effort to walk the last block. Enough of playing house, already. Rose was ready to go home.

Barrett said she'd gone down to Jersey for Thanksgiving. Practicing the piano was the only way to quell the worry that she might not come back. Making his fingers follow the music and trying to incorporate all of Mrs. Salerno's admonitions—to think about the shape of the hand, to anticipate the next note, to think in phrases, to remember dynamics—these tasks so occupied Percy's mind while he sat at the keyboard, they crowded out the thoughts of Rose that filled every other moment of his day. He didn't want to be condemned to playing the piano. It was just supposed to be a hobby.

Had he missed his chance? And if she did return, what would happen? Percy was still worrying these two possibilities like a sore tooth as December dropped its first snow. He shoveled the drive, cleared files at his desk, sorted the greeting cards that arrived in the mail, always looking for an answer.

Maybe he should send her a Christmas card? But what would he say? Did she even celebrate Christmas? No, she'd take one look and think he really was stupid about things like labor and God. He wasn't going to insult her again, not if he could help it. Best to lay low.

Laying low didn't mean not thinking about her, and Percy kept up a steady conversation in his head. He'd see her at the store, maybe, and say, "I'm sorry, Rose. I didn't mean to hurt your feelings."

She'd frown at first.

Then he'd explain, "I just never thought of you as one of the oppressed. It seems to me, you do pretty good taking care of yourself."

No. He'd better not open that can of worms again. Clearly, he didn't know about labor. Not firsthand, not the way she did. But she didn't seem like the needy type, the type who holds out a hand for government relief. From what Percy could tell, Rose had made something of herself—on her own. He admired that.

Laying low also didn't mean not looking about for her. Once he'd learned she'd returned from New Jersey, it was just a matter of time before they'd run into one another. He had to be patient, that's all.

12 | christmas eve

It wasn't until Christmas Eve that he saw her. She was standing two pews ahead, on the other side of the aisle. The candle she held illuminated her face with light as soft as her hair. Just the sight of her filled him with—well—with music. His bass voice boomed with a rounder tone than he'd ever sung carols before, and the words of the familiar holiday songs rolled out of his mouth like fat, shiny bubbles of joy. *The First Noel.* Had he ever celebrated Christmas before? Could he be the King of Israel? She was like a star, standing shoulder to shoulder with his neighbors. A star that didn't sing. Rose stood, a candle flickering in one hand, and the hymnal closed and hanging by her side in the other. Her eyes were closed too. *God Rest You Merry Gentlemen. Little Town of Bethlehem—and Orton—the hopes and fears of all the years are met in thee tonight. Not a Silent Night, but O! A Holy One. It came upon a midnight clear, that glorious song of old.* Percy filled with gladness just seeing Rose again. He sang in a round, ringing tenor, *Hark! The Herald Angels Sing! Deck the Halls!*

The congregation filed out, still holding their candles, then turned back to face the church as the bell in the illuminated steeple tolled midnight, and everyone burst into a final chorus of *We Wish*

Percy approached as Rose blew out her candle. "Merry Christmas, Rose."

"Percy!" she grabbed his hand in both hers. "It's so good to see you! Merry Christmas!"

The skin on her hands was warm and soft.

"Oh," she said, letting go. "You probably want to put your gloves on." She looked at the stub of her candle. "What do I do with this?"

"I'll take it." He pocketed it and pulled out his gloves. She wound a scarf around her neck.

"What did you think of our service of carols?"

"Oh!" Rose looked away and wiped her eyes on her scarf. She fanned her hand in front of her face and glanced back at him, eyes full again.

"Here." Percy reached inside his coat and extracted a pressed handkerchief from his pocket. "Please."

Rose started bawling, and Percy simply put his arm across her shoulder and led her away from the crowd.

"I'm sorry," she hiccoughed in jagged breaths.

"Shh. Shh." Percy comforted her in a voice that soothed distressed horses and cows.

"I don't know what's the matter!" Rose wiped her eyes again.

Percy said nothing, but let the weight of his arm press on her shoulder. The fragrance of her hair mixed with the wool of her coat and the clarity of the midnight air.

"It's just—" She took a deep breath and regained her normal speaking voice. "It's been so long since I've heard any music." Her eyes fell to the ground, as if she'd said something shameful. "Since Marlboro." Rose blotted her eyes and stepped from under Percy's arm to face him. "And I've never been to a Christmas service before." Her eyes dropped to the ground again. "It's the first time I've ever been inside a church."

Her snowy head fell under his chin and he pulled her to his chest, as if they were longtime lovers whose touch was solace itself.

"No music since Marlboro?"

Rose shook her head against his wool coat.

"No radio?"

"No phonograph?"

"No piano?"

Rose kept rocking her head back and forth.

"Would you like to hear some music tonight?"

"You mean more? Another church service?"

"No. I mean angels and trumpets and voices all singing the Glory of God."

She shook her head ever so slightly.

"Let me take you to my house, and I'll play you the *Messiah* on the phonograph." He paused. "Would you like to do that?"

"Very much."

Percy told Sally Boyce he was bringing Rose home. Sally smiled and wished him a Merry Christmas; Percy steered Rose by the elbow to his car. At his house, he led her to the solitary wing chair, but he didn't turn on the light. Instead, he lit the oil lamp that he saved for power outages, and all the candles that Addie had insisted on setting about as part of her relentless interior decor. It was Christmas, after all.

As he moved about the room, Percy saw it as it must have appeared to Rose: lived-in but tidy, the clutter confined to the side tables piled with books and magazines. And the stereo cabinet with the new components he'd just bought himself, a combination gift for Christmas, retirement, and his birthday. He blushed at the expense. But look, already he was getting a return on his investment.

"Just a moment," he told Rose, who sank back into the chair with her eyes lidded, as if even the half-light of the candles was too much. He pushed the self-loading button, which responded with a series of whirs and clicks before the music filled the parlor with sound.

Percy stood in the middle of the room, unsure where to sit. Aside from the armchair, where Rose was enthroned, there were two side chairs flanking the window and a ladder-back at his desk. None looked inviting. He wanted to sit near Rose.

He disappeared and returned with a cushion from Addie's couch. Hesitating only a moment, Percy dropped the cushion on the polished wood and sat on the floor by her feet.

What was he doing, playing Christmas music for her? He tried to calm his breath to the sad, slow overture, only he didn't feel sad, just nervous, like the violins. Courage. Comfort. *Comfort ye, my people.* Who were Percy's people? He had none. Rose was his comfort. Would she hear his cry in the wilderness? That's what she calls Vermont, the wilderness. Make Orton her new Jerusalem. *Exalt every valley.* But was Percy saying he was God? God to Rose? Didn't she have a God of her own? He could just see it, Rose talking to God, giving Him a piece of her mind. He almost chuckled. Pity the God she scolds!

So, Percy wasn't God, but he could help make *the crooked straight and the rough places plain.* He could help her live more easily in Vermont. What did she call the man who took care of her apartment building? The super. He could be her super, fix things around her house. As clever as she might be with a needle—and he'd heard she was a fierce seamstress—he also gleaned from the stories Eamon Boyce told him that Rose wouldn't recognize a screwdriver if she were handed one, or know which end was used for business.

Percy shook his head, not knowing if Rose's coming to Vermont was God *shaking the heavens, the earth, the sea and the dry land* of his universe, or if Rose was the *desire of his nation?* Who did Percy think God was? And would it matter to Rose that Percy was Christian? And what did that mean? That he celebrated Christmas? It was an ancient story, the miracle of birth. Maybe there was truth in it—in Joseph and Mary traveling to Bethlehem to be counted. It had that ring of plausibility, the sort of thing that tax collectors would do. And mistreating the poor, that's been going on a while. Was Jesus God? Percy couldn't honestly say. But he liked Christmas. What else was there to do in the darkest days of the year but renew fellowship with song and light? It probably goes back further than Christ. Maybe as far back as the invention of the sun. That's it: this is all about the Sun, not the Son. Wouldn't that be just like humans to mistake the power of a star for a man? No wonder He was magical. How else to explain that power?

Percy shook his head. What did he know? Rose had leaned against him and cried into his chest. She'd used his handkerchief to wipe her tears. She was here with him, in his house, this Christmas Eve, sitting in his chair, listening to his music! Wasn't that miracle enough? Nothing else really mattered.

By the time the music ended, Percy was leaning against Rose's legs, her hand on his shoulder. The turntable made its mechanical clicks, and the two of them continued to sit in the silent room. At length, Percy groaned as he stiffly rose to his feet. "It's three a.m."

Rose frowned. "I'm too comfortable to move."

"Stay here. I'll make up Addie's guest bed for you."

She just nodded and closed her eyes.

Percy crossed to Addie's side of the house, which was cold. He'd find flannel sheets, fill a hot water bottle to warm the bed.

After the dusk of the lamplight and candles, the electric hurt

Percy's eyes, and the doilies and dolls appeared as fussy clutter in Addie's spare room. He wanted Rose to be comfortable, so he piled all the dolls from the bed into the armchair, followed by all the lace and embroidered cushions that seemed to have multiplied since he was last there. And when was that? When was the last time anyone slept in this room? Over a year. Percy stripped the bed. Rose needed fresh sheets. And what to do for a nightgown? Percy blushed. Nothing of Addie's. He wouldn't have Rose sleep in a dead woman's clothes. Knickknacks crowded the dresser. Maybe it was time to clean up after Addie, to redecorate. Another project for retirement. Retirement, only a week away.

Just as the music at the church had filled her till she overflowed with tears, the music at Percy's stirred her as if the blood in her veins were flowing backwards and forwards at the same time, swirling around till she had to lean back in the chair and close her eyes. The candlelight flickered, and her heart swelled.

Except for the "Hallelujah" chorus, she'd never heard Handel's *Messiah* before. It sounded like a cathedral, music rising to the vault of heaven. *Comfort ye.* Rose felt safe, warm, cared for. *Comfort ye*, sang the tenor. The music did. She sighed and listened to the voice that cried in the wilderness. The landscape of summer passed before her eyes, all the green of it, the exalted valleys, the green mountains, the bare rocks, even the dark woods with their mysterious large animals lurking in the underbrush. The blaze of fall foliage appeared in the lamplight. Rose relived her glorious walks in the brisk October sunshine. The way the clouds sailed overhead, the way the yellow and red vibrated against the blue sky.

Perhaps it was the glory, the glory of the Lord. The music made her want to sing.

Rose sighed. Percy leaned against her legs. This kind man. She patted his shoulder and he took her hand, and her heart raced. *All the flesh shall see it together.* This was too much. Unlooked for. Unasked for. An earthquake, and at her time of life. Rose closed her eyes again, trying to empty her mind even of the words. The music washed over her and she relaxed into a tide of fatigue. Maybe she didn't have to be alone. Shhh. Just listen.

She was a virgin and bore a son called Emmanuel, *God with us.* Was that the problem, then? She'd treated her son as The Son. A good Jewish boy who thinks he's the Messiah? A son who brought her to the high mountains which just may be the one place God does exist, in the glory of the mountains, in those maple trees that burned up with beauty, those mornings of mist rising off the meadow.

For unto us a Child is born, unto us a Son is given. She and Sam had a child. He was wonderful. But Manny is Manny. A man. A man who maybe they made too much of. Who was to tell? She did the best she could. Did she make Manny into who he is, or did he come that way? Life's a mystery. The older she got, the less she knew. At least she knew she knew less. Maybe that was wisdom, knowing how little we know? Anyway, Manny, her son, he was a grown man. There was nothing more she could do.

The music erased words from her mind. Even though they were singing in English, all she heard now was sound, lovely sound. Soothing sound! *Rejoice! Rejoice, O daughter of Zion!* She was a daughter of Zion. And she did rejoice. Greatly but quietly. She was so tired. She could use a little peace. This was lovely, sitting here and listening to music in the quiet light.

Rose drifted in and out of dreaming wakefulness. The King of

Glory—that was all the wonderful sound filling her heart. Sound climbing mountains and viewing the vast horizon beyond. Not the endlessness of ocean, that cold ocean that squeezed her heart when she was a girl setting out, but the endlessness of the mountains rolling off to the edge of the earth. And the white steeples peeking up in the foreground. Godhouses. Okay, for those who needed them. She? All she needed was a view: a meadow, a hillside, a valley. It didn't have to be gigantic or endless. She'd be sixty-five in January, three weeks. The end was coming, though not yet in sight, *kayn aynhoreh*. A good view was good enough; a distant horizon maybe more than she wanted.

A good view, and maybe someone to stand beside her. *Hallelujah!* The famous chorus washed over her. And she saw it! She saw the gates of the future open before her: the rolling hills, the blue sky, the glorious sun! With this man standing beside her. Yes, she could love again. She could. But she was too tired to move.

"Some of those dolls of your sister's," Rose said when she came down in the morning, "They're quite valuable."

"Are they?" Percy handed Rose steaming coffee.

"I'm sure of it." She sipped the hot brew. "There's a German doll with a porcelain head that's worth something, if I'm not mistaken. But it's the American one with the clay head that would probably fetch a small fortune."

"How do you know?"

"I read a book once, on account of an article in the *New York Times*."

"Well, maybe I'll sell 'em. Or give them to a museum. I think it's time I cleaned up that side of the house." Percy cleared his throat. "I hope you slept well?"

"Like a baby." Rose laid her hand on Percy's forearm. "Thank you for taking care of me last night."

Percy stood still and let the electricity pass through him. Slowly, he leaned forward and pressed his lips into Rose's forehead. "Thank you," he whispered.

He straightened. "How about waffles and syrup for breakfast?"

"I'm expected at the Boyce's for dinner at noon."

"Scrambled eggs and toast, then?"

"But it's already after ten."

"I can't let you leave hungry."

"Another time?"

Percy considered. "That's fair."

"Thank you, Percy."

His heart wobbled. He cleared his throat. "Well, I guess you'd like to go now." And he drove her home.

Now that Rose had been to his house, Percy viewed it with new eyes. He walked through the kitchen. Serviceable. Better than when Addie was queen, as he'd rehung the antique sink on the wall. Well, it might be more suited to his taste than those confounded double ones, but the wall itself was a sorry sight. He'd patched the holes when he rearranged the plumbing, but he'd never repainted. And there was a cloud of soot behind the woodstove, and a dark smudge around the doorknob and all up the edge of the door.

He wandered into his parlor, where they'd listened to Handel. It wasn't just a plain room—that he'd known all along—but it was as dingy as the kitchen, which was a surprise. When was the last time he'd painted these walls? And it was fine to have just a single armchair if you lived alone and never had company, but it wouldn't do if you had friends.

Percy ran his fingers along the armrests of the wing chair, where the fabric was worn. Maybe it was time to do a little rearranging. Addie'd been gone more than a year, and in any case, he meant no disrespect for the dead. He could move the stereo into Addie's parlor, which was more comfortable. He was about to retire and spend a great deal more time at home. He might as well make it pleasant.

He'd start upstairs, in the room where Rose had slept. He went to look, and found the bed neatly remade, with all the dolls sitting in a neat line. New wallpaper and curtains would spruce it up. He'd ask Rose.

What would he ask her? He sat down amidst the doll population on the bed. To marry him? At his age? She'd laugh him into the next county. He picked up one of the dolls wearing a white lace christening gown. It had a cherubic face and pudgy hands, complete with a ring of fat around the wrist, just like a real baby. But much smaller, and much better dressed. He sat it back against the wall and picked up another, this one with coarser features, probably on account of the material it was made of, like Rose said. Funny, she should know about dolls, like Addie. But it was a peculiar thing for a grown woman to collect, baby dolls. Could have been Addie's way of making up for not having a baby of her own, though she never did seem to lament not having children, nor being a widow, either. No, widowhood seemed to suit her. And baby dolls, too. They didn't require much attention. Maybe once or twice Percy could recall Addie pulling the clothes off all the dolls and laundering them all in mild bleach, then hanging the miniature dresses and tiny bloomers in the sun to dry. Addie, she ironed all those clothes, and then she had the damnedest time getting them back on. Not only was it hard to maneuver those little limbs into the tiny sleeves and leg holes, but she lost track of which clothes belonged to which doll, and in the end she had an extra pair of drawers but no one to claim them. Put her in a bad humor over a week. So maybe, if that's how frustrated baby dolls made her, maybe it was a good thing she didn't have any babies of her own. She just wasn't the maternal type, that's all. But like Percy always said, it takes all kinds, be it cattle, dogs, or people.

Maybe he'd ask Rose to come over again tonight, listen to more music?

No. He shook his head. Too soon. And they were too tired. He glanced at the dolls to see if they agreed. The one at the head of the bed, all golden curls, blue eyes, and pouty lips, winked at him. He looked back, to make sure. He shifted his weight and made the mattress bounce, and the doll's eyelids blinked again. It seemed to be telling him something, so he picked her up. Was this the one Rose admired so much? He'd give it to her, as a Christmas gift. He'd take it over to her house this afternoon, and he'd invite her to his birthday party.

What was he talking about?

He was going to be sixty-five. It was about time he had a birthday party.

Late that day, Percy stopped by her house and handed her the doll. "For your first Christmas," he said.

"Oh, Percy! This is too much!" Rose took the doll into her arms. "She's lovely! Look! She has pierced ears! What a wig!" She turned to Percy and said, "She's so elegant." Then Rose flipped her over. "S & H—It's a German company, but I can't remember the name. Shoulder headed, see." She showed Percy how the head and shoulders were molded together. "The head was made in Europe, but the body is probably American made. Born in Europe and put together in America," she laughed. "Just like me!" Rose sat the doll on the couch. "What a lovely gown." She faced Percy.

"I don't have a gift for you."

He stepped close. The smell of the cold outdoors lingered on his sweater, but underneath was that warm odor of him—a musk that made her heart race. "Last night," he said, brushing hair away from her eyes. "Spending Christmas Eve with me was a gift." His eyes searched hers. "Rose, Rose." He held her face in his hands. Without thinking about what she was doing, she raised herself on tiptoes and kissed him, full on the lips. His arms wound around her and he covered her mouth with his.

"Oh, Rose," he sighed. "Rose, Rose, Rose." He held both her hands in his. "Will you marry me?"

Rose stood a moment, looking into his kind face. Finally, she said, "I've been thinking about it."

Percy threw his head back and laughed.

"What? What's so funny?" She tugged on his hands. "Tell me, what's so funny?"

Percy pulled his hands away to wipe his eyes with the back of them, but he couldn't stop laughing. "It's just—" He was still shaking. "It's just—" He was slowly catching his breath. "I don't know," he said, grabbing her hands again. "Your answer is just so *Rose*." She tilted her head to the side. "I was afraid you'd say no."

She shook her head. She liked it when he grinned.

"But you've been thinking about it?"

She nodded.

"And what have you been thinking?"

"Come, sit down." Rose moved the doll out of the way so she and Percy could sit side by side on the sofa, where they could hold hands. "First of all," Rose lifted Percy's hand knotted in hers and thumped it down on her leg, "After Dory died, I wasn't ever going to marry again." Rose frowned, remembering the bewildered widow she'd been, sitting by candlelight for weeks on end, wondering what was to become of her.

"I'd heard as much," Percy said.

"You heard as much what?" Rose asked, not comprehending.

"I'd heard you'd said you'd never marry again."

"How in the world?"

"It's a small town," Percy shrugged. "Word gets around."

"But," Rose sputtered, knitting her brows together. "I didn't think the Stitch and Bitch ladies would blab."

"I'm sure no one did," Percy said, unhooking his hand from hers. He stretched his arm across her shoulders and pulled her back into the couch. "Oh, it must have been way back, early fall. I heard it from Barrett, back when we all thought Wilson Nye was putting on a full-court press."

"*Oy.*" Rose rolled her eyes. "I didn't realize what a rich source of gossip I was."

"Hey, you're not sore, are you?"

She had her arms crossed over her chest.

"C'mon. You didn't expect to just fade into the woodwork, did you? No one around here gets away with that. Maybe in a big city, your neighbors don't care what you think or do, but this is a small town. It's not every day we have a new character like you move in among us." He squeezed her shoulders.

His breath warmed her ear as he whispered, "Back when I heard that you had no plans ever to marry, neither did I." He nuzzled her neck. "So, maybe we've both changed our minds."

She slid her eyes sideways to see the light in his eyes. Rose sighed.

Percy squeezed her again. "So, what do you want to talk about?"

Rose sat up and rearranged herself, with her legs folded under her, so that she could face him. "First of all, I've been married before. Twice."

"I know," Percy nodded.

"And you've never been married?" she asked.

"That's right. I expect someone's told you the story of me and Lila. But that was long ago. A lifetime."

Rose didn't say anything.

Percy turned sideways to face Rose. "I never expected I would marry, or want to. Believe me, Rose. And I ain't saying this to boast, but there's been any number of women around here who've set out to catch me, and maybe one or two who I thought fondly of. I only want to get married on account of you."

Even though she was smiling, her eyes watered, and he leaned over to kiss the tears away. He kept leaning over, until he was lying on top of her. She accepted his weight, his warmth, sighed into being sandwiched between him and the couch. It was delicious, his body pressed into hers, their bumps pressed up against one another. Rose put her arms around Percy and chuckled, then laughed and laughed and sobbed. It felt so good to be held. Rose floated into a warm sea of sensation that had been slowly leaking back into her life and now gushed forth with a flood.

Percy slid to the floor and knelt by Rose's head. "You look beautiful lying down." He rested his elbow on the couch and cradled his head against his arm; with the other hand he softly traced her features until she trapped his hand and held it close to her chest. His eyes were so blue, so kind, so full of smile. She smiled back.

"What do we have to talk about?" Percy asked.

"Where are we going to live? What are we going to live on? And what are we going to do about religion? I'm Jewish, you know."

Percy smiled, "I know." He heaved himself back onto the couch and held Rose's hands. "Does it matter to you that I'm not?"

Rose sighed. "It bothers me that it doesn't bother me."

Percy waited for her to continue.

"All my life, until I moved to Vermont, I've lived among Jews, only Jews. And you know what? When you only live among Jews, you don't have to think about it, about being Jewish, that is. All the thinking is done for you." She paused and gestured to the door. "But here—here, I'm the only one. It makes me think about it a lot more. I mean, I have to explain why I do things the way I do—things I've done my whole life without thinking, like not eating bacon or ham, or *milchedig* and *flayshedig* together."

Percy squeezed her hands to interrupt. "Translation please."

"Dairy and meat."

"Thanks." He smiled.

"I've lived here what? Seven months? And I've thought more about being Jewish in that time than during my whole life before this."

"So?"

"So, it's a big deal, that's what!"

"What about God?" Percy asked.

"God?"

"Yeah, God. Isn't that what religion is about?" Percy asked.

"Is it?" Rose asked. "I don't know. Maybe. Do you?"

Percy sighed. "No. I don't know. But I suspect religion gets in God's way."

"So you believe in God?" Rose asked.

"Sometimes," Percy answered. "In the purest sense of there being something bigger than us out there, yes, I do. When I'm outdoors, I believe God exists."

"What about indoors?"

Percy frowned.

"What about in church?" Rose insisted.

"I can't honestly say I've ever met God in church," Percy said, slapping his hands on his thighs. "But then, I'm not a church-goer, by the way."

"No?"

"No." Percy shook his head. "I'm not even baptised, you know."

"How come?"

"My folks just didn't get around to it, I guess."

"Didn't they go to church?"

"Not much. Nope." Percy thought a moment. "Mother, she was active in the Grange. Still, she didn't like that my father didn't even observe the sabbath the way most farmers did back then. Still do, most of 'em. Father, he'd just as soon start a big project on a Sunday, if the weather was good. Maybe that's what wore him out, finally. Most farmers, whether they go to church or no, they make Sunday a day of rest, meaning they only do the necessary chores—the milking, the mucking, caring for the livestock. But no fencing or haying or building a new shed. Even the Whites—I don't believe you'll see them inside any church most Sundays, but they won't be out in the field, neither. No, Bob and Mary eat a big dinner Sunday noon—everyone's welcome to join them—and Bob and Mary, they've taken to bowling every Sunday afternoon. Keep trying to get me to join them," Percy humphed. "But I don't think so."

"So you weren't baptised and you don't go to church or go bowling?"

"None of the above."

Rose was silent.

"Anything else?"

"There's one more thing, Percy." Rose could feel her face turn red to her hairline. "There's something I need to know. You'll forgive me?"

"What is it you've got to know that makes you blush like that?" He leaned forward so that her question had less distance to travel, but Rose leaned back, so the question could hang naked between them.

"Are you circumcised?"

Percy stared at her.

Rose raised her eyebrows.

He leaned into her ear and whispered, "You want to find out?"

"You're teasing me!"

"I'm teasing you!" Percy held Rose by her shoulders. "Who keeps saying no?"

"I haven't said no." Rose couldn't meet his eyes. "I just haven't said yes yet." She could feel his eyes bearing down on her. The whole weight of his desire lodged in her chest. She'd never ask him to convert. No, that wasn't necessary. But all her life—her life among Jews—men were all a certain way. She stared into her folded hands, shaking her head. Could she ask him to do it? Would he do it? For her?

Percy covered her hands with his. "This matters to you, doesn't it?" His voice was gentle.

Not trusting herself to speak, she shook her head and shrugged, hoping he'd understand she didn't know why.

"Well, not to worry. I may not have been baptised, but I was circumcised. All the boys around here were. Or most of them. Anyone whose mother was attended by Doc Pingree. Who knows, maybe she was Jewish?"

"She? You had a lady doctor?"

"Before Doc Stoddard. She was a horse and buggy doctor. Stoddard, he always had a car. Went through a car a year until he built the hospital over by Waterchase."

Rose tried to imagine what Doc Pingree looked like, and how she could thank someone like that, someone she never knew, but to whom she was indebted for a personal service, nevertheless. Rose deflated, like a balloon with a leak. "I don't know why it matters," she sighed.

"Hey." Percy lifted her chin with his hand. "It's okay."

"Okay that I'm so—so tribal?"

Percy chuckled. "It's who you are."

"Amen."

13 | new year's eve

Percy was pleased that the scruffy walls and the shabby furniture faded into the background when the rooms were filled with people. Aside from funerals, there'd never been so many in the house before, not even in his parents' time. Maybe at haying, his mother would put on a giant feed for the farmhands, or when they cut ice on the pond. But it wasn't so much the number of people present at these events as it was the quantity of food his mother laid on.

Percy had a fair bit to offer himself, even though he invited his friends over for ten p.m.—not exactly a meal time. But on New Year's Eve, anything goes. He had a tray of ham salad sandwiches, a relish barge with carrot and celery sticks, some salted nuts and pretzels, and mulled wine, seeing as how everyone had already had their seasonal fill of eggnog. For midnight, he had champagne and birthday cake.

"Hey, Percy!" John Ready slung a heavy arm across Percy's shoulder and lifted a cup in his face. "This is a bang-up gathering, Old Man!" They surveyed the crowded parlor together. "Didn't know you had so many friends!" John punched him playfully in the shoulder again. "Just kidding, Old Man."

"Hey, John," Percy asked. "How much of that mulled wine have you sluiced your gullet with?"

"It's mighty fine!" John drained his cup.

"Well, it must have addled your brain some."

"How's that?"

"You keep calling me 'Old Man' but I'm only just turning sixty-five. You're a fair bit older than me, and if you keep calling me 'Old Man,' I'll have to call you 'Grandpa.'"

An enormous guffaw exploded from deep in John's giant belly and filled the room with a howl of laughter that claimed everyone's attention. "Oh, you're a rare bird, Percy, you are!" He wiped tears from his eyes with the back of his great paws.

"What's going on?" someone asked from across the room.

"Percy—here," John's words were chopped by his gasping for breath, "it's—his—birthday!"

The noise in the room rose then fell, and someone started a chorus of "Happy Birthday" followed by "For He's a Jolly Good Fellow," and finished with a great cheer.

"Why thank you. Thank you," Percy said, clearing his throat.

"Speech! Speech!" someone called up from the back.

"Well, I was going to wait for midnight for this." He pushed the knot of his tie.

"It's close enough, Percy," someone said. Another exclaimed, "It's already after eleven!"

Percy checked his watch. "So it is. So it is." He pulled his cuff down on his wrist. "Well, then," he cleared his throat. "First, I want to thank you all for coming."

"Hear, hear!"

"It is, as John says, my birthday tonight." Percy held his hands up to stop another chorus of the birthday song. "And as I'm turning sixty-five, I'm also officially retired starting today."

A low "boo" rumbled around the room. Percy again held his hands up.

"And it's also New Year's Eve, a good time to start a new phase of life."

Now people were listening.

"I guess most of you know I go to the Marlboro Music Festival every year, but I don't guess many of you know I started learning piano. And now," he looked around at the serious faces, "now I'm going to test the strength of our friendship, and play for you."

Applause.

Percy held up his hands again. "I'm just an amateur," he warned. "And I've never played for anyone other than my teacher, so I'm not making any promises. I'm not Rudolf Serkin, I can tell you that right away." He coughed. "And I can tell you I've also never been so nervous in my life."

His friends laughed, also nervously.

"So, the piano is in the other parlor, through the kitchen. And if you want to come listen, why please do." He turned to the other room, relieved that it was a mite cooler on account it being further from the woodstove.

Percy rolled up his shirtsleeves and removed his wristwatch. As he set it on the ledge just beyond the last note in the bass, he caught a glimpse of Rose's white hair.

He was just going to pretend he was practicing, playing for himself. He wasn't going to think about the people listening to him play. He certainly wasn't going to let himself be distracted by Rose at the edge of the sofa, fiercely attentive. His hands were damp. He wiped them on the top of his pants, and opened the Bach. He'd start with the piece he knew best, the C-Major Invention. He'd played it hundreds of times. The trick was to start slow enough. The beginning was easy, but the middle section—he could play it note perfect, if only he started off at a reasonable tempo and didn't speed up. He exhaled a deep breath and thought through the first phrase. He was going to play it. He wasn't going to think about all the ears tuned to the movement of his fingers; he'd think only of his fingers and what they had to do. A vision of Rose sitting in his wing chair, her eyes half lidded as she listened to the *Messiah* in the semi dark, crossed his sight and Percy had to blink to restore the notes to the page. He took another deep breath, placed his hands on the keys and to himself uttered a brief prayer, "Here goes!"

His right-hand fingers sounded the melody, which he echoed in the left, then picked up again in the right. In the third measure, the left-hand melody slowed in half while the right cascaded down the scale by thirds, then climbed by thirds, then the end of the first segment and he'd done it without flubbing, but he was hotter than haying, which is saying something, especially the last day of December and the thermometer outside down around zero. No time to hesitate, his left hand echoed the eight-note phrase deep in the bass and he just had to keep the tempo even because the hard part was coming up but he had the rhythm inside him and as long as he didn't think about Rose sitting just behind his left field of vision he could anticipate the shift of his left hand into the treble clef and the C-sharp that was coming up in the right, and the B-flat in the left, a tight cluster of notes with an F-sharp and a G-sharp and a C-natural. A man could trip over his hands here, but he was getting through—oops! Never mind, just keep going. He was almost through the tight spot where his hands were all on top of each other and he had to keep his two hands out of each other's way. Whew! A rest in the left hand. A sustained note in the right. Remember pianissimo. Pay attention: Here comes the B-flat again, now B-natural, now B-flat and a decrescendo at last to the final broken C-major chord. He bowed his head over the keys a moment, before lifting his hands from the keyboard, relieved to have made it to the end.

Applause interrupted his trance. He sat up and turned. There were people in his parlor! He nodded slightly, but he was floating and not really there, watching a movie of people applauding. A movie of people he knew. And then he saw Rose, sitting back on the sofa, just beaming. Percy's face cracked into a wide grin and his friends cheered some more. "Encore! Encore!" they called. Percy nodded and cleared his throat.

"That little piece I just played," the room quieted as he spoke. "It might just have taken Johann Sebastian Bach an hour or two to write that little ditty, but it's taken me about three-and-a-half months to learn how to play it." Titters fluttered through the room. "So, I don't have a large repertoire," he frowned and rubbed his hands as if he were washing them. "But I am learning this new piece. It's by Chopin, and it's real short." He turned back to the keyboard and switched to Chopin's Opus 28, most of which looked like rivers of ink with an impossible number of notes running down the page. Percy took his time to readjust his thinking from the clock-like motion of the Invention to the rippling eddy of the Chopin Prelude. He rubbed his thumb along the binding of the music, to flatten the pages and to look at the notes, like blueprints—instructions for how to build a house of sound. He cleared his throat and over his shoulder he said, "This is Prelude No. 7 in A Major."

The house hushed. Percy could sense they were nervous for him. Well, he was nervous too! This one was hard. It didn't have the regularity of the Bach, no clear sense of rules and exceptions. But when he'd practiced it, when he'd taught his fingers to learn the shape of the notes the way Mrs. Salerno kept stressing, he could find the melody, which was the sound of his heart singing. This piece was Percy's anthem to joy. Not raucous, like Beethoven's Ninth, or any of those grand symphonies he always listened to, full of the bombast of timpani and horns and as voluminous as the sky on a clear night. Those were all very well, those great, hulking pieces. They were like what he imagined the great cathedrals would be, or the skyscrapers in Manhattan. But this piece—he lay his fingers on the keys, ready to play—this piece sang as sweetly as a bird in springtime. It was the chapel of shade under a tree, a moment of repose while wind rippled through a field of grass. It was the sound of hope, the promise of a fair day, the possibility of love.

Percy hesitated with his fingers above the notes. This was hard. There weren't a lot of notes, but the ones that were there weren't easy to play. Maybe he was attempting too much, trying to perform a piece he'd really just started to learn. But he could feel everyone at his back, waiting for him to begin. He tried to recapture the image of the sound—the sunny meadow and the singing lark—but all he could see was the cream colored page with the black notes and Mrs. Salerno's penciled numbers, where she changed the fingering from what was printed in the book. Fingerings she recommended worked so much better than what was printed; if he'd tried to play the piece without her guidance—well, he probably would have given up long ago.

He let out a deep breath. The worst he could do was botch it. Inhale, one, two, and exhale. The notes sang. He could hear them planting themselves in his neighbors' ears. He came to the half note at the end of the first phrase. So far, so good. He took up the melody again. It rose from his fingertips through the hammers and vibrated across the room, against an eardrum, worming its way to her heart. The music started to build; the sound piled up and up, like a kite on a string. Could Rose see it? Did the string of this music tug her heart? The music wavered, the kite started to sink. Percy played the great gust up to the enormous, impossible, chord. Nine notes across two-and-a-half octaves. At Mrs. Salerno's suggestion, he played it as a broken chord. Even broken, the nine-note chord could break your heart with glee. And then the final phrase, those deep tones. He had to stay calm to find them. "Calm" wasn't what he thought of as the sound of joy when he was younger.

Years ago, he would have dismissed this music as subdued, even melancholy. But he now found this melody filled with the kind of joy that ran deep. He let the last notes waft into the air, then lifted his hands from the keys and placed them in his lap. The room was quiet for a moment. Someone sighed, "That was beautiful!" and applause broke out.

Percy turned on the stool and faced his friends, who were all clapping.

"Take a bow!" someone yelled.

"Go on," a neighbor nudged him.

Percy glanced over at Rose, who wasn't applauding, but smiling. She nodded. He stood up, and friends clapped louder, stamping their feet. Percy bowed, once. Then he held his hands up, trying to get the crowd to stop. Mary White, closest to him, took his hand and tiptoed up to plant a kiss on his cheek.

"Happy Birthday, Percy!" Her eyes glittered. "That was wonderful!"

"Well done," Robert White said, gripping Percy by the hand and slapping him on the arm.

Slowly, Percy circulated the room, shaking hands, stooping for kisses, taking the congratulatory slapping across his back.

"It's almost midnight," Irma Bassett reminded him after giving him a peck on the cheek. "Shall I open the champagne?"

"Please do. It's in the fridge. And there's a cake in the pantry. Would you be so good?" The room was emptying out, and Percy was slowly working his way back to Rose, who was still sitting on the sofa, waiting for him.

Only Rose and Percy remained in the room.

Rose patted the seat next to her and Percy nearly collapsed into the sofa at her side. Fatigue blew out of him like air from a leaky tire. "Whew!"

Rose took his hand in hers. "That was wonderful!" Her voice was as smooth as the mulled wine. "I could sit and listen to you play forever." She squeezed his hand.

He picked her hand up and rubbed it against his cheek. "No you couldn't," he chuckled. He looked at her with a new glint in his eyes. "Because those are the only two pieces I know how to play!"

They both laughed. Just then, Irma came through the door holding a cake alight with so many candles it looked like a torch as she led the parade of all Percy's guests back into the parlor singing another chorus of "Happy Birthday."

Barrett Greenwood followed with two bottles of champagne, and behind him Shirley carried a tray of stemmed glasses.

"You have to blow all the candles out!" Irma said. She held the cake before him. "But hurry, before it melts!"

"Well, there was no need to use a hundred candles," Percy said, leaning forward to get a breath.

"There aren't a hundred," Irma quipped. "Only sixty-six. Now come on." She repositioned herself so the cake was now between Percy and Rose. "Rose can help."

Rose pushed herself to the edge of the couch.

"Ready?" Irma asked.

They nodded.

"Okay. Make a wish!"

Percy and Rose blew until they were both red in the face and all the candles were out, leaving a mass of smoking wicks.

"Hooray!"

"And it's almost midnight," boomed John Ready, who was holding up a fat pocket watch in one hand, and counting out the numbers with his other. "Ten, nine, eight, seven, six!" He opened his hand again and started pulling in his fingers one at a time as the group joined him, "Five! Four! Three! Two! One! HAPPY NEW YEAR!!!"

"The champagne!" Shirley tried to get Barrett's attention. "Open the champagne!"

Irma set the cake on top of the piano. "Who has the plates?"

The room was pure pandemonium, with people trying to cut and serve cake and pour and distribute champagne.

"Uh-oh," John Ready's loud voice brought the house to silence. He held two glasses of champagne and was standing with them in front of Percy and Rose, so that everyone in the room could see Percy relaxed back on the couch, with his arm around Rose. They both blushed.

Percy unwound his arm and stood up. He handed one glass to Rose, who stood next to him, and held on to the other. "Thank you, John."

"You're a sly one, Percy. That's all I got to say!" John winked at Rose.

"Does everybody have a glass of champagne?" Percy asked. "I'm not paying close attention to my job as host here. So thank you for taking over." He cleared his throat. "I'd like to propose a toast." He paused while a few more glasses were poured and passed around. Everyone was quiet. Percy cleared his throat again.

"This may be harder than playing the piano." Everyone chuckled. "So, I'll, uh, I'll keep it brief." He looked around at all the familiar faces of his friends. "Thank you." Percy nodded and held his glass high. "That's all I have to say. Thank you, and God Bless." He tipped his glass back and drained it.

Percy sensed people were expecting more, but he'd promised Rose not to say anything. No general announcements. Not yet.

"What's to announce, Rose?" Percy teased, as they'd waited for the guests to arrive.

"That we're considering—"

"Ladies and gentlemen," Percy interrupted, holding up an invisible glass in a mock toast. "I'd like to announce that Rose and I are negotiating marriage."

She had to laugh, "But it's not funny!"

"I promise," Percy said, with a sober face. "Not a word." The kiss that followed left her speechless.

But he didn't have to say anything, it was so obvious. Everyone, when they walked in, said, "Hello, Percy! Hello, Rose!" as if seeing them together in Percy's house was the most ordinary and unexceptional thing in the world, as if they'd expected it. And everyone was so sly, saying things like, "It's so nice to see Percy so happy!" and "It's about time Percy—" and then they'd change the subject, or stuff a sandwich in their mouth, stopping up whatever else it was they were going to say.

Sally gave Percy a hug and said, "I'm so glad Rose decided to stay!" And Mary White said she'd like to have him and Rose over for Sunday dinner, maybe they'd join them for bowling afterwards? But most people weren't so obvious. They just smiled and slapped him hard on the back, congratulating him on turning sixty-five, on retirement, on the turning of the new year.

14 | january cold

After the party, Percy asked her to stay.

"I need to sit with these feelings for a bit, Percy."

Percy said nothing.

"I rushed into my other marriages. I don't want to rush into this." Rose tried to explain. "This seems somehow different. More significant." And when he folded her inside his embrace, she didn't understand why she was removing herself from this comfortable haven, but something inside her insisted she go home and be alone. She accepted a ride from Sally and Eamon and woke up in the New Year in the narrow bed in the chilly room off the kitchen of her son's summer house.

It wasn't her own house, and it rattled about her. She became aware of how much she wanted to rearrange things, like pushing the sofa against the wall and moving the armchair to the window, but she didn't dare. The only thing she'd actually changed was the sewing machine under the window, and the machine didn't even belong to her; it was borrowed. No, this was Manny's summer place, not her home.

How was she ever going to tell him she was going to marry

again?

She'd tell him, that's all.

But not until she told Percy. She still hadn't said yes.

And she hadn't given him a birthday gift, either. She was going to knit him a vest.

Rose knitted into the new year, as if making the stitches were a kind of rosary, each stitch a prayer for Percy, for keeping him warm and well and preserving his love for her, though she continually shook her head, wondering how it was that she deserved it; hadn't she had her share of happiness and husbands already?

But this was different. Sam, they were children. Babies having babies. Raising Manny. The Depression. The War. And Isadore. He followed Sam like a natural progression, feeding her brain after all those years of scrubbing and needlework. And then taking care of him, helping him from a chair to a walker, onto the commode. Helping him dress. After the last stroke, feeding him. It was like having a baby all over again, only more work.

What was to stop Percy from getting sick, from having to take care of him?

Who knows, maybe he'd have to take care of her?

Rose finished a row, switched needles, and continued knitting. Maybe they'd have a few years before either of them got sick. Maybe they'd get sick together. Maybe they'd just get old together. They were nearly the same age. Three weeks' difference.

Rose shuffled back and forth, from one needle to the other, Percy's birthday vest lengthening, and with it, the shape and determination of Rose's decision. Was it a sin to be happy? She'd tell him tomorrow. She'd spend one more Sunday on her own, with her newspaper. At the end of that day, she'd let him know.

Walking up Wheeler Hill was always hot work, but this Sunday, it seemed harder. She was sweating under all her layers, despite the cold. She carried her *Times*, anemic without all the holiday advertising and very little news, which was a relief. Rose liked that the whole world rested in a post-holiday stupor, as if even governments were hung over. Rose wasn't hung over—not from a single glass of champagne three nights before, but she was tired. She hoped she wasn't getting sick.

As soon as she stepped indoors, she felt it, like a curtain of cold water washing down inside her and settling in her feet. Blocks of ice, they were. She pulled on another sweater, wrapped her throat in a scarf and her shoulders in a shawl. Too tired even to build up the fire, she collapsed into her armchair with the magazine section in her lap, and started to sneeze. She couldn't read a sentence without wiping her nose, so she gave up.

Who knew it could get so cold? The wind, it whistled through the house, like the walls were Swiss cheese. Drafts at the windows, under the doors. Before Christmas, Sally had shown Rose the door snake she used to stop the wind from coming in, and Rose had gone home and made long, stuffed pillows for each of her doors and all the windows on the ground floor. It made a difference, all the snakes in the house.

And the fire made a difference, when she could get it going, but Rose and the woodstove were not friends. Sometimes, she'd get a great blaze started, and could keep the place warm as long as she didn't let it burn down. But if the fire went out—sometimes, when she woke up in the morning only the faintest of embers languished—it was a trial to get the thing started again. What she needed was kindling—dead sticks from the forest floor—but how was she to find it, now that the world was covered in snow? And today she felt so awful, she didn't have the energy to file through the wood pile searching for the skinny pieces that burned first. Well, the only way to get better was to rest, so she pulled another blanket over her and dozed.

Percy was more tired than he ever could have imagined. It couldn't all be from staying up late. He hoped he wasn't coming down with a cold, but what else could it be that made it so hard to get up in the morning, and once up, so hard to get going? The day after the party, he could understand. How many times in a man's life does he stay up past midnight drinking champagne? Precious few, that's for sure. And given how fatigued he felt, maybe he understood why.

But New Year's Day was Friday, and here it was Sunday, and he still didn't feel up to snuff. In fact, he just finished putting away all the dishes. He hardly felt ready to face the first Monday of not going to work. Whose idea was it to start retirement in January? What was there to do?

He stood at the window and looked out at the cold. January cold. It was the kind of cold you could see, it was so still. At least a fresh blanket of snow covered the ground, keeping foundations and the roots of sleeping, living things warm. Well, January was supposed to be cold! He'd go out. No good hiding from it, not as far as he could see. Hiding only made it worse. You had to embrace it. Bundle up and go out, cut wood, shovel a path, walk to Greenwood's for a paper or a quart of milk. Anything to be outdoors and active.

So Percy went out and did all those things, and he felt better for it. Something about cold air that got into your system different, maybe on account it was thinner, so that when you breathed in, the air went past your lungs and right into your bloodstream, straight down the network of blood vessels until it filled up even the tiny capillaries at the tips of your fingers and toes. Cold air: it made the mucus in your nose freeze and sometimes it just seized

262

up your lungs, it was so sharp and you had to cough to get them going again. Like priming them for cold air, same as changing the oil-to-gas ratio in small-engine fuel.

He thought about maybe walking down to the church, but sitting through a sermon would only make him mad. Never failed, except on Christmas Eve, when all they did was sing. No harm in singing. It's the palaver of sermonizing that bothered him, and the rigmarole of responsive reading and standing up and sitting down, as if somehow that was what God expected.

It's not that Percy wasn't a religious man. He was. He just didn't think you had to wear a starched shirt to tell God your concerns. Besides, the way Percy figured it, Sunday was God's busy day. All those prayers and services. Folks from all over all clamoring for God's ear. Why not make your prayer, say, on a Tuesday, when God might not otherwise have anything to do? And maybe outside, for a change of scene. God must get tired of the sameness of churches after a while, it would seem.

But Percy hadn't seen a soul in three days, and that didn't seem quite right, either. For all those years his whole job was one of visiting. After all those weekdays, it was a pleasure to spend a quiet weekend at home. But now his life was turned around, and he was alone all day. How did Rose spend her time? Well, he'd pay her a visit to find out.

She answered the door bundled in a shawl over her sweater. "Oh, Percy! It's nice to see you, but I'm not sure you should come in. I have a bad cold." She stood blocking the door and blew her nose on a handkerchief.

He hesitated. "Do you have everything you need?"

Rose nodded and sneezed. "I just came back from the store."

"You walked to the store?" She must not be feeling too bad. But maybe it fagged her out. "What about firewood? Can I bring some in for you?"

"That would be very nice." She didn't shut the door until he'd started out back to the shed.

All she had were big, split logs. How in the world did she ever get her fire started without kindling, he'd like to know. Nor was there an ax to be found, so Percy knocked on the door again and told her he was going home to fetch one, to split kindling, he explained. Could he pick up anything for her on the way back?

"Does Barrett have a chicken, do you think? And some carrots and celery and parsley and a parsnip or two?"

"If he doesn't, I can get them for you in town tomorrow. What do you want them for?"

"To make soup."

"I can buy you a can of soup."

Rose blew her nose. "It's not the same, but it will have to do."

Percy returned with an ax, a maul, and some wedges. He filled a wooden crate with finely split kindling, and carried it in. "This will make fire-starting easy," he explained. "A little newspaper underneath three or four pieces of kindling, and your fire will start right up."

Rose just nodded.

Next he carried in a stack of medium-sized split logs, which he piled next to the kindling. "This here is birch," he explained. "It catches fast. Use this on top of your kindling, and you'll have a blaze roaring in no time."

Rose sneezed.

Every time he walked from the front door to the wood shed, Percy knocked down snow from the sides of the path and packed it, making it wider. He should have brought a shovel. He shook his head. It sure was plucky for a city girl to come live in the country. Winter wasn't a season for amateurs.

Finally, Percy carried in a load of split maple and oak. "These here," he dumped them on the far side of the stove, "these are your long burners. This is the stuff you want to put on after your birch has burned down. This here is hard wood, you see, and it will burn all night and keep you warm no matter how cold it gets outside."

"Who ever knew there were so many different kinds of wood?" Rose shrugged.

"Every different kind of tree has a different kind of wood," Percy said.

Rose nodded, sneezed, and wiped her nose.

"Now, if you give me a list, I'll get what you need at the grocery tomorrow."

He followed Rose into the kitchen.

"Excuse the mess," Rose said, though when he looked around, all Percy could see were a couple of unwashed dishes in the sink. "I haven't felt like cleaning up."

Percy was already rolling up his sleeves. "I'll wash up while you make that list."

"Don't—"

But he was already filling the basin with suds.

"Okay, now let's see what you've got," he said, taking the list from her when he finished drying his hands. He nodded at each of the items until he came to the bottom. "What's matzoh meal?"

"Matzoh meal?" Rose had a way of making statements like questions. "It's matzoh ground into fine crumbs, but not as fine a matzoh flour. That's different."

"Okay," Percy scratched his head. "But what's a matzoh?"

"What's a matzoh? You don't know from matzoh? *Oy!*"

"Rose," Percy chuckled. "Just tell me what it's like and I'll find something you can use instead."

"Matzoh. There's nothing like it. It's the unleavened bread that the Jews brought out of Egypt when Moses led them into the desert. It's the Bread of Affliction, because the Jews had to flee before the bread could rise. It's what you eat during *Pesach*—"

"Rose! Rose! What does this mythical bread look like? How does it come? Is it kept in the freezer? Where should I look for it in the A&P?"

"The freezer? No! It comes in a box. It's like a cracker—with no salt."

"Ah, the bread of affliction." That's when she looked at him. His heart beat. It was a moment before Percy could again find his voice. "Do you think crackers would work, like Saltines?"

"Saltines?"

"Well, what do you want them for?"

"To make matzoh balls!"

"Matzoh balls?"

"*Knaydlach*."

"Kay-nay-da-lack?"

"Dumplings. What you *goyim* call dumplings."

"Okay, so cracker crumbs would be a workable substitute?"

"How should I know?" Rose shrugged. "But in the wilderness, you have to make do. That's what the Jews did in Egypt. It's what I'll do in Vermont."

"Anything else?"

"Parsnips. Do you have parsnips in Vermont?"

"Of course we have parsnips. We're not barbarians." Percy wrote it on the list.

"And dill."

"Dill." Percy wrote that down. "All this for chicken soup?"

"Chicken soup with matzoh balls. It will cure my cold, just you see."

266

"I'm not doubting it. But do you need anything else? Regular bread? Milk? Eggs? Butter? Things like that?" He looked around. "Do you have enough tea? Sugar? Toilet paper?" She was grinning at him. "What about candles? Do you have candles and matches in case the power goes out?"

"Why should the power go out?" Rose wiped her nose.

"It happens. Sometimes, a limb falls on the line. Or if we get a big storm. Do you have any supplies in case of a storm?"

"Supplies? What kind of supplies?"

"Well, you should keep a bottle of water, for drinking. And a bucket of water, in case you want to flush. And a flashlight with fresh batteries. And candles, because batteries can only last so long. But if you keep spares in the refrigerator, they last longer. The cold keeps them fresh."

"Keep my batteries in the Frigidaire?" Rose sounded doubtful.

"But you don't want to open the fridge if the power's out. It will keep things fresh longer if you don't open it."

"Percy, tell me." Rose put her hand on his sleeve. "Is this really going to happen? I'll be here without electricity?"

"Probably. But you'll have some warning. Usually, we have an idea when there's going to be a storm, though not always how severe."

"You're serious." She frowned.

Percy put his arm around her.

"Careful. You shouldn't get sick." Rose tried to push him away, but Percy held on.

"Rose, you'll be fine."

"Maybe in the Old Country, where we didn't know from electricity. But here?"

Percy had never heard her be uncertain before. He squeezed her shoulder. "I'll come over if the power goes. I'll stay here with you, or I'll take you over to my place. No need to worry."

"So I won't worry."

"Good." Percy put the shopping list in his pocket. "I'll be back with your groceries."

"Thank you."

"Let me just build up the fire, so you can rest."

"You're very kind."

Percy loaded the stove, then stood by the chair where Rose had herself wrapped up in blankets and shawls. "Are you snug? Is there anything I can get you before I go?" He stroked the top of her hair, and she didn't seem to mind. Her smile warmed him more than any woodstove would ever do. "I'll check back later." He leaned over and kissed her forehead. It was cool, not hot. Just a head cold. A nuisance, but not alarming. She'd be well with a few days' rest.

Rose lost track of the days, sleeping and waking without reference to time. Whenever she woke, it seemed, Percy was fixing the fire. At some point, he told her how the size and shape and type of wood made a difference, like the difference between using silk or cotton or worsted thread, depending on the fabric you were sewing. Or the difference between cornstarch, flour, and tapioca. They all thickened a sauce, but with different results. So maybe he didn't know from *knaydlach*; he knew from wood. The house had never been so toasty. And he must have slept on the sofa, because there he was whenever she opened her eyes, wakened by the dreams of fever and chills.

Daylight returned, and she could smell chicken soup cooking. Real soup, not from a tin. The aroma was of health, and the soup itself an elixir and cure.

"It seems that all I do is thank you," Rose said as she took the cup of tea Percy handed her on a saucer. Sun streamed in the windows. "Thanks for the firewood, for bringing my groceries, for making the soup." Rose sipped from the cup. "You know, you're the first man I've ever met who knows how to cook. Most men, they're scared of the kitchen."

Percy poked the fire and loaded it up. "Are you warm enough?" he asked.

"You're not listening!" Rose scolded.

"I heard you," Percy said, standing.

"Well?" she asked.

"Well what?" he replied.

"Where did you learn how to cook?"

"Rose, I've lived a bachelor all these years."

"But didn't Addie cook for you?"

"Yes. Some."

"And where did you learn to make such good chicken soup?"

"From you."

"Me?" Rose raised her eyebrows.

"Don't you remember? You told me to buy parsnips and dill."

Rose was almost afraid to ask, "How long have I been sick?"

"Today's Wednesday. You took cold Sunday."

"And you've been taking care of me ever since?"

"Shh." Percy stood by her chair and stroked her hair. "I'm glad you're feeling better."

Rose took his hand. "Percy."

"Mmmm?" He covered her hand with his other.

"Where are we going to live, when we're married?"

Rose loved that he didn't whoop and holler or even press her hand between his. He just said, "I'd like you to come live with me, at my house."

Rose wandered through her memory of the double Cape, from the spacious kitchen to Percy's parlor, where they'd listened to the *Messiah*, back through the kitchen to Addie's parlor, where the piano was. She wandered up Addie's staircase, past the guest room where she'd stayed, past Addie's room and bath, through the narrow hall that connected Addie's side with the original house, where Percy lived. She was trying to see down the passage into Percy's bedroom and whether he had a double bed or not when he said, "I want you to help me redecorate. Change it around. Make it ours, instead of mine and Addie's." He cleared his throat. "I thought maybe I could stay here while we tore the other place apart."

In a dreamy voice, Rose said, "I sleep off the kitchen. There's only a single bed." She turned to look at Percy. Their eyes locked, and they regarded one another for a long time, holding their gaze steady and deep, so that by the time Percy did squeeze Rose's hand it was as if she'd stood naked before him and he before her, and now it was just a matter of her getting better and them figuring out logistics.

15 | fresh paint

Rose had to reorient herself. From Percy's house, she was still two miles from the store, but they were relatively flat and entirely paved miles east of the village, making for a much easier walk, which was good, since it took a while before she regained enough strength to do it even in one direction, her illness having punched the stuffing out of her. The road crossed meadows, open to the sunshine, and free of the torturous undergrowth of forest and goblin that shaded Wheeler Hill. But the openness invited the biting wind to tug at the seams of her coat, slap her face, and even push against her on the way home, so that in some ways, it was just as hard as walking uphill.

The cold stole her breath, and the snow squeaked beneath her boots. On windless days, Rose expected the air to crack, it was so brittle; on overcast days, it was the brook running under the snow that thrummed in her heart. It was this sound that Percy imitated in the new Chopin prelude he was learning, water rumbling under the frozen ground. And above it, in the treble, the song of unspeakable sorrow rising in her own throat. Sorrow? Tenderness? A feeling so full and new that Rose didn't recognize it until that first night Percy led her upstairs to bed.

It was in her house; his was pulled apart and covered in the dusty mayhem of stripped wallpaper and boxes of goods to be sorted and sold. As had become their habit, they returned to Rose's place for dinner. But this day, they'd dismantled Percy's bedroom, as part of a massive makeover, prepping and painting all the walls at one go. White walls with white, semigloss trim.

"You want only white?" Percy asked, to make sure.

"I'm in love with the winter. I want the house to be as pretty as snow. Besides," Rose added, "we can always repaint a room later on. After all this patch work, repainting won't be so much trouble."

Percy nodded. "For a city girl," he said, reappraising Rose in the overalls he'd bought her, "You sure do catch on quick."

Rose shrugged. "What's to catch on? So far, all we've done is clean. When do we get to paint?"

"All in good time."

Their lives had become such an array of cardboard boxes, that Rose didn't question what was in the one Percy was taking to her house that evening, nor did she really register his footsteps making the floorboards creak overhead. She stepped into the shower, eager to rinse the dust and fatigue from her limbs before starting dinner. Potato soup. It just needed reheating. And coleslaw. Percy drank milk with his supper. Rose preferred tea.

It wasn't until Rose had pulled on her nightgown and tied her robe around her that the butterflies fluttered. She slid her feet into her slippers, telling herself, this is what she always did when they came home from working on the house. This showering at her house at the end of the day was how their laundry had come to be commingled in just over a week. But this was the first time that Percy was staying over, and when Rose emerged from the bathroom, she saw the same thought in his eyes.

As she set the table, she kept an ear tuned to his noises, to the percussion of the water bouncing off his skin, like the sound of wind lashing rain against a window.

Dinner was ready. What else could she do?

Rose cleared the few dishes in the sink, using the water from the kitchen faucet to drown the muffled sounds of Percy toweling dry. But he didn't come directly into the kitchen. Rose placed her cool palms against her hot cheeks. Where was he? And what was he doing? She paced the width of the kitchen, feeling caged. She could go see what he was up to, but. But. She waited. She stirred the soup. She filled the kettle and put it on the stove. She was just adjusting the flame when Percy appeared in the doorway.

He, too, was wearing a robe over pajamas.

She stared at him. He stared right back. Could he see how nervous she was? Was he?

"Do you have a tray?" he asked.

"A tray?" She echoed.

"A tray. We can carry our meal into the parlor. I built up the fire. It's warmer in there."

"I think there's one over the fridge." She couldn't move, but watched as Percy pulled the tray from the overhead cabinet and sponged it off at the sink. He collected the cutlery and napkins from the table, stacked the bowl of coleslaw on top of the salad plates, and filled two bowls with soup. "All set?" he asked.

Rose nodded.

"Follow me."

Like a sleepwalker, she did.

The room twinkled in candlelight.

Percy set the tray on the low table, miraculously cleared of papers and books. "Have a seat," he nodded, indicating the cushions he'd tossed on the floor.

Rose took her seat, tucking her legs beneath her.

"That's right," Percy said, laying the dishes out and serving out the salad. He lowered himself on the cushions and leaned over, close to Rose's face.

Rose just stared at him. If ever there were such a thing as a human jack-o'-lantern, Percy was it. "Your face is all lit," she murmured.

He smiled. Then he picked up a soup bowl and offered Rose a taste off his spoon. He alternated, feeding himself, then her. When he offered her a forkful of coleslaw she shook her head.

He nodded. "We've had enough to eat." He took her hand and helped her to her feet. "Let's go upstairs."

"Upstairs?"

Percy pinched out all but one candle.

Rose started to gather the dishes.

"Just leave them."

He guided her to the staircase.

"But it's freezing up there!"

"Shh. You'll see." He urged her up the stairs. She stopped at the top. "This way." He led her into Jeannie and Manny's room, where the big bed was freshly made.

"But there's no heat up here!"

"Yes there is." He placed the candle on the night stand and beckoned her.

Rose came to him. He turned down the covers for her to slide in. "Flannel sheets," he said. "And a hot water bottle."

It was like magic, sliding out of the cold. Percy climbed in beside her, raising himself up enough to blow out the light.

Rose lay in the dark, eyes open and unseeing. Percy dove under the covers to pull the water bottle out. She heard it thud on the floor.

"My nose is cold," Rose said, blowing into her palm to direct warm air to her nose.

Percy took her hand and kissed it. "Keep it under the covers, and you'll stay warm." He scooched next to her. "I'll keep you warm." He kissed her neck and whispered, "Rose, I've never done this before."

"Never?" she whispered back.

His head rocked back and forth against her shoulder.

"It's okay," she said, placing her palm against his chest, to slow his racing heart. "You've imagined it, right?" she whispered.

His head bobbed up and down in the space between her neck and shoulder.

"So show me what you've imagined." She held his face between her hands and kissed him long and deep. His hands swept across her back, down her side and up her front. He broke from her mouth and slid down to her breasts.

"We're overdressed," Rose said, and they shed their nightclothes to the delight of skin.

"Oh, Rose!" It was a sigh that unmoored her. She was a floating continent, and he its first explorer. She'd never felt so naked before, nor so breathless and wound up.

They rolled in the soft folds of down and flannel, arms and legs, kisses and touch. Adrift in sensation, they orbited the moon. It was nearly full and shone through the window when she rested along the length of Percy's flank and nestled in the corner of his arm.

"Oh Rose! It's like music!" He rolled to his side, stretching an arm and leg over her. "Oh, Rose!"

"Shh." She hugged him.

"Oh, Rose!"

Was he sobbing or laughing? "Percy?"

He rolled on his back, a goofy grin aross his face.

"Percy?"

"Ummm?"

"What's today's date?"

"January sixteenth. Why?"

"Today's my birthday."

"Is that so? Well, Happy Birthday, Rose. I'm afraid I don't have a gift for you."

"Oh, you just gave me one." She rolled over and curled into him. "That was the most magnificent birthday gift ever." She tapped his chest. "You have no idea." No, she wouldn't tell him about groping, of almost getting there, of being only nearly satisfied so many times. "Oh, Percy. You're a natural. I'm going to hold on to you."

"Shh." He stroked her head. "Let's get some sleep. I need to rest, so we can do that again."

Every day at noon, Rose would pull out a thermos and sandwiches for their lunch; after, Percy would practice the piano amidst the chaos of all their work. It was Chopin's Prelude, Opus 28 No. 4 that Rose always waited for. To her, it was the story of winter: life pulsing deep underground while the trees wailed mournfully, their trunks creaking in the cold. Then came the excitement of the February afternoon sky. Now Rose was thinking of pastel paint instead of white, of trying to capture the magic of the pink twilight as it faded into a bluer and bluer blue before night's black set in. But white is what they'd decided upon, and white is what they painted the entire interior of the house. Percy rolled the ceilings and walls; Rose brushed the windows and trim.

Sometimes they talked, often about how they thought they should use each of the rooms. Rose would have one just for sewing, and they'd use another just for guests. That left one room upstairs completely unused. It would be a place to store Rose's stuff. They would go to Florida after the wedding and close her apartment. A working honeymoon, rather like what they were doing now, before the main event.

The main event. Rose was undecided about how and when they should get married. For all her marriages, she'd never had a wedding, just a ceremony in the rabbi's chambers. This time, there'd be no rabbi, but there was a whole group of friends who dropped heavy hints that a party was in order.

"It's entirely up to Rose," Percy said to whoever inquired.

"I'm thinking about it," was all Rose would reply. "And I'll let you know."

Meanwhile, room by room, they moved furniture back into the house. Rose bought a sewing machine and made curtains. In her workroom, she hung dotted Swiss, so that it always looked like it was snowing. In their bedroom, she hung curtains of lace. On the ground floor, she sewed rick-rack on white cotton for the kitchen, and made curtains of white-on-white jacquard stripes in the two parlors.

Finally, they restocked the kitchen. Percy didn't see why, just because they were going to be married, Rose should be the only one to cook. Rose wasn't quite so sure about sharing a kitchen, but she was willing to try.

"Rose," Percy said, as they moved down the aisle of the A&P, filling the cart with fresh tins of herbs and spices, flour, sugar, salt. "Rose," Percy said, as she studied the different kinds of cooking oil. "Don't you think we should be married before you move in?"

"Do I hear my desperately conservative husband worrying over propriety?" Rose teased without interrupting her study.

"But I'm not your husband!" Percy protested. "At least not yet."

Rose lifted a bottle of corn oil off the shelf.

"When are we going to get married?" Percy insisted.

The poor boy was love sick. Rose moved close to him and laid a palm against his cheek. "You've got it bad."

He rolled his face so that he could plant a kiss in her palm. "I know I do."

"Do you think it will last?"

"Is that what you're afraid of?" Percy asked.

"I don't know." Rose hated her indecision. "But I'm working on it. I am."

Percy pressed his lips together, to stop any more words from coming out.

When they returned from the supermarket, and argued—nicely—about where things should go, Rose stopped and said, "I know!"

"What?"

"Do you have a calendar?"

Percy showed her the one hanging inside the basement door.

Rose flipped it over to April and scanned. "Oh," her voice fell. "It doesn't say."

"Doesn't say what?"

"When's *Pesach*."

"*Pesach*?"

"Passover."

"What's that?"

"That's when I want to get married."

Rose enclosed cash with the shopping list she sent Jeannie, enough to cover postage as well as the matzoh, the matzoh meal, and Passover wine. She also asked for one copy of the *Haggadah* they used every year, the book they read at the Passover service. Jeannie and Manny had six, and Jeannie's sister had the same. Surely, they could spare one. What was one copy? She'd make do. They'd pass it around the table. They'd manage. Meanwhile, she splurged on a textured turquoise wool and a Vogue pattern for a smart suit with a single-breasted jacket, notched collar, contour pockets, and a slim skirt. She bought enough fabric to make a hat. A Jackie hat. And she'd dye shoes and a handbag to match. She also told Percy that she'd spend the days at his house, but until they were married, they would sleep at hers. She wouldn't move until after the wedding.

Percy, he was off helping the Whites sugar. It had something to do with trees and maple syrup, but Rose didn't know what, only that everyone was talking about a sugar-on-snow supper coming up Saturday night. Then she'd find out. And Percy wanted to take her to the sugar house and see the boil. She kept busy, sewing. Not only was the suit to be fitted, but lined. These were her last wedding clothes, of that she was sure. And her finest. Once the suit was finished, she'd make herself nightclothes. Not flannel—too hot with Percy next to her. And not satin—she was sixty-five! But some lovely lawn with eyelet lace. White, like the sheets and the walls and the curtains and the new towels they'd bought for the house.

The snow was no longer pure white, but mixed now with grey. March snow fell wet and sloppy, and the banks alongside the road were dusted with dirt. It was a new season, these days of sunshine and melt followed by nights as cold as any in January. Colder, maybe, after smelling the earth's mud. Rose was so engrossed with the gradual shift from winter and her preparations for spring, for marrying Percy, that she was unprepared for the heat of Manny's temper.

"What do you mean, you're not coming here for *Pesach*?" he shouted over the phone.

"I'm celebrating Passover up here," Rose said, forcing her voice to stay calm. "That's why I need Jeannie to send me supplies. I can't even find Sabbath candles up here. Please have her add those to the list."

"Ma—what's gotten in to you?" Now he was whining, not yelling.

"Manny, is that any way to speak to your mother?"

He answered with silence.

"You're being very childish, you know. Besides," Rose paused, "You're the one who told me come to Vermont. It wasn't my idea."

"For the summer. I invited you for the summer. I didn't expect you to stay the whole year."

"Well, I'm here."

"We wanted you to come live with us."

There, he finally admitted it. "I know," Rose said. "But God had other plans."

"God? What has God got to do with it?"

Rose held the receiver away from her ear. "I can hear you just fine. Don't shout!"

Manny's voice went steely. "Well, I hope you're happy."

He didn't mean it. Rose took a deep breath and said, "As a matter of fact, I am." There was tense silence between them. Rose forced herself to go on. "Manny, this seder is very important to me."

"If seder is so important, why aren't you going to be here, celebrating it with your family?"

"Please watch your tone of voice. I'm trying to tell you something."

"What? What are you trying to tell me?"

"Will you listen?" Rose asked.

"I'm listening," he said.

"And promise not to shout."

"Okay," he sighed. "Shoot."

"I will be celebrating *Pesach* with my family." Rose couldn't help smiling at her plans.

"You want us to come to Vermont for Passover? Jeannie's parents and her brother and sister? And all their kids? All those people? Where will you put them? It's easier if you just come to us."

"Manny, you're not listening. Let me finish."

"So finish."

He was bored with the conversation, she could tell. It was always like this when he didn't get his way. Maybe she let him get his way too often. She did the best she could. Who teaches you how to be a mother? Who decides what child you're given to raise? Manny was Manny. He wasn't going to like what she was going to say.

"Manny, I'm getting married. I'm making a seder to celebrate."

Silence.

"Manny? Did you hear me? I said I'm getting married at *Pesach*. Then I'm moving over to Percy's house. We'll close up this one. We've got his all fixed up. We're just waiting for *Pesach*."

Silence still.

"Manny. This is your mother speaking. I'm telling you something. Something very important. Are you listening to me?"

She could hear him breathing. Then he was yelling for Jeannie to come to the phone.

"Rose? Rose? What's this? Manny says you're getting married?"

"That's right." Rose scrambled to make a connection with her daughter-in-law. It was the only way this was going to work. "Remember Percy Mendell? The announcer at the parade? Fourth of July Parade? White hair?"

"I remember."

"Well, we're going to be married on April sixteenth. In the afternoon. Right here, at the house." Somehow, Jeannie's silence was friendlier than Manny's. "And we're inviting a few friends over for a meal. A seder." Before Jeannie could say anything Rose added, "And I asked Manny to tell you I also need candles. There are no *Shabbes* candles to be found around here. I'll send you more money."

"That's all right, Rose. I'll buy you some candles. It will be my pleasure."

Good. A woman understands. A man—a son—Manny, he's selfish. He doesn't like change.

"But what a surprise," Jeannie said. "You've been very sly. You haven't said a thing."

"What's to say?" Rose paused. "Besides, I never expected it myself. Not at my time of life."

"Well, congratulations, Rose."

"Thank you."

"I'll send you the things you need."

"Thank you, dear. Thanks a lot."

"And Percy?" Jeannie asked. "Is he Jewish?"

"No," Rose smiled. "He's not."

16 | exodus

"No butter on the table, please. This is a *flayshig* meal. No dairy!"

"No butter with dinner? No butter with bread?" Percy stood, holding the butter dish indecisively.

"No bread, Percy. Passover is the Feast of Unleavened Bread. We eat matzoh."

"Right. No bread." He replaced the butter in the fridge.

She could feel his hopelessness.

"Rose, are we going to keep kosher?" he asked.

She stopped fussing over the soup pot and replaced the lid. "Kosher? Do you want to keep kosher?" This man was full of surprises!

He let his empty hands fall by his sides. "I wouldn't know how to begin. But Rose." He looked at her. "I have to understand a little bit, in order not to make some terrible blunder."

This was the man she was about to marry. So thoughtful, it was almost past bearing. "Percy, I don't keep kosher. To keep kosher, you need two sets of dishes, for meat and *milchedig.* Different soap for each. Different towels. And two more sets just for *Pesach.* It's a major bother."

"But some things—like the butter—some things are important?"

"On account of it's *Pesach*," Rose said, checking on the roasting lamb in the oven. "For *Pesach*, I get a little fussy, that's all."

"Well, tell me the basics, so I know."

Rose glanced at the clock. "Percy, it's a quarter to three! We're getting married in two hours! There's still a lot to do!" She bustled from stove to sink.

"Just the basics, Rose."

She turned off the faucet and faced him. "The basics: No meat and dairy at the same meal. No shellfish. No pork."

"No pork?"

"No pork. I've never eaten it in my life."

"Rose?" Percy stood stock-still. "You have."

"I have what?" She turned and glared.

"Eaten pork." Percy's voice was quiet.

"When?"

"At the sugar-on-snow supper. And at my birthday party, if you ate the sandwiches that Shirley made."

Rose flipped back through the months. She hadn't eaten anything at the party, she was too full of feeling to eat. At the sugar supper, she passed the meat platter, not taking any of it. "But I didn't take any of the ham."

"But you ate the baked beans."

"Beans are beans! Vegetables are *parve*, neutral. Not dairy or meat."

"But baked beans are made with salt pork. Pork fat."

"I thought you said they were made with maple syrup?"

"Maple syrup's what makes them sweet. Salt pork's what gives them their flavor."

Rose pressed her lips together.

"Are you okay?"

She nodded.

"You're sure?"

"Well, God didn't strike me dead, did He?"

"Did you think He would?"

Rose wrinkled her nose. "Those beans were delicious!"

"Pork is tasty."

"Don't ask me to cook it for you!"

"Never."

"Okay."

"But may I cook it for you? Or do I give up bacon and ham and baked beans from this day forward?"

Rose put her hand to her mouth. "What else have I eaten? That's pork, that is."

"Sally Boyce's apple pie."

"How can apple pie have pork in it?"

"Lard. In the pie crust. It's what makes it flaky."

Rose put her fingers to her lips. "Pork fat?"

"I'm afraid so."

"What else?"

Percy shrugged. "Did you taste the sausage at the sugar house, the ones we boiled in the sap?"

Rose nodded, remembering the sweet meat washed down with the cold, bitter beer. "I had no idea."

"If I'd known, I would have told you."

Rose said nothing.

"If it makes you feel any better, I've never eaten gefilte fish before, either. Or matzoh balls. Or—what's that stuff you had me chopping for the seder, with nuts and apples?"

"*Haroses.*"

"Haroses." Percy nodded. "Doesn't my trying new foods count for something?"

Rose tilted her head to the side. So, she'd eaten pork. She'd enjoyed it. And instead of being struck dead on the spot, she hadn't even known. Not only that, but she hadn't suffered! She'd been blessed, instead. "Yes. Trying new foods counts for something." The sparkle of her eyes was reflected in Percy's. "After all, when Moses led the Jews out of Egypt, they'd never eaten matzoh before." She chuckled. "Or manna." She laughed. "How can you expect to wander in the desert, to live in the wilderness, and not try something new?" Rose asked. "It can't be done."

"So you're okay?" Percy asked.

"Okay? Percy, we have company coming in two hours! I have dinner to prepare! We have to finish setting the table! We have to get dressed! I'm frantic, I'm not okay!" Rose threw up her hands, but stopped in mid-air. He was shaking with laughter, trying hard not to make any noise. Tears leaked out his eyes.

With a hand gesture, he coaxed her to approach him. "Oh, Rose," he gasped when she finally let herself be folded into his arms. "You are too okay."

"Okay!" She pushed herself away from him. "But let's finish up here."

"Do I have time to go home?" Percy asked.

"Go home? Didn't you bring your suit? What did you forget?"

"It's something I just thought of—for setting the table."

Rose squinted, trying to understand.

"I'll be right back. You'll see."

He returned carrying a large, wooden chest. "Here," he said, setting it on the kitchen table. "You said you used special dishes and whatnot for seder?"

Rose looked at him.

"Go on. Open it up."

Rose lifted the lid.

"It was my mother's silver. Then Addie's. It hasn't been used in years."

Rose lifted a spoon with a tapered bowl, a slender neck and a plain handle. "What does it say?" She held the spoon for Percy to read.

"G. R. F. and B. E.—initials." He pointed at the top line. "Grace Richards Franklin, my grandmother, and Burton Ells, my grandfather." Percy flipped the spoon over, and showed Rose the engraver's mark. "1854. That's the year they were married. Burton Ells was killed in the Civil War. I don't know much about him. My mother was a little girl when he died." Percy replaced the teaspoon and removed a tablespoon. "Now this: I remember Sunday dinners at my grandmother Ells's house, and trying to wrestle dessert into my mouth with this monster. It was quite a trial for a youngster, let me tell you."

"Are you sure it's a tablespoon and not a serving piece?" Rose handled the large utensil.

"Oh, yes." Percy lifted the top tray off the case. "These are the serving pieces." The ladle, two spoons, and two giant forks fit into their own felt-covered slots.

"Percy." Rose clutched his arm. "Your family goes back to the Civil War?"

"Longer than that," he shrugged, replacing the top tray in the box. "My mother's family, they came over early."

"Pilgrims?" Rose squeaked.

"Almost."

"You're a real American!" She paused. "And you're going to marry me?"

"But you're an American—unless you lied when you filled out the marriage license."

"Yes, but naturalized. I wasn't born here."

"So?"

"So? It's just strange, that's all. Like I've finally arrived, marrying an American."

Percy interrupted their brief silence. "Rose, we have a lifetime ahead of us to get used to it. Meantime, I'm going to set the table."

"With this?" She indicated the silver.

"With this," Percy affirmed.

"But it's tarnished! It needs to be polished!"

"Another time," Percy said.

"But—"

Percy held his hand up. "Just like the Jews didn't have time to let the bread rise, we don't have time to polish the silver."

Rose shook her head. How could you argue?

John Ready served as justice of the peace, and their friends understood the seder better than Rose expected.

"The Last Supper was a seder," Shirley Greenwood told Rose. "And today is Good Friday, when Jesus ate it," she explained.

Rose had no idea.

She sat at one end of the long table, and Percy at the other. Happiness overtook her. "Friends," she cleared her throat. "Friends," her voice was louder. "We'd planned to have a traditional seder tonight." Percy cocked his head. She nodded to reassure him everything was all right. "But," Rose took a deep breath. "But I think we'll have a short version, instead."

All eleven faces were turned toward her. "Basically," she continued, "Passover is about freedom." She swallowed. She could do this without crying. She wasn't going to cry. "To celebrate freedom," Rose continued, "we have to remember slavery. So tonight, we say our usual Sabbath prayers over the light, the wine, and the bread, only instead of bread we eat matzoh."

Rose lit and blessed the candles, translating for her guests,

Praised are Thou, O Lord our God, King of the Universe, who hast sanctified us by Thy commandment and hast commanded us to kindle the Sabbath and festival lights; who has kept us alive and sustained us and brought us to this season. May our home be consecrated, O God, by the light of Thy countenance, shining upon us in blessing, and bringing us peace!

"Amen!"

Rose was startled by the vehemence of the word, spoken so wholeheartedly. She paused; Percy nodded encouragement.

"Here." Rose pinched a piece of parsley and passed it to her left. "Take some, and dip it in your salt water. That's in the small dish." Rose indicated the saucers by everyone's place. "Slavery is bitter, full of tears. We dip parsley in salt water to remember the bitterness of being enslaved." Rose dipped hers and ate. "There's a blessing for it. In Judaism, there's a blessing for everything. Some things we can skip. But this," Rose held up a giant cracker. "This is matzoh. Called the Bread of Affliction, it is what the Jews carried with them out of Egypt when they fled. Here." She passed a square of matzoh down each side of the table. "Everyone, take a piece." She waited until they were served. Rose held it up and read from the Haggadah, *This is the bread of affliction which our fathers ate in the land of Egypt. Let all who are hungry come and eat. Let all who are in want come and celebrate the Passover with us. May it be God's will to redeem us from all trouble and from all servitude. Next year at this season, may the whole house of Israel be free!*

Rose watched her friends munch the matzoh.

"Tastes like affliction, all right," John Ready said, and everyone laughed.

Rose felt her heart swell. When the table returned to attention, she said, "There's more: There's horseradish and *haroses*." She pointed to the ceremonial foods in front of her. "There's a shank bone." She held it up. "There are eggs. And they all mean something." She paused. "Usually, we read the story of the Exodus. That's what's in the Haggadah." She thumped the book closed. "But just as the seder is supposed to be a reenactment of the Jews' escape from Egypt," Rose continued with growing confidence, "maybe we should conclude it with the same haste that they left Egypt in!" Everyone laughed. Rose lifted her wine glass and waited for their attention once more. "So, one more blessing. *Praised art Thou, O Lord our God, King of the Universe, who has created the fruit of the vine.*" Everyone followed Rose's example and drank their wine.

"That's all," Rose said. "We can have dinner now."

"Hear! Hear!" It was Barrett Greenwood, struggling out of his chair. "Not so fast!" He stood, nodded toward Percy and bowed toward Rose. "If you're all done, Rose, some of us have a thing or two to say!" Everyone laughed. "First of all, thank you for inviting us to this wonderful feast and celebration. We've all waited a long time for someone to come along and free Percy from being a bachelor!"

Eamon Boyce raised his glass, "Out of the pan and into the fire!"

"Yoked at last!" John Ready swallowed his wine.

"You have a peculiar sense of freedom, Barrett!" Rob White piped.

"Shh. Shh," Barrett said, knocking his spoon against his glass. "Order!" When the jibing subsided, he recommenced. "Rose," Barrett held up his glass. "We're beholden to you, and we wish you the very best!"

Noise broke out all over the table and everyone drank. Then Percy stood up. "If I may be allowed to speak," he cleared his throat. "I just want to thank you all for helping us along, so Rose and I could get to this place. Maybe, if it weren't for some of you giving a nudge here, or a push there, well—" People started telling their Rose and Percy stories. Percy and Rose exchanged a long-distance smile the length of the table. "Please, fill your glasses! Everyone, fill your glasses! Before my wife changed the agenda here and shortened this service, she instilled in me some of the protocols of a proper seder, one of which is to drink four glasses of wine. So fill up! Fill up! And please, join me in a toast—To my wife, Rose Mendell!"

Rose bit her lower lip. Rose Mendell! Well, it was something to get used to. But if they didn't stop all this toasting and drinking, dinner would never be served. Rose raised her glass to Percy's and sipped.

The meal was a smashing success. And the ladies all pitched in; the kitchen was spotless by the time everyone left.

"What shall I do with all these leftovers?" Rose asked Percy, as they were getting ready to go.

"We'll come back and get them in the morning. We'll come back tomorrow to close up." She liked the way his hands on her shoulders directed her toward the door.

"And you're sure you know how to shut off the water so that the pipes don't freeze, and all those other things Manny told me to do?"

"I'm sure." Percy held her coat.

"And everything's turned off on the stove?" Rose peered around him toward the kitchen, just to make sure.

"Eveything's turned off. The fire's out. The house will be fine." He placed his hands on her shoulders again, this time facing her, and looked deep into her eyes. "Do you have everything you need?"

Rose nodded.

"And you're ready to come home with me?"

Rose nodded again.

"Our home, Rose." Percy searched her eyes.

"I'm ready, Percy. Are you?"

He nodded and opened the front door. Together, they stepped out into the night.

Breinigsville, PA USA
01 March 2010
233366BV00001B/11/P

9 781935 052203